Praise for
The Night Archer

"Historian and diplomat Michael Oren has at long last returned to fiction with an extraordinary collection of stories that sparkle with wit, intelligence, tenderness, and penetrating honesty. The luminous prose is best savored slowly, but most readers will undoubtedly devour *The Night Archer* in a single sitting and then eagerly await Oren's next offering."

— DANIEL SILVA, *New York Times* #1 bestselling author

"That hum you hear when you read Michael Oren's gorgeous short stories is the song of humanity pushing against all of its innate limitations. Oren delivers a heartfelt and heartbreaking account of who we are as a species— flawed, fearful, and lonely but always open-hearted, always trusting that transcendence is possible, if not imminent. This is what optimism for adults looks like, and this is the book you should read if you need a dose of unfettered hope."

— LIEL LEIBOVITZ, author of *A Broken Hallelujah: Rock and Roll, Redemption, and the Life of Leonard Cohen*

"Thank you Michael Oren for a delightful book. And the scope of it! There are ghosts, Upper West Side Jews, Biblical figures, aliens, 16th-century Spanish explorers, plenty of love, sex, regret, revenge, forgiveness, and on and on—all written with Michael's empathetic, realistic, (and often very funny) voice. Highly recommended."

— A.J. JACOBS, Author of *Thanks a Thousand: A Gratitude Journey*

Also by Michael Oren

Fiction
The Night Archer: and Other Stories
Sand Devil: A Negev Trilogy
Reunion

Nonfiction
The Origins of the Second Arab-Israel War: Egypt,
Israel and the Great Powers, 1952-1956
Six Days of War: June 1967 and the Making of the Modern Middle East
Power, Faith, and Fantasy: America in the
Middle East, 1776 to the Present
Ally: My Journey Across the American-Israeli Divide

To All Who Call in Truth

a novel by Michael Oren

WICKED SON

A WICKED SON BOOK
An Imprint of Post Hill Press
ISBN: 978-1-64293-580-6
ISBN (eBook): 978-1-64293-581-3

To All Who Call in Truth
© 2021 by Michael Oren
All Rights Reserved

Cover Design by Matt Margolis

Post Hill Press
New York • Nashville
posthillpress.com

Published in the United States of America
1 2 3 4 5 6 7 8 9 10

For Leslie,
who every morning pointed at my desk and told me,

"That book isn't going to write itself."

With deepest gratitude and love.

Adolescents are not monsters. They are just people trying to learn how to make it among the adults in the world, who are probably not so sure themselves.

Virginia Satir, *The New Peoplemaking*

There may be many lies, but there is only one truth.
Rabbi Nachman of Breslov

Prologue

It wouldn't be the first time he'd used his fists, his belt, and car keys, too. They left lavender bruises, crosshatched scratches, and welts anywhere they landed, especially on the face. He'd learned that in the POW camp where his captors beat him for the flimsiest infractions. Yet still he bowed and thanked them. A serious crime—rifling through the garbage—could have cost him his head.

And yet he had survived. He returned to a country dazzled by its own victory. An adolescent land where even a damaged vet could start his own business, build a big house, and fill it with art, imported furniture, and the town's prettiest wife. He could have a son to teach the most effective ways to defend himself, the same techniques his captors had once inflicted on him.

He never forgot his captors. His walls were decorated with their handicrafts—testaments to their taste—as well as their weapons. The deadliest of these was slung in the den where any visitor could view it. Lacquer-clad, pleasingly curved, its blade could slice through any substance softer than metal and effortlessly through a human skull.

The sword reminded him of the cruelty of the world and perhaps also his own. It was a cruelty he had either acquired as a prisoner of war or was born with—he was never quite certain which, only that the violence still roiled inside him. Harnessed, it gave him an advantage on corporate boards and tennis courts. Unleashed, it could easily kill.

And kill it might, as life for him became unbearable. The once-spry country he once returned to grew up decadent. Fat, fractured and drugged. And his wife and son came to love one another far more than either loved him.

He would punish them for that, repeatedly, aiming for the face. He no longer heard the screams for help or the swish of unsheathed steel. The pain, if he felt it, was fleeting.

It wasn't the first time he had used his fists, yet it'd surely be his last.

Autumn

1.

Beneath the castle façade, the costume rack, and random dusty props, his outlines were barely visible. A curved back and a protruding butt that couldn't be hidden was all that Sandy saw curled beneath the curtains. Yet he could feel him there, as palpable as the audience outside. He felt ashamed for the kid and sorry for having to humiliate him this way. But there was no choice. This was just another rung in the ladder of growing up, he consoled himself. Someday, at a bar, he'd laugh about it. And besides, this was Sandy's job. His duty.

"You're going to have to come out of there eventually, son," he said gravely.

A whimper. "No."

Sandy tugged on his half-knotted tie and folded up his shirt cuffs. He glanced at the watch on his inner wrist. Time was a factor here. It took the school principal, Dr. Steinseifer, ten whole minutes to silence the uproar, long enough for Howard's guidance counselor to try and reason with the kid, but it couldn't last. Any crowd, much less this one, would riot.

Of the several options—dismissing the assembly, sending Howard home sick—this alone seemed reasonable. And educational, teaching about resilience and life. Yet Sandy couldn't help speculating what he would've preferred in Howard's place. He remembered a similarly mortifying incident in his own past: that Thanksgiving game when, while being hauled from the field with a corkscrewed leg, he caught sight of his father. That look of withering disappointment still rattled him. But this was a different order of embarrassment. This was devastation of a type attainable only by Howard Weintraub.

Overweight and ungainly, with glasses, braces, and zits, he was shunned by classmates who called him fatso and pizza face and, worst of all, faggot. And so he joined the Drama Club. There he played old men and monsters and, in this performance, a middle-aged prig. His opposite, cast as the innocent maid, was the petite Chrissie Esposito, the most popular girl in school. The two took the stage at the end of Autumn Assembly, part welcoming ceremony for incoming students, part football rally, and generally a bore. Except for the sketch, intended as comic relief. But nobody expected bedlam.

It began with a hug, Howard nuzzling Chrissie. But he kept holding on to her, making not only Chrissie but the entire audience squirm. Only when she managed to twist free of him was the effect of the embrace displayed. Chrissie, a hand over her dainty mouth, gasped at first then giggled while Howard merely froze. He stood there, mid-stage, blinking into a spotlight. Finally, shielding his crotch, he fled from the proscenium and barrel-rolled under the rear curtain.

Chuckles were already flying spark-like through the auditorium, igniting jeers here and there and ultimately a firestorm. Sandy had never heard roars like that before, not even after touchdowns. Sheaves of notebook paper were swirling along with balled-up candy wrappers. Feet stomped, fists pounded armrests. The students seemed possessed by a pubescent frenzy that threatened to explode. Before it could, though, the principal sought out Sandy and, with a flick of his fingers, ordered him backstage.

"Let's go, Howard," Sandy said. "Time to take it like a man."

A long silence, followed by a sniffled, "Okay."

"Need a hand?"

He extended one, but Howard refused. Instead, he crawled out from under the scenery and stood, a quivering shadow.

"What now?" Sandy heard him ask.

"What now?" He hadn't thought it through. "Walk back out there, I guess. Pick up just where you left off."

"But they'll all make fun of me."

"Yeah, so what? People make fun of me, too."

Another silence. Bully bait, Sandy thought. Even his shadow is fat. "Nobody makes fun of you, Mister Cooper."

"Yeah, right."

He held up the curtain just enough to reveal to the cast loitering awkwardly on stage and, below them in the orchestra pit, the marching band roiling in hysterics. Beyond that stretched row after row of howling students. Still, he turned to Howard and said, "Go."

With a whiff of makeup and fear, the boy stumbled passed him and out through the folds.

A moment later, alone in that lightless place, Sandy felt it. Enveloping him and for a second threatening to shatter him. It pursued him through the emergency exit, down the hall and the stairway to his office. Only with the door shut and hands clapped over his ears did the laughter finally cease.

* * * * *

It resumed an hour later in the teachers' lounge. Mr. Bronowski, mean and anvil-headed, was the first to enter snickering, followed by McGonnigle. He also taught some kind of math but contrastingly affected nape-length hair, Peter Max ties, and bellbottoms. In seconds, the dingy room with its announcement boards and secondhand furniture bustled with teachers. All were eager to share in the joke and hear the details from Sandy.

"Come on, Cooper, tell us what you told him. That we all get 'em? That it's just part of being a man?" That was pumped-up D'Angelis, fresh from gym class, needling him. And Stevens, the science teacher who failed to become a real scientist, chortled, "Not bad for an eighth-grader. Gonna make some girl real happy someday."

"Hey. *Hey.*" The protest came from Charlotte Fox—Foxy, behind her back—who taught Social Studies, whatever that was. Said to be a refugee from some Sixties commune, she was rock poster pretty with an upturned nose and shaggy blonde hair that she still wore parted in the middle. Her peasant shirts were translucent and her skirts so short that Dr. Steinseifer repeatedly upbraided her, "Teachers cannot be beatniks."

Teachers, in fact, could be many things, Sandy knew, from rednecks to bookworms, closet radicals to bigots. In the lounge, though, they were mostly just adults fleeing their students' madness. The girls' trailing tissues out of their training bras and boys whacking off into lockers. Hormones like static in the halls. The cliques, the gangs, the brutal battle to be "in" and "cool" and "popular." Like soldiers ribbing each other after combat, the teachers needed a release from the rawness, the torment and cruelty of adolescence.

"Imagine what he's going through right now," Brooks, the frumpy shop teacher opined. "Imagine sitting through class."

Sandy didn't have to. He knew exactly the indignities inflicted on Howard, the ruthless wisecracks, the punches that would numb his upper arms. Perhaps he was wrong by not sending him home, providing him with a note from the nurse and an excuse to tell the poor boy's parents. But would that be doing him a favor? After all, it was Sandy's responsibility to help these young people learn to grapple with life, not dodge it. How else could they ever emerge as adults?

"Whatever happens to him, it won't be enough," ruled Wendell Barr, formerly of the Phys Ed department and, before that, of the U.S. Marines and minor league baseball, a man who, at every step in life, fattened his satchel of hate. Now, as Vice Principal for Discipline, he hunted the hallways for gum chewers and dress code violators, doling out detentions and spite. Roughly Sandy's age but with a steel-gray buzz-cut and leathered cheeks. With hobnail eyes, he drilled the guidance counselor. "Oversexed, over-pampered, over everything. That's what's wrong with you people."

"People" referred to Jews like Howard and Sandy, and Wendell was betting that no one would challenge him, not even Charlotte. They didn't. But neither did Sandy. As much as he longed to, he didn't shoot up with the right hook he learned in high school and unhinge the vice principal's jaw. What example would that set for students? Instead, he remained seated on the sofa, with his mug and bitter coffee, until the bell rang for class.

"A bunch of Archie Bunkers, don't listen to them."

He gazed up at the apple-shaped face of Jeanne Pagonis.

"You did the right thing, Mister Cooper. Someday that boy'll thank you."

Still seated, Sandy stared at this short, slight woman—they were almost eye-to-eye—and tried to remember if he'd ever heard her voice. Even her name was a stretch. Dark brown hair cut hood-like, a boyish body in an unflattering pantsuit, unadorned except for a gold Orthodox cross. The youngest faculty member, she ate lunch alone on the lounge's stained Formica table, too shy to join in debates.

And yet here she was standing up for him. For Howard. He didn't know whether to hug her or cry, but as a man inclined to do neither, he toasted her with his cup.

"Maybe thank me, maybe resent me. The main thing is he survives."

"Don't be so gloomy, Coop," Jeanne said. Sandy flinched, as much from her use of his nickname as from the sudden touch on his cheek. Her fingers were tiny, but their tips felt enormously warm. "The world is a beautiful place."

* * * * *

The memory of that touch, much more than her observation about life, remained with him as he wheeled through the rest of the day. This was typically busy with students, seventh to ninth graders, streaming in with a blinding range of complaints. The pressured kids already obsessing about their futures, the creative ones who couldn't fully read. There was a girl gone uncommunicative because of her parents' divorce and another caught smoking twice in the bathroom. A fifteen-year-old afraid to admit that a closet existed much less come out of one. The counselor listened or at least appeared to. Still careening through his head were doubts about his decision to keep Howard in school that day and his desire to break Wendell's face. He nodded "yes" to his advisees when he was really dwelling on Jeanne Pagonis, and "no" to drive such thoughts from his mind.

Between consultations, he browsed through the paper. Not the front pages with its reports of war and campus unrest. As a rule, Sandy kept to the sports section. Though a lifelong Yankees fan, he'd taken to following Pittsburgh in the playoffs, fielding the first all-Black team, or the A's, for the joy of finding names like Catfish Hunter and Vida Blue. Football was less interesting lately, with Miami and Dallas predictably on top. Yet he read the NFL news as well—anything to pass the time until four.

The final bell sounded loudest, followed by a mass slam of lockers and the rataplan of feet. Sandy waited for the ruckus to subside and silence to return to the halls. Only then did he rise from the cork-walled cubicle that served as his office and swing through its frosted glass door. He stiff-legged past the principal's suite and down a stairway to the gym, across the parquet overhung with climbing ropes and into the coaches' room. There, surrounded by game balls and old rosters, he donned a ratty gray sweatshirt. That, along with the half-knotted tie, the pushed-up sleeves, and the Timex worn inside his wrist, was his trademark.

The defense was already going through its drills and the offensive line stretching by the time he gimped out to the field. The Appleton Rams would likely win only half of their games, yet still Sandy treated them like champs. There were plays to memorize and techniques to master along with the team spirit and sportsmanship he felt responsible to instill. He loved the smell of sweat beneath shoulder pads and of freshly churned-up turf, the smack of body armor and the hollow thump of punts. Above all, he cherished coaching his quarterback, Russel Pressman.

Or less like coaching than nurturing, for Russel's talent—he could toss a forty-yarder and sprint the hundred in full gear—only had to be honed. A smart kid, too, capable of remembering multiple patterns, a leader whom others quite naturally followed. Strawberry-haired, freckled, and tall, he was unanimously ranked most popular in school and relentlessly pursued by girls. Sandy saw his task as keeping him focused and not letting his abundant gifts get in the way of winning. Someday, when Russel was an all-star, Sandy could say—so he fantasized—"I forged him."

But rather than forging Russel, Sandy found himself repeating counts for the center, Tony Metallo. A lug of a boy, bell-headed and empty-eyed, he couldn't remember the calls and kept hiking late, throwing the entire line off-sides. Sandy tried marking the codes on Tony's knuckles, even making them rhyme. He shouted them through the faceguard, a rant of numbers and nouns met with desperate sighs of "Sorry, Coach, sorry."

Outside, an Indian summer still burned. Even Sandy's sweatshirt was stifling. Still, the sun setting over the goalposts cast a pumpkin-colored light and withering leaves crisped the air. These Northeast autumns always made Sandy feel wistful. Though not the reflective type, he nevertheless grew aware of time's passing, of a present already preserved in an amber-like past.

Now, hollering at Anthony but eager to return to his quarterback, Sandy found himself thinking about Howard again. What would he tell his parents when they asked him about the school play? How would he explain their son's refusal to come out of his room? Perhaps he should have spent more time talking to the kid, got down on a knee and tried to comfort him as he lay curled. Maybe he should have told him what it was like getting injured in front of his father or about his own son, who Sandy would've given anything to see up on that stage, even humiliated.

It was dark when Sandy blew his whistle, signaling the end of practice. He huddled with his players, promised them they'd crush Edison next week, and whistled them off to the showers. Then he was alone on the field.

A breezy night brought every blade to attention and crowned it with moonlight. The school, even the goalposts, disappeared. He stood, in the same brand of khaki pants and gum-soled shoes he favored in high school, the face of his wristwatch worn under his palm where he once grease penciled plays. Apart from an extra inch of sideburn—his sole concession to the seventies—and the peppery temples, his hair was just as short. And yet, for a second, Sandy saw himself not as he was but as he might have been. His legs unbroken and sprinting downfield. The wind singing in his helmet, hashmarks flashing past. He dashed with the football clasped to his ribcage with nothing but triumph ahead.

But the vision quickly passed. By the time he deposited his sweatshirt back in the gym, Sandy had nearly forgotten it. He was, as always, the man good at counseling others but never in need of advice. Uncomplicated, unheroic, not quite happy, perhaps, but safely hovering over sad. Sanford Cooper. The Coop.

* * * * *

Coming out of the Appleton parking lot, Sandy could have turned left and passed by Sobotnik's Deli, Wexler's Drugs, and Hershkey's Bakery. The road then rose sharply through an upscale neighborhood of duplexes, sprawling lawns, and the Hartmont Country Club. Appleton's Jewish section. But instead he veered rightward, downhill, toward the Starlite Pizzeria and Vinny the butcher, through a series of sharp, poorly paved S's to an even grid of row houses.

These had been built a half-century before, in the 1920s, by the master bricklayers and machinists whose skills had lifted them out of city life and deposited them here, on suburbia's frontier. The area was still rural back then, checkered with family farms. But the farms had disappeared, displaced by yet more row houses, and instead of journeymen came small business owners and salespeople. And teachers, enough to staff several schools.

The Cooper residence was identical to the rest, whitewashed with a screened-in back porch. The same one-car driveway and carriage house garage that once held Model T's and Packards, the same thin toupee of grass.

The sole distinction was the absence of any images, decorative or divine. No jockeys or Virgins, not even a gnome. Esta hated them. "Narishkeit," she said, dismissing the figures with the Yiddish word for nonsense. "Who needs them?" she asked. "We have each other." And Sandy went along.

Esta's car, a secondhand Corolla, already took up the garage, so Sandy left his Impala outside and entered through the front door. Supper, he smelled, was ready—or, rather, burnt. Strange, he sometimes thought, that a woman tasked with preparing young girls to be housewives was such an incompetent cook. Yet he never complained, grateful that Esta's job in another junior high allowed her to get home before him. The scorched odor, even the scrape of a frying pan in the kitchen, comforted him as he slumped at the dining room table.

A second later she bounded out with plates of flank steak and onions. She laid one in front of him and, in the same motion, pecked his forehead. "Tough day, sweetie?" she chirped. Esta often called him that, sweetie, while she was always "sweetie pie." But tonight he was too bedraggled for affection.

"Had better."

"Eat, then." She pushed the plate closer to his chest. "Whenever down, eat up."

That was Esta: energetic, buoyant. And usually right, for even her scorched-earth meals often brightened him. But not tonight. While saw-ing the steak into slivers, he revisited the Howard Weintraub incident, the tension in the teachers' lounge, his near altercation with Wendell. So, too, he remembered Jeanne Pagonis's touch. He thought about it all but said nothing, chomping industriously instead. Inwardly, Sandy assured himself that he would get around to all of that before they went to sleep. With her one unpillowed ear, Esta would listen to him and maybe pat his cheek. Her last wakeful words would be, as they often were, "No worry, sweetie. Everything's great."

Sandy set to chewing, mumbling as he did, "Metallo...Not the bright-est bulb...Couldn't get a minute with Pressman."

"Russel will be there tomorrow," Esta said as she poured him some kind of juice. "And the tomorrow after that."

While his jaw revolved, Esta went on about her day teaching Home Ec. As in all junior highs, the boys took shop and the girls Home Ec where they learned how to bake, iron, and sew. But now the course was being eliminated. No more recipes and patterns, Esta lamented, but Drug and Sex Ed. "And what do I know about drugs?"

Mid-gnaw, Sandy gaped at her and she glowered back before they both burst out laughing.

Esta Cooper was faintly Nordic-looking, with the turned-up nose that other women paid for and watery blue eyes. Though nearing forty, she was as attractive to him now as she had been as Esta Lapidus, a year behind him in high school. It didn't matter to him that she still wore prim cream blouses buttoned to the neck or her platinum hair in a beehive. While he maintained his youthful wiriness, her body filled out beyond her once-enviable bust, her pert features gone fleshy. Still, he cared for her. They shared a lifetime together, struggles, let-downs, intolerable sorrows, and even the occasional joy. They traded affections, made twice-monthly love, and each night sat down to an overdone dinner.

Later, in the small living room that doubled as a den, Sandy slouched in his recliner. The detective on TV solved crimes in a wheelchair but, with Esta again scraping the kitchen, he could barely hear how. His eyes drifted from the screen to the walls. There was the photograph of his father standing double-breasted and Stetsoned in front of his Plymouth and his mother on her last trip abroad, posing beside the Louvre. There was an old family clock from whose family exactly Sandy forgot—and a vase of some Eastern origin. Also displayed was a black-and-white snapshot of himself, circa seventeen and suited up for football, a helmet hugged in one hand and, in the other, a cheerleader.

Though often told that the looked just like he did as a kid—the same pug nose, the features as tight as a T-formation—he was otherwise unrecognizable. The grit, that scarcely contained aggression, could have belonged to a stranger. Looking at that photograph taken close to the day when his life would change, he couldn't help noting the irony. Esta, though physically aged, was internally unaltered. Only he was a different man.

While still studying the picture, he remembered the sensation he'd experienced at practice. As if a curtain had parted and quickly closed, but not before he caught a glimpse of himself as he was and might again become. The image saddened him, excited and frightened him, and he was almost relieved when it vanished. He would have to tell Esta about that, too.

At some point he must have drifted off because she was shaking his knee and saying, "Come, sweetie, time for bed." Hauling himself up the newel post and then the narrow, creaky stairs, massaging his bad thigh, he reached the second floor. He turned toward their bedroom at the back of the narrow hall and then paused. At the opposite end there was another room, and while he promised himself not to visit it more than necessary—it was never necessary—tonight he couldn't resist.

The overhead light illuminated the shelves lined with his old trophies. A stuffed bear with "Joey" stitched on his chest. Esta's megaphone and a single bed painstakingly made. And silence. Still, he stood there for a while, disheveled and groggy, feeling like a quarterback who'd been sacked.

Esta was already under the blanket and breathing dully by the time he got undressed. The sheets were heavy with her smell. He didn't read much, just the occasional *Sports Illustrated*, but he was too tired even for that. Instead, in the dark, he inched as close to his wife as he dared without waking her. Tomorrow he'd fill her in about the school play and the chaos it almost ignited. He'd tell her about how he'd told Howard, "You're going to have to come out of there eventually, son." And he'd tell her about that luminous moment on the football field. Tomorrow, he promised himself, as he curled his body ball-like and rolled under the safety of the sheet.

2.

The girl was a gnarl of contradictions. Sweet and resentful. Courteous and curt. Dressed as if for parochial school in a pleated skirt, stockings, and tennis shirt but sporting a worldly manner. Her problem was incongruous as well. What fourteen-year-old ever complained about getting too much attention from boys, the overindulgence of teachers, about being *too* popular?

"I mean, really, Mister Cooper, my locker is filled with love notes. On exams, I can't even get an A *minus*."

"I understand, Rae, but what do you want me to do? Tell you to dress more modestly? Purposely blow some test?"

"Tell me?" she glared at him. "Tell *me*?" She pointed through the frosted glass door of his cubicle, presumably past Dr. Steinseifer's office to the hallways and classrooms beyond. "Tell *them*!"

Sandy massaged his almost bridgeless nose. "Tell them what, Rae?"

"Tell them, Mister. Cooper…." Rae leaned toward him. Her onyx eyes, almost Asian in shape, betrayed vulnerability. "Tell them to leave me alone."

A reasonable request, Sandy thought, but impossible to meet. In a school that was roughly divided between Italians and Jews with a few pale WASPS thrown in, Rae Henderson inevitably stood out. Dressed as she did unobtrusively, nothing could divert attention from Appleton's only African American student. And nothing could dilute the need of classmates and teachers alike, in the wake of the Civil Rights movement, to show tolerance.

It didn't help Rae that she was everything adolescents hanker to be: bright and athletic with lustrous skin and well-off parents who lived up the hill where the affluent neighbors worked even harder to accept them. Even

Wendell Barr showed deference, grunting in the lounge, "Well, at least she's not a spic."

Sandy yanked his tie once, twice. Frustrated by not having answers for her, he was bothered by the sense that he, too, was treating her differently. "Well," he tried, "you could start by you being you."

Rae shook her head.

"I mean, you could stop trying to live up to everyone's expectations. Figure out who you are and go with it."

"Go with it...."

"Wear what you want, talk like you want. Let your guard down a bit."

"Let my guard down...."

Sandy choked. What he was suggesting, he realized only too late, was that Rae should stop acting so white. He considered taking it back, began stuttering, but it was too late. She stood and yanked down her tennis shirt, jammed a book under one armpit, and stretched a defiant neck. Short of the cubicle's frosted-glass door, though, she paused and glanced over her shoulder.

"And you, Mister Cooper, do you ever let *your* guard down?" Rae affected a smile. "Do you ever just *go with it?*"

*   *   *   *   *

Why had she come to him? Sandy asked himself. Why did any of them? Sometimes he felt like a phony, prescribing tips that could just as easily hurt as help, pointing kids in directions that he, himself, would never tread. Other times, though, he recalled that young people only needed a neutral place to air their anxieties and a nonjudgmental adult to hear them. Other times, he was reminded of his duty.

That duty was pasted everywhere on his cubicle walls. Letters from students who, though washouts in junior high, went on to graduate college. Postcards from players he coached who now worked far away. Thank-you notes from grateful parents, a citation from the Chamber of Commerce. Such mementos inscribed a universe in which Sandy's place was secure. A place where he could still bring some good to the world if only he did his job.

He was thinking about his job and his inability to help Rae when he heard a sniveling sound. Somehow, Sandy knew who it was before he even looked up: Howard Weintraub. He stood in the entrance, his hair mussed, clothes rumpled, a bloody tissue clasped to his nose.

"Aw, Jeez," Sandy muttered as he pulled the kid inside by his wrist. "What happened?"

He already knew the answer. Up close, Howard looked even fatter than on stage, crammed into too-tight pants and a shirt he could barely button. The braces, the acne, his eyes muddy puddles behind glasses—all spelled misery. And there was something even more repellent. Sandy had a hard time pinning it but Howard, he sensed, *needed* to suffer. As if the humiliation during the school play, the embrace of Chrissie Esposito and its tumescent result, were pre-planned by Howard, intended to cause him shame.

But bullying was one thing and beating someone up was another. "Alright, don't tell me what happened. Tell me who did it."

Sandy offered him a fresh tissue and watched as Howard applied it first to his red-rimmed nostrils and then to his glasses, smudged with what looked like snot. Only then he said, "I'm no stoolie, Mister Cooper."

Where did they get words like that, Sandy wondered? TV, probably. "Of course you're not, Howard. Still, I think it might help you to tell me."

"Promise you won't do anything to him? Bad enough they call me a fag." Even his voice, a nasal singsong, was grating.

"Not a word."

"Okay…" Howard sighed. "Arthur Warhaftig."

Sandy groped mentally to place him—a new student, recently transferred from another school. Some mention of problems there as well, and family issues, but the exact ones remained vague. "Yes, of course, Arthur Warhaftig," Sandy lied. "What are we going to do about him?"

"Nothing."

"Nothing?"

Howard sobbed, "I can't tell on him. I can't stop him. I can't…" He abruptly paused. The tissue dropped and the eye-puddles froze. "I want to play football."

Sandy struggled not to laugh. A boy who had difficulty surviving recess, he wouldn't last a minute on the field. But could he tell him that? No, he preferred to let students make their own decisions, no matter how awful. Ultimately, hopefully, they'd grow.

"Okay. Come to the gym after school today. Tell the manager you want to suit up. I'll try you at…" Sandy thought for a minute. "Offensive guard."

The one position that required almost no skill, only a body big enough to stop a tackler—Sandy congratulated himself on the idea. Then, an instant later, regretted it. How could he be certain that this wasn't just another of Howard's set-ups, a plot in which he played both victim and trap? And was his guidance counselor foolish enough to fall for it?

But, once made, the suggestion could not be retracted. Already Howard was jubilant. "Great! Can't wait to hit and hit hard." He smacked a pudgy fist into his palm. "See you at practice, Coach."

Several moments passed before Sandy, alone again in his cubicle, registered that Howard had called him Coach. The thought of it made him queasy. So, too, did the prospect of another break in the teachers' lounge. Lunchtime, he took the sandwich that Esta had bagged for him and wandered out into the hall. He stood there, pylon-like, as students streamed toward the cafeteria.

Conformity and contradiction, that's how Sandy saw them. From an undifferentiated flow of high-energy, minimally attentive juveniles, adolescents diverged into categories. The blemished and the creamy-skinned, the strait-laced and the drugged. The ex-virgins too young to talk about it and Romeos too egotistical not to. The one or two who would later drop out due to pregnancy, succumb to overdoses or illnesses or drunken driving, or who, like Vincent Delgado, a competent linebacker Sandy once mentored, would be killed in some overseas war. But the bulk would go on to high school and maybe college and from there to marriage, children, affairs, crises, holidays, work, and, if they were lucky, old age.

Sandy watched as they stampeded past him and wanted to bark at them, "Stop! Stop and grab hold of a locker or a fire extinguisher, anything to keep you in place." Beyond the pizza burgers and mac n' cheese or whatever crap they were serving today was the gristly potluck of life. As tough as junior high school could be, he longed to inform them, it's kindergarten compared to what's next.

* * * * *

Preparing students for what's next was the purpose of Appleton. Erected in the late 1950s, the school provided sixth graders with a three-year runway before taking off for the tenth. The building was rectangular and broad but with constricted windows to discourage daydreaming. Orange brick outside and beige linoleum within, sepulchral bathrooms and echo-haunted halls. Scents of bubble gum, Palmolive, and Prell. An institution that presented itself precisely as it was: an interim stage between hopscotch and road rallies, hide-and-go-seek and proms. A holding pen, a no-age land, no sooner exited than forgotten.

From the flow of pupils surging to lunch, a single voice called out, "Hiya, Mister Cooper!" And another, "Mister Cooper, hey!" Less benevolently, from somewhere behind him, came, "If it ain't the Roach Coach," and "Coop the poop."

These were the most onerous years, when kids were deprived of childhood's innocence, yet expected to show grown-up restraint. If pubescents ran the world, atrocities would be commonplace. That barbarism was on display as Sandy crossed the cafeteria and headed outside to a yard. Footballs and frisbees lacerated the air and curses poisoned it. Girls bickered, boys brawled. Disturbing, yes, but still Sandy needed to see it occasionally to witness the malice firsthand. It gave context to the suffering he encountered every day in his cubicle. It helped to rekindle his compassion.

The sky was overcast and the wind had picked up in the season's first chilly day. Wishing he had brough his jacket, Sandy nevertheless remained in the fray of the recess yard, searching for someone in particular. It took a few minutes but he found him, finally, standing in a patch of weeds the janitors had forgotten to mow.

Not standing, really, but whirling and kicking, hands slicing in movements Sandy recognized from a popular television show about Kung Fu. His clothes were fancier than those worn by most of the students, even the richer ones, but oddly large for him. His long hair hung in greasy strands. More than recognizing him, Sandy intuited who he was. Whatever his problems at home, they were enough to drive Arthur Warhaftig to this place, beyond the realms of popular and unpopular, outside the cliques, alone.

"Good moves," the counselor, approaching, observed.

Arthur merely shrugged and continued chopping.

"You make that up or are you taking lessons?"

Another shrug followed by a hand motion that, for a split second, pulled back his hair. Sandy caught sight of a clean jaw and delicate lips, a nose finely crafted—a beautiful face in the process of becoming handsome. Only his eyes seemed out-of-place, at once distant and fixed but with vibrating pupils, as if they were seeking escape.

"My dad showed me," Arthur offered. "He learned it in the war." The boy's voice was pre-pubescent and high, so soft that Sandy strained to hear it.

"A hero, then."

"Yeah. A *big* hero."

"And you want to be like him."

A roundhouse kick. A punch. His movements, unlike his voice, were potent. "Someday."

"Someday, I'm sure. People aren't born heroes, you know, they become them."

Just where was he going with this conversation, Sandy wasn't certain. The difficulty here wasn't self-image, he gathered, but something much deeper, a trauma perhaps. Though Arthur looked like one of the hippies, he wasn't part of their circle, nor of the egg-heads' or the jocks'. No friends that Sandy noticed, no one to invite him to confirmations and Bar Mitzvahs.

No, Sandy's goal was simpler than figuring out who Arthur was. He needed to learn what brought this seemingly harmless boy to beat the crap out of Howard Weintraub. Discover what—or who—made Arthur mad.

"You're new here at Appleton, yeah? People treating you okay? Teachers? Classmates?"

Arthur dropped into a feline crouch, tried and failed to lunge. "Fine."

"Good. Good. And you're not getting into any fights? I mean, I wouldn't want to be on the receiving end of those chops."

In a carryover gesture from grade school, Arthur raised a shoulder to his cheek, and in a child's voice he protested, "I never hit anybody."

"Glad to hear," Sandy humored him. "But what say you come in to see me sometime? Any time. We can just talk things over, you and me. Man to man."

But Arthur just went on jabbing and felling imaginary foes. Sandy was about to leave him when he thought he heard a whisper. Between grunts, "Okay," the eighth-grader said.

Though nearly shivering, Sandy was not ready to return to his cubicle. He continued, rather, beyond the yard to the football field. Standing between the hashmarks, he tried to remember being Arthur's age more than a quarter-century ago, before the concept of "teenager" fully crystallized. Those years were still considered a dry run for adulthood, when college was not a certainty and marriage between sweethearts understood. That was especially true for working class kids like Sandy whose father, while hardly laboring in a sweatshop, still put in long hours selling suits. Sure, there were milkshakes at Wexler's Drug Store and knishes at Sobotnik's. There were senior dances and homecoming games and getting pinned. But much of these experiences were considered ultimate, not preliminary. After them, linear and predictable, lay life.

He sauntered toward a goalpost. How many times had he galloped under one of those uprights, planted his knee, and raised the ball in triumph? The answer was twenty-three and Sandy remembered each one. The delirium of sensing defensemen pursuing futilely behind him, the cheers, the drums booming—this in the days before marching bands, just drums. Esta bouncing on the sidelines and his father bundled in his houndstooth coat, silent but proud.

Sandy laughed at himself, bitterly. Fool, he thought, giving in to this autumn wistfulness. And yet for a second he couldn't help wondering if the passage of time was not, in fact, illusory. Maybe he was not so altered but remained as he was—as he saw himself in that moonlit moment—unchained?

The end of recess bell sounded but Sandy lingered on the field. He ate his sandwich—tuna fish, not the way he liked it, slathered in mayo with a dollop of mustard, but as Esta preferred, mostly dry. He was down to the crust and attempting to swallow when he felt someone approaching his back. Reflexively, he swerved, only to confront Jeanne Pagonis.

She appeared even smaller than she did in the lounge, almost stunted. Wrapped in a brown trench coat, her cropped hair tucked into its raised collar, she seemed to draw into herself even as she neared. "I didn't mean to startle you," she began. "I just wanted a word, you know, in private."

Sandy nodded and swallowed. But if he thought Jeanne had come to flirt again, her next remarks disabused him. "I saw you talking with the Warhaftig boy. He's in my homeroom class and I think there's something wrong."

He tried to recall what subject Jeanne taught—English literature, Algebra? History, perhaps. "Wrong?"

"Well, not wrong exactly, but…different. He acts out a lot but otherwise keeps to himself. A loner. Until somebody or something lights his fuse. Then…" Her tiny hands flew up and splayed. "Bam!"

"Bam."

"And I've heard there's trouble at home. Part of why he trans-ferred schools."

The wind flipped Sandy's tie into his face. He whisked it away and at the same time took a hard look at Jeanne. She was dark, exotically so, with an overbite and mole-studded cheeks. Pagonis was her last name—Greek most likely, which would explain the Orthodox cross. And this softness, a fragility that needed guarding. Hugging? In the split-second that it took to smooth out his tie, Sandy calculated that Jeanne was far closer in age to their students than to him. His own body had thickened and his sideburns turned white. The hitch in his leg had worsened. He pictured himself pining for his old football glory and fantasizing about Jeanne and thought once again, "You fool."

Jeanne was still talking. "I tried looking into it but nobody in school seems to know. Or wants to tell. Maybe you could…" Her words were lost in a gust.

"What?"

"Investigate!" Jeanne hollered.

"Okay. Sure."

"Okay. Sure," Jeanne awkwardly repeated. She seemed aware suddenly of the impropriety of cornering a senior staff member outdoors. But that didn't prevent her from reminding him that the bell had rung and chiding him, "Really, Coop, you should wear a coat."

* * * * *

The word "fool" needled him throughout practice that afternoon. Jeanne, he realized, was not interested in him romantically but only filially, a girl perhaps spurned by her own parents. And like so many young people, she perceived his need to mentor. Esta often joked with him about that. "You don't have to be everyone's father," she'd laugh, though behind the chuckle he discerned a lament. After all, he *had* been somebody's father.

Fortunately, Sandy had Russel Pressman to distract him. Though Tony Metallo, the slow-witted center, still couldn't memorize the counts, he could be occupied with showing the basics—the three-point stance, body block-ing—to Howard Weintraub. The fat kid had indeed reported to the gym and received his uniform, pads, and helmet. He wore them clumsily now, gagging on the mouth guard, as Anthony sent him careening into a dummy. The sight was pathetic but at least it freed up the coach to focus on his quarterback.

Russel was not only Sandy's favorite, but the prize of several prep schools scouting him. It's wasn't just his arm or his sprinting abilities, but his cool headedness under pressure. In the huddle, in the locker room bucking up his team, Russel was unflappable. On or off the field, Russel led.

And Sandy's job was to let him. Like the sculptor who liberates his statue from stone, he saw himself chipping away at the last chunks of encumbering doubt. He wanted to help him emerge fully formed and resplendent, a classic at age fourteen.

Russel seemed to know it. He reveled in it, his eyes almost level with Sandy's. "Yes, Coach! You got it, Coach!" he would snap, crisp as a new recruit.

The coach put him through his drills: passing, open-field running, changing plays mid-count. He pressed him hard, near to the breaking point, Sandy sometimes feared. But Russel never broke or even came close. Instead, he received each instruction with a wag of his strawberry hair and a freckle-scattering grin.

Licking the back of his fingertips—another trademark—one set after another, Sandy sent Russel out deep. The kid could also catch, and not just footballs. He could dribble, pitch, bunt, and shoot—a triple-letter athlete who shone equally on courts and diamonds. His report cards were matchless, his parents well-off. An up-the-hill kid with everything going for him, he now ran a sweeping deep hook as Sandy cocked back his arm and planted his good leg forward. The result was a pass arching well beyond reach until Russel suddenly shot skyward. He hung there, frozen for seconds it seemed, before making the catch while Sandy looked on, awestruck.

Later, when he'd whistled the boys to the locker room and even Howard Weintraub managed to lumber off the field, Sandy remained. In the breezy dusk, he hoped for another glimpse of the self he had seen on that first autumn night. Even a peek. But no, all he saw was a star demanding attention and an airplane's lonesome wink. He was just Sandy Cooper, guidance counselor and coach, wiping his hands on a ratty sweatshirt.

*   *   *   *   *

Tuesday evenings after practice, Sandy joined Esta at Temple Beth El. Located down Union Street from the junior high, across from the fire house, the synagogue marked the halfway point between the up and downhill sections of town. Its design was median as well, gray cinderblock halls. Here, the Coopers attended High Holiday services and the occasional wedding, and here they augmented their income by running the post-Bar Mitzvah youth program. Yet more early teens.

Fortunately, they did not have to teach sewing or guide them in life, but merely keep them occupied with recreational games and crafts. No competition, no violence certainly, and minimal oversight, requiring a single supervisor—most often Esta—which left her husband to wander if he liked, browse through the library or poke around in the kitchen. It was the night that Sandy liked best. Thinking time.

He thought about little questions, not big ones. Like what, for instance, was he to make of Jeanne Pagonis, and what trouble had brought Arthur Warhaftig to Appleton? How would he keep Russel Pressman focused on his game and avoid unnecessary injuries? He pondered these issues while passing the booze-scented door to Rabbi Isaacson's study and the Hebrew school drawings—shofars and Torahs, a floating Moses—tacked to a board. Sandy wondered what Moses was really like, a man who, though overwhelmed with difficulties, pressed on. And what had turned a learned man, by contrast, to drink?

Fleeing the echoes of Esta's dodgeball game, Sandy paced deeper into the hallways. Not raised religious in any way, reading his Bar Mitzvah in English letters and earning his father's frown, he now guiltlessly ate bacon and shrimp. And yet here, in the temple, Sandy felt reverent. As if the corkboard ceilings and cold vinyl floors were somehow sanctified, the antiseptic smells an incense. He shuffled solemnly on his gum-soled shoes, even when entering the kitchen.

With its monolithic freezers and altar-like tables, this space seemed especially divine. And blessings could indeed be found in the form of a bagel and whitefish platter left over from the Men's Club or an orphaned wedge of wedding cake. Sandy went scrummaging and came up with a bowl of egg salad and some saltine crackers, a respectable snack. He shoveled and crunched, squinting in the neon.

"There's some grape juice in the pantry."

Sandy flinched. "Jesus…."

"Unless you want some schnapps. In which case, it's under the sink."

He didn't know which was stranger, the sight of a large Black man emerging from the shadows with a dustpan and a broom, or the presence of any Black man in a synagogue, at night, offering him schnapps. Either way, Sandy gulped. "You nearly choked me, Louis."

"Wouldn't want to do that, would we, Mister Cooper?" Louis laid his cleaning tools in the utility closet and wiped his hands on a rag. "To think, entire generations of young people left guideless."

Louis, the custodian, had worked at Beth El for as long as Sandy remembered, and reportedly had been there before. The kids loved him, the adults respected him, a bulky yet warmhearted man who remembered everyone's name and issues. "How's your mother feeling today, Mister Zimmerman?" he'd inquire, or offer, "Don't look so anxious, Dougie, I'm sure you'll ace that test." Yet nobody, Sandy included, knew where Louis came from or where exactly he lived. Wife, children, any past—all were mysteries that the congregants never probed. If he'd been white, perhaps, some might have wondered why a man wearing Oxford shirts and chinos, so eloquent and kind, was cleaning the bathrooms in a *shul*.

"Guideless?" Sandy's eyebrows rose. "I don't know. Maybe better off."

"Give yourself more credit, Mister Cooper. There are people who owe you their life."

Sandy studied him. His broad face contained lips that were big but delicately defined and a nose that, though never broken, was even wider than Sandy's. His lichen-like hair was clipped close to the scalp. His deep-set eyes eluded scrutiny.

"Christ, Louis, you make me want to retire while I'm ahead."

Reaching into a cabinet, the custodian produced some wine. "You're always ahead, aren't you?" Louis asked, not expecting a response. Nor did he wait for one before filling two paper shot glasses and proffering one to Sandy. "L'chaim," he toasted.

"L'chaim," Sandy repeated, noting that Louis's pronunciation was better than his. The wine was ceremonial and tasted like cough syrup, but the guidance counselor was grateful. It had been a long and confusing day, and he wished he could share his dilemmas with Louis. He wished he could quiz him about Rae Henderson. What did it feel like to be a person of color around people who weren't, and a colored person who—how could he frame this?—dressed and spoke like him? Instead, Sandy noted, "You're here late."

"I prefer to be on my own now and then. Like you." Louis swigged and scowled. "Only I do it and clean up."

"Oh, I do some cleaning alright, Louis. I'm just not as good as you."

The custodian indulgently smiled. "Might I suggest, Mister Cooper, you go and get yourself a broom?"

Sandy laughed and washed the last of the egg salad down with wine. Then, with a shake of Louis's hand, he continued his wanderings. Not much of Beth El remained, though. Invariably, he found himself standing before huge, wrought-iron doors that might've required a giant to push. Yet they swung open easily enough, soundlessly, into the temple's sanctuary.

Pine wood pews, stained glass depictions of biblical scenes too abstract to identify, a blood-red Eternal Flame burning electrically in its sconce. If the kitchen were hallowed, this was the holy of holies. Not that he frequented it much outside of the High Holidays or understood a word of what he recited. Nevertheless, alone at night with only the sound of his breath and his heartbeat in his ears, Sandy could almost feel spiritual.

He entered solemnly and sat. Around him were walls lined with three-inch plaques, each one etched with a name. "In Loving Memory of Max and Silvia Eisenstein," one said, and another, "For My Sister, Freda Hirsh, Who Died in Auschwitz." There must have been hundreds. Sandy tried to imagine their lives, their joys, and ultimate suffering. But his attention drifted from the memorials and up to the pulpit that still reeked of Rabbi's Isaacson's Scotch, behind the lectern to the ark.

Framed between American and Israeli flags, this too was inscribed, with lions rather than words. Rolling back the panels revealed velvet curtains and, behind them, the scrolls with their silver crowns and satin. Sandy found something spooky about it, all that wisdom trapped in darkness. Someone should let it out.

Only one wall was empty except for a quote. From the Bible, Sandy figured, probably a psalm, in wooden letters painted in gold. "*The Lord is Near to All Who Call on Him,*" it said, "*To All Who Call on Him in Truth.*" He questioned whether *this* was true. How many people called but remained unanswered? How many called and died?

Sitting upright suddenly, he realized how long he'd been wandering. Esta would be irked. He cast one last glance upward toward the ceiling, at the plexiglass bubble in its center. This supposedly supplied a glimpse of God, but the surface was too weather-stained and the sky beyond it blackened. Still, he considered praying—for his late mother, maybe, or Joey. A prayer for Russel Pressman's success or even for Howard Weintraub's survival. But instead Sandy rose from the pew and escaped through the wrought-iron doors. Down the corridor he trundled, to the reception hall that doubled as a gym.

The screams and bongs of dodgeball had been replaced by silent scrawling. The youth group participants—the nerdiest in their schools, not an athlete among them—were on their knees drawing autumn landscapes. Esta strolled between them, oohing. The platinum beehive, the pantsuit let out in the rump, she still looked precious to him. Coquettish and spry, as if she might at any moment throw off her dumpiness and leap up cheering, "Touchdown!"

He lingered at the entrance and waited for her to notice him. And she did, eventually, her eyes rising to meet his, her lips still pursed in an O. The expression hung for a second before reconfiguring into others—a smirk, a frown, a succession of smiles. A display as sparkling as fireworks.

3.

It happened too fast for even Sandy, his reflexes still keen, to prevent. A second after Tony Metallo snapped the ball into the V of Russel Pressman's hands, the tackles burst through the offensive line. Sandy blew his whistle, calling off the play, and already knew who to blame. It didn't help the quarterback, sacked by his own teammates. His coach had to peel them off, yelling, "Enough! Enough already!" and all the while checking if Russel was hurt. He wasn't, fortunately, just shaken up, but Sandy fumed. His eyes hunted the culprit.

He stood apart from the line, self-incriminating. Helmet lowered, Howard Weintraub all but advertised his guilt. Sandy glowered at him. All he had to do was stand there with his tub of a body and stop the rush, but the kid didn't block at all. He merely collapsed into a lump that was easily vaulted or sidestepped. What did he care if his captain, receiving the ball only a few feet away, was crushed?

Sandy cared. He stomped toward the guard who trembled and tried to step back. "Goddammit, Weintraub! Are you going to play or you going to pussy out?" He hated losing his temper this way, but seeing Russel flattened infuriated him.

"I'm sorry…Coach."

And he hated hearing Howard call him Coach, a privilege reserved for athletes. "Okay. Okay. You want to know what it feels like? I'll show you what it feels like." He flipped Howard the ball.

The boy glared at the parabola in his hands as if it were ticking. "You want me to…?"

"Quarterback," Sandy informed him. "Snap's on five."

The players fell into position. Tickled by being included in the coach's joke, they traded winks and giggled as Howard rattled off some numbers.

"Thirty...twenty-six...eighteen...."

Russel, standing in for Tony, didn't wait for the "five" before hiking the ball. Howard took it, hugged it, and began running—backward, away from the onslaught of tacklers let purposely through the line. First to the right and then backwards the husky boy scampered, but not for long before all eleven defenders pounced on him. Tore him to the ground and heaped on him, a mound of body armor.

Yet Sandy didn't blow his whistle. Rather, he let a long second pass and then another, all the while gazing up at the reddening sky pierced by an arrowhead of birds. This wasn't about revenge, he persuaded himself, but about Howard's education. And it almost worked, until he heard the cries.

"Okay. Everybody off," he ordered, but the team took its time obeying. Even when freed, Howard remained spread-eagled on the turf. Sandy looked down at him with an expression of disdain before hauling him to his feet by his shoulder pads. Howard's whole body was shuddering and the eyes behind his glasses drizzled. The boy, Sandy realized, was sobbing. But still, he was curt. "Know how it feels now, son?" He slapped Howard's helmet. "Now get back into position, goddamnit, and block!"

* * * * *

The incident left Sandy unnerved. Long after he left the gym, driving home in his Impala, it stayed with him. In truth, he was uncertain what bothered him more: his tantrum at Howard or his fear that Russel was hurt. They were linked, he knew, but that knowledge only further unsettled him. Yet he didn't mention it that night at dinner—a pork-and-rice casserole rendered Chinese by duck sauce—or even when roused from his recliner for bed. He lay awake thinking about it, replaying it in his mind while the wind buffeted the house.

Only that Sunday, after handball at the Y, did he bring it up with Saps. Arnold Saperstein, his friend since grammar school, who attended the same regional high two towns over and still lived on the same street they grew up on. Who didn't go to college but instead joined the Appleton police, making sergeant and remaining there, content. A dowdy wife named Marjorie, a bookkeeper, and two boys interested only in model cars. Tough and dependable, no bullshit and kind. Saps.

So kind, in fact, that he let Sandy win at least one game per week. Usually the last, when Sandy was limping and hard-pressed to reach any ball. It didn't surprise him when, after licking his hands and serving, the cop made a show of tripping and missing the shot completely.

"You threw that away!"

"Like hell I did," Saps protested.

Bent over his knees and huffing, he tried to hide his smile, but Sandy caught sight of it. Over the smack of rubber on walls, footfalls, and grunts, he blew a kiss at his best and only real friend. "Go fuck yourself," he said.

The topic of Howard and Russel had to wait, though, until after they removed their sweat-darkened Appleton Rams and Appleton PAL t-shirts, showered, and drove to Sobotnik's. Located on Union Street halfway between the school and the temple, the deli had always been there, a magical source of halva and fat sour pickles for kids, and, for adults, the Sunday special. There, in a rear alcove crammed with two-customer tables, over pastrami on rye and sodas, Sandy felt secure enough to speak. Was wanting success for one student obscuring his responsibilities toward another, he asked? Was he being selfish or even negligent?

"What you're being is a guy who does his job," Saps responded between chews. He didn't so much eat as assault his sandwich, gutting it between his fists.

"You wouldn't go that easy on a suspect."

Looking up with one closed eye, a strand of coleslaw stuck to his lower lip, Saps drilled him. "Suspected of what, exactly? Being a hopelessly decent guy with an outdated sense of duty?"

Sandy picked at his meal. Beneath that receding hairline and a head so narrow that service caps wobbled on it, he knew, lay Sap's incisive mind.

"Okay, you want to know the truth? I'll give you truth," the policeman went on while shaking out more salt. "The quarterback, Pressman—he's what you were. What you wanted to be. And that other one, the fasto…"

"Weintraub."

"What you're afraid of becoming."

"Brilliant." Sandy slapped the table. "You should have been a shrink."

Brandishing a pickle spear, Saps agreed, "And you should've been my patient."

A silence followed that neither of them, friends for so many years, felt compelled to fill. Not that there was a shortage of noise—of plates clanging in the kitchen, knives chopping, calls for more chopped liver. Behind the counter, Bernie, a man so obese he strained his apron, served tubs of white-fish to customers carrying newspapers from Wexler's Drugs next door or a babka from Hershkey's Bakery. A Manischewitz calendar on the walls, the miniature vats of mustard, relish, and *chrain*. A fan, frozen as an old clock, on the ceiling.

Sandy lamented, "Someday, this world will disappear."

"Yeah, well," Saps swallowed, "they all do."

* * * * *

Sandy had said goodbye to Saps, scarcely expecting to see him the very next morning at school. But there he was behind its back wall, uniformed and scribbling in his notebook. Sandy wanted to rib him about his too-big hat, remind him that he still owed him two bucks for brunch. All he said, though, was "Shit."

He spoke softly so that Dr. Steinseifer, standing on the recess field nearby, wouldn't hear, but Saps announced, "Shit it is!"

They were both looking at the wall and words spray-painted across it. The scrawl was magnified by a coat of frost—the season's first—and by the color: flaming pink. Yet, even without embellishment, the message was stark. *Fuck the Jews.*

"Kids, yeah?" Sandy surmised, but Saps withheld judgement.

"Kids or someone trying to make it look like kids."

Sandy immediately thought of Wendell Barr who should have been the first on the scene. But the vice principal for discipline was curiously missing, and only Steinseifer showed up, dour as ever. Buoy-shaped, bespectacled, he observed the scene from within clouds of his own breath. His only movement was a flick of the wrists indicating, once again, that Sandy had to act.

"And who would do such a thing?" Sandy asked. "For Chrissakes, it's 1971."

The comment earned him another of Saps's one-eyed leers. "Grow up, Coop," he snarled.

They both remembered what it was like in the neighborhood with the Italian and Irish kids who detested one another but allied in fighting the

Jews. They both had learned early to use their mitts—Sandy took boxing at the Y—picking out the biggest bully and bloodying his nose so that the rest could see that the Hebes meant business. By high school, though, those same enemies became pals and the fistfights gave way to sports and double dates. And then prejudice went out of fashion. Except for throwbacks like Wendell Barr, bigots belonged to the past.

But now this graffiti and the prejudice it spelled. Jacketless, pushing up his shirtsleeves, Sandy looked dispirited. "I suppose you could check the hardware stores. See if anybody bought this shade."

"Suppose I could," Sergeant Saperstein concurred. He removed his cap and drew a sleeve across his narrow forehead. "And I suppose I could tell Captain Rizzo that I'm off for a week in Bermuda."

Saps laughed acidly but his friend barely nodded. He was already calculating what kind of solvent, if any, removed spray paint from brick. And it would have to work fast. In only four hours, hundreds of students would charge out on the field expecting recess only to be met by hate.

The incident should have dominated the conversation in the teachers' lounge that day but didn't. Garrulous about everything except his inability to get into graduate school, Stevens, the seventh-grade science teacher, said nothing. Neither did the math instructors McGonnigle and Bronowski. The first seemed choked by the psychedelic bandana around his throat, the second compressed by the weight of his own anvil-shaped head. D'Angelis, freshly inflated from his workout, mixed his power lunch of bone meal and Ovaltine, and even Charlotte "Foxy" Fox who, as the resident sixties holdover, might have been expected to protest, remained mute. No one wanted to mention much less denounce the perpetrator, as if doing so would affirm his existence.

Sandy, too, preferred not to talk. His hands smarted from the turpentine he and three janitors used to scrub the wall, and his thigh still ached from the cold. He preferred to dwell on that Saturday's opening game against South Central. The only mostly Black junior high in the conference, an athletic powerhouse, they were slated to trounce Appleton, but Sandy wasn't concerned. His only thought was of Russel Pressman and how many yards he'd might pick up. Prep school scouts were expected to be watching and maybe even a far-sighted college recruiter. Irrespective of the final score, his quarterback had to shine.

"I'm sorry, Coop."

Shaken out of deep contemplation, for a second Sandy was unsure of where he was. Then the lounge came into focus along with the awkwardly silent faculty. A half-empty coffee cup quivered in his hand. Lastly came Jeanne's face—warm, comely—looking down at him on the sofa. Sincerely, he asked, "Sorry for what?"

Jeanne's eyes sought out the floor, an overbite took in her lip. "You know. The desecration." The word was reduced to several syllables and whispered.

"But why be sorry for *me*?"

Belatedly, he realized that she was asking forgiveness for all the gentiles on the staff and that his question embarrassed her. Her face darkened as she anxiously fingered her cross. Now it was he who wanted to apologize.

Before he could, fortunately, Jeanne changed the subject. "Did you ever get a look at Arthur Warhaftig's record?" Sandy looked blank. "In my home-room class, remember, the new boy? That family trouble—did you ever look into it?"

"Damn, I've just been so busy with the team and everything, preparing it for the game...Totally slipped my mind."

"No problem. No rush." They were taking turns apologizing. "He's acting out again, that's all. One day sitting by himself in some corner, the next picking fights. When you get a chance, let me know."

"Of course, Jeanne. I'll make a mental note of it."

He did, only to have displaced by fantasies of Jeanne, of Russel Pressman out-sprinting defenders downfield. And hovering over them all, the memory of those three venomous words—*Fuck the Jews*—shouted in pink.

After lunch break, drifting out of the lounge, Sandy noted the black-and-gold banners emblazoned with "Go Rams" and "Beat South Central," the cheerleaders chanting "A-P-P-L-E-T-O-N, spell it louder, spell it again!" He watched the ebb and flow of students on their way to class, a current not even hatred could stem. And finally, he caught sight of Wendell.

Illuminated by one of the school's few windows, he stood strategically at the juncture of several hallways, handing out detentions. The vice principal noticed the guidance counselor looking at him and trawled his fingers over his buzz-cut. His eyes, today the color of gun metal, narrowed, and his strop of a mouth grinned. Sandy wanly smiled back while recalling that Wendell alone had been absent from the lounge. Had he also spent the morning scouring, Sandy speculated, cleansing his hands of paint?

* * * * *

Such suspicions virtually disappeared by Saturday, though, along with the memory of that wall. Replacing them was the field, freshly limed, and the stands teeming with parents and schoolmates and local residents who had nothing better to do on weekends. A home game, the scoreboard declared, "Welcome South Central," though their fans could hardly have felt snug. Bused in from the county's poorest neighborhood, they stood out from across the fifty-yard line as a somberly clad mass, chanting in a syncopation alien to Appleton's fight songs. Their cheerleaders rocked, the players strutted.

The image was intimidating, but Sandy fought to ignore it. So, too, he resisted the urge to think about those watching from the bleachers: Saps and Dr. Steinseifer, Wendell and much of the staff. He didn't search for Esta, discernible in her fake rabbit fur coat and hat, and Jeanne seated inconspicuously nearby. Why should he feel guilty, he asked himself? So what if they met? But then another question intruded, this time from the ref: "Heads or tails, Coach?"

He lost the toss and, returning a flaccid kick, the visitors ran for a touchdown. Sandy displayed disappointment but not shock. As he had told the team in their pre-game prep talk, the defense should do its best, no more, but the offensive line would have to excel. Give Russel time to launch one of his bombs or to end-run into the open, he promised, and Appleton would make the board.

And they did, twice, by halftime, though South Central scored as well. Sandy scarcely cared. Russel was in ultimate form, handing off and lateraling, charging up the middle and, of course, passing. His arm was a catapult. Though down by twenty points, he never lost his composure. On the contrary, adversity sparked him. His coach's eyes, meanwhile, darted between the scrimmage and the stands where scouts were no doubt scribbling.

By the last quarter, the lopsided lead had widened, but so did Russel's repertoire. With nothing to lose, he experimented with fakes and sneaks, even a pooch punt, to Sandy's joy. Pacing just out of bounds, he had removed his team jacket and unfastened his tie and cuffs. Already he saw Russel at the Rose Bowl and then on some professional roster. He saw him leaving Appleton and never once looking back, except to visit his mentor.

A whistle exploded his reverie. Player down on the field. Sandy hitched out to where Metallo lay, grunting and clutching his knee. "Shit," the coach started to hiss but managed to stretch it out to "Sheet." Still, the ref barked at him and told him to send in a replacement. The only one available was Amster, the right guard, who had some hiking experience. But this meant resorting to the bench.

Sandy squinted at the side lines. Here was the chance, he now allowed himself to think, to make amends for that pile-on in practice, and for the boy to redeem himself. And, with only five minutes remaining, what harm could he cause?

"Weintraub," he shouted, tossing a thumb over his shoulder. "You're in."

Perhaps for the first time looking up from his knees, the boy was nonplussed. Again, his coach's thumb pumped. "Waiting for an invitation? Now!"

With coronation-like pomp, Howard donned his helmet, yanked on the facemask, and lumbered onto the field. Sandy slapped him on the butt and spat, "Give 'em hell!" What he meant, though, was "Please, for once, keep him safe."

The "him," of course, was Russel, but from the first down, Sandy suspected, safety was not realistic. A full second before the snap, Howard flinched forward, off-sides. He then found himself on his back and flailing while a player half his size stretched on top of him elbowing and kneeing. Behind the whistles and boos, Sandy clearly heard, "Honky, I'm gonna make your ass look like grass!" He paced miserably while the refs pulled the defenseman off his guard. That scene was mortifying enough. The next would haunt him.

The following play, a simple draw, began without incident and even augured some gain. But then, in a splintered instant, disaster. That same fire plug of a tackle blitzed through to Russel, caught him midsection, and lifted him off the ground. The quarterback folded and collapsed.

Sandy didn't wait for the whistle. He didn't wait for the volunteer doctor to accompany him but burst onto the field hollering, "Time out!" He arrived to find Russel conscious but winded and dazed, requiring two sets of hands to upright him. They staggered off with Russel leaning on Sandy, to the home crowd's applause. With her fake rabbit fur hat in her fists, Esta hopped to her feet. Jeanne and Wendell, Saps and Steinseifer—all united for a single moment, cheering.

But Sandy didn't notice. He was fixating on whether Russel had sustained a concussion or some other injury that would force him to sit out the season. Or worse. But these emotions competed with another, no less overpowering. Stomping into the shower room, it was all he could do to keep from punching a locker, so immense was his anger at Howard.

* * * * *

"Stop beating yourself up, sweetie," Esta exhorted him later that week. "The doctor said he was fine. Kids get the wind knocked out of them now and then—you know that—and then they snap back. Like rubber bands." She was serving him fried scallops from a can and spinach patties topped with processed cheese, placing a napkin in his lap and a fork in his hand, irrepressibly chipper. But Sandy was having none of it, the food nor the glee.

He sat, rather, fuming as he had for two days now, ever since the game. His anger, he knew, was irrational, disproportionate to the crime. Crime? That Howard couldn't block and Russel got sacked? That was life. Failure and downfall were followed, one hoped, by resilience. Why then the funk? Esta was right, Sandy conceded. He had to let it go.

Yet at regaining composure, Sandy failed as well. After stewing in his recliner for a while, he pushed past the newel post and stormed up the creaky stairs to the bathroom, furiously brushing his teeth. From there, he plowed into the bedroom but then, abruptly, turned back. "No," he ordered himself, only to be ignored. More irrepressible than his anger was the draw of the room down the hall.

The trophies, the megaphone—all appeared frozen in the sudden light. Only the bear appeared larger in some way, as if only recently stuffed. Sandy violated his long-standing rule and lifted it. The eyes were buttons and the mouth a crescent of beads, yet the toy possessed a human spark or so he imagined. Holding it up, he questioned whether it was really a bear or some other animal, maybe a groundhog or a chimp. And was that mold on its paws or was Sandy only obsessing? One thing, though, remained unaltered. "Joey," spelled the Yankee-blue stitching on its chest. Joey.

For how long exactly he cradled that bear wasn't certain. Only that at some point he made a vow. Not to let the tragedies of the past cloud his present thinking. Russel Pressman was not the young Sandy Cooper, nor was Howard his fate. They were just junior high schoolers caught between the shoals of growing up, and his job was to help them navigate. His duty, Sandy reminded himself as he returned the stuffed animal to the shelf and switched off the light, was sometimes just to step back.

The conviction lasted three days, until the morning when he woke from turbulent dreams. These featured familiar images—the back of Sobotnik's Deli, the trophy room in his house—but also people he couldn't quite place, distant and marginally hostile. The only known figure was Jeanne Pagonis but not the Jeanne he knew from school. In place of the demure young woman in boyish clothes was a vamp. Naked, her enormous breasts tipped upward at the nipples, and her pubic hair appeared woven from silk. He pressed his body against her, groping and panting but unable to penetrate. "One more chance," he kept begging. "Just one."

Thrashing awake, Sandy became aware, first, of the sheets and pillows mangled on his side of the bed, and then of the erection tenting the covers. He considered putting it to use with Esta, snuffling in the darkness with her jaw slackened and hands folded over her paunch. But then he remembered the dream and felt guilt-stricken. Curling toward the wall, he waited for the alarm to ring.

He arrived at school in a sour mood that only blackened when the volunteer sports doctor called. Russel could not suit up for a week. Though he checked out just fine, the physician explained, a still-growing boy should not be taking chances. Sandy thanked him, inhaled, and slammed down the phone.

In the lounge, later, he avoided contact with the other teachers, especially Jeanne Pagonis. He couldn't look at her without seeing that dream and so averted his eyes. She, too, kept to herself, as if hurt by his indifference, lunching on the Formica table.

So the afternoon dragged on. Eighth and ninth-graders talked about the usual fourteenand fifteen-year-old fears only to receive absentminded answers. He listened with upturned palms, affording a view of his watch. Even football practice plodded. With Russel in his school clothes and watching from the endzone, the drills seemed lifeless. Sandy wished it were over with so that he could drive out of the parking lot and head home, but then again, to what? Another underdone or overcooked meal, another nap in his recliner until Esta woke him for bed?

Nevertheless, entering the coaches' office, Sandy rushed to remove his sweatshirt and retrieve his tie from a hook. Perhaps tonight he would make love to Esta, if for no other reason than to repent for the sins of his dreams. The thought excited him enough to send him hurrying out of the door, but just then Howard confronted him. In his uniform, padded and fat, he blocked the exit. Sandy could not even squeeze by.

"What is it now?" he snapped.

"I quit. I'm quitting the team."

Not tragic, this news. Still, Sandy asked, "Why?"

"I got beat up."

Only then did Sandy notice it. The swelling behind Howard's lenses, the blood showing between his teeth.

"Where did this happen?"

"In the shower room. He said I was a sissy. So he threw me into a locker and lifted up my shoulder pads to my neck. 'I hate you! I just hate you!' he yelled at me and punched me all over."

Howard clearly relished relating his story, but suddenly Sandy fretted. "He?"

"He? Who else could it be, Coach?" The fat boy feigned surprise. "Russel Pressman."

Surprise or, maybe, triumph. It occurred to Sandy that, for Howard, getting bashed by the Arthur Warhaftigs of the world didn't suffice. For a lover of suffering, only the finest oppressor would do. For that reason, rather than showing sympathy, Sandy fumed.

"You know what, Howard?" he grumbled. "Next time somebody lays a hand on you, I don't want you coming to me. I don't want you coming to anybody. I want you to lay a hand on *him*. Got it?"

Howard beamed. "You mean you want me to hit back? Get into a fist-fight?" Rather than frighten him, Sandy's advice promised just what he wanted: fresh opportunities for pain.

"You heard me, Howard. Time to take it like a man."

Pushing past Howard and into the gym, the coach waited for his quarterback to emerge from the showers. Then he pounced.

"Are you out of your mind?"

Exiting with several players, Russel cast a half-querulous look toward the office and motioned the others to go on. He stood on the parquet, under a canopy of ropes, confronting Sandy.

"Risking everything, just to rough up some miserable kid?"

Sandy was red in the face, but Russel remained calm. Unnaturally, disturbingly calm, his on-the-field obedience replaced by a sudden hubris. "He had it coming. You know that."

"I know that you're being scouted and all it'll take is one expulsion to blow it." Sandy's protests reverberated around the gym. "And, Jesus, Russel, you could have hurt yourself."

Beneath the huge aluminum-cupped lamps, Russel's hair looked scarlet, his freckles backlit. Though roughly Sandy's height, he glared down at him with a mixture of imperiousness and pity. "The scouts don't care what I do when I'm not playing or who I beat up," he responded. "And as for hurting myself, I don't think so. Not with that piece of shit."

The quarterback smiled wanly, an expression that said many things. That, at fourteen, he knew precisely who he was destined to become and could already make or break most of the rules. "Someday I'll leave Appleton and I'll never look back," the smile told Sandy, "Not even at you."

*   *   *   *   *

Knuckles white on the steering wheel, streetlights bleaching his face, Sandy drove home. He wished he was going anywhere else. If only he could've met Saps for a knish or chatted with Louis at Temple Beth El. He even fantasized about calling Jeanne, rendezvousing with her over coffee, taking a late-night stroll. But he didn't have her number and even if he did, would never really call. Sandy Cooper had many faults—an over-protective manner, a too-vulnerable heart—but shirking duties wasn't among them.

He pulled into their single-car driveway, crossed the cracked pavement and the scraggily lawn free of any statuettes he might trip over. Acrid smoke wafting from the kitchen signaled supper ready and, sure enough, Esta emerged in an apron and oven gloves presenting something torched. She nearly dropped it, though, when she saw his downcast look.

"Poor boy, tell me about it."

He did. To Sandy's surprise, he told her everything. About Howard Weintraub getting clobbered by Arthur Warhaftig and Russel Pressman, about the incidents on the football field, and his fears for his all-time favorite quarterback who clearly couldn't care less. He even told her about the "Fuck the Jews" spray-painted on the school wall and the turpentine it took to remove it. Everything spilled out except for Jeanne Pagonis, but what was there to tell, really? Some off-color feelings? A dream?

Esta listened and waited for him to finish before reacting. A woman of rare reflections, those she offered were wise. "If anybody's getting beaten up here, sweetie, it's you. *By* you. What do you say we call it a match?"

She reached across the table and shielded his hand with hers. A subtle squeeze communicated more than empathy, but Sandy replied with an anemic smile. Once exhilarating, back in high school when they were both virgins, lovemaking with Esta had long since grown predictable. Affectionate and reassuring and occasionally necessary if only to reconnect with the past.

He no longer felt the urge. All he wanted tonight was to retreat to the den with its familiar vase and clock, its black-and-white photographs of his parents as younger people and of those more distant relations—him and Esta at seventeen. He longed only to coil in his recliner and watch some mindless TV police show, to doze off peacefully, and be wakened when it was over.

* * * * *

Esta was right, of course, as usual. He had to stop living vicariously through Russel and taking his anger out on Howard. Once again, he vowed, no more assigning his own emotions to others, students especially. Each had their own life and his job was not to live it for them. His duty, on the contrary, was to keep a distance.

He sustained that detachment throughout the morning and even during lunchtime in the lounge. The teachers prattled and Jeanne waved "Hi," but he kept to himself on the sofa. Back in his cubicle, Sandy listened dispassionately to the complaints about grades and peer pressure. Then came the commotion outside.

Emerging into the corridor, the first person he ran into, literally, was Rae. Impeccably dressed as always, stature regal, she nevertheless seemed unnerved. Tears clung to her ducts. *The bastards*, he thought, first "Fuck the Jews" and now this. Heat gushed through his temples and his hands furled into fists. He was already poised to fight back, if only he knew against who, until he noticed the stain. A spur-shaped blot on her cashmere sweater.

"It's not mine, Mister Cooper," Rae rushed to assure him. "I just brought him to the nurse. He's really bleeding."

"He?" Who could she mean, Sandy worried, Russel? His rage was replaced by dread.

Later, he would remember how he walked then, more like a jog but in a motion so slow it seemed to take minutes to reach the infirmary. Spread out on the examining table was indeed a bloodied boy. Torn lip, scored forehead, a rip at the earlobe that might require a stitch. The term "worked over" occurred to him even as the victim's identity took time to register.

"Arthur?"

Hidden behind long, greasy hair, the boy's face was hard to recognize. Sandy came closer, peeking over the slightly humped back of Nurse O'Shanassy, a quiet former nun. She did not look up from her work but kept dabbing at the wounds with a washcloth.

"Arthur Warhaftig?"

His discolored eyes blinked.

Though it didn't happen often, whenever he was caught off-guard, Sandy's face contorted. His cheeks constricted while his mouth fell open and his eyes bulged. That face now emitted a gasp, "My God," followed by the now-familiar question: "Who did this?"

He expected Arthur to mention some ninth-grader known for roughhousing. Still, he braced for the outside chance that it was a decent kid who would have to be suspended. In the half-second it took Arthur to answer, Sandy again thought of Russel.

"Howard Weintraub."

"Howard?" He asked this incredulously, as surprised as he was relieved. "Why would he do that?"

"Because, Mister Cooper..." Arthur sobbed violently now, blowing red-swirled snot into a tissue. "You told him to."

Sandy stumbled backward. Out of the infirmary he fled and down the corridor where much of the staff had crowded. McGonnigle and Bronowski, D'Angelis and Stevens. All of them apparently knew. Reluctantly, they parted for him while treating him to withering looks. Charlotte Fox shook her beaded head. Only Wendell Barr stood his ground and spat, "Nice work, Cooper. You really fucked it up this time."

The last to confront him was Jeanne Pagonis. Hands clasped to her mouth and her eyes peering over them wetly. "Doctor Steinseifer wants to see you in his office immediately," she informed him, but then practically wept, "My God, Coop, what did you do?"

4.

Merely seeing him sufficed to make people cry. Thread-like body, lifeless clothes, hair in a half-deranged wisp. He described his once-peaceful *shtetl*, the *aktions* and deportation, in voice that sounded pressed through a strainer, the gas chambers and the death march. Perched on a wooden stool and coned in sooty light, he read from his memoirs and the entire congregation wept. Everyone except Sandy Cooper.

Esta had dragged him to the event, if only to haul him out of depression. After years of silence, she said, people were now talking openly about this new word, Holocaust. Here was a man on a stage. "We have to go," she insisted. "*You* have to."

He did, joining the other congregants in Beth El's sanctuary where the walls—the memorial plaques, the Eternal Flame, even the ark—bore witness. That biblical quote, "*The Lord is Near to All Who Call on Him, To All Who Call on Him in Truth*," could've concluded with a question mark. Esta was mangling her third Kleenex and already groping for a fourth, but Sandy's eyes remained dry. He looked at the survivor and heard his words but all he saw was Steinseifer earlier that morning warning of his possible dismissal.

"If the mother insists on it, we'll have no choice," the principal announced matter-of-factly. Everything about him was lackluster: the colorless suit and tie, the steel-rimmed glasses. His doctorate, rumor had it, was in auditing. "She's threatening to take you to court."

Sandy considered begging. His job was his life, the reason he got up in the morning and why he bothered to sleep. But the situation was hopeless. He and nobody else had instructed Howard to punch the next kid who picked on him. He, more than any fourteen-year-old, was responsible for what happened to Arthur.

"I understand, Doctor."

"I'm sorry about this, Sandy. You're a good man, I still think." This, too, was pronounced without intonation, yet the counselor believed it was true.

"Thank you, Doctor."

"Thank you, Doctor," he repeated out loud, but his words were lost in the applause. The man had just related his liberation at the hands of courageous G.I.'s. After years of bitterness about Vietnam, anger at presidents, people were on their feet applauding and breaking into cries of "God Bless America."

Sandy also rose but didn't sing. Esta glowered at him. Ever since he told her about the incident, she had been understanding, assuring him that all would be forgotten in a day or two if only he stopped fretting about it and stuck to his job. But she seemed fed up. With a nod of her tear-streaked face toward the stage where the man now stood, feeble but erect and joined the congregation's song, she hissed, "Really, you should be ashamed."

* * * * *

The next day, cloistered in his cubicle and avoiding the lounge, he pondered the options. Resign before his was fired? Find a job like his father, selling suits? But the hurt of leaving the school he had served all his adult years, the humiliation in town, the thought of no longer coaching—it all seemed insufferable. Dilemmas careened in his mind as he read and reread the thank-you letters pinned to the walls.

Looking back on that day, he couldn't remember the exact moment when the idea materialized. Was it after Howard Weintraub traipsed in to complain about his three-day suspension?

"But you told me to hit him." His protest was tinged with pride.

"Yes," Sandy wearily agreed. "But I didn't say you wouldn't have to pay for it."

No, Sandy determined, it must have been after recess, when Jeanne Pagonis stuck her head in to see if—she quipped—he was still breathing. By that time, his mind was settled.

"We talked about Arthur Warhaftig once, didn't we, Jeanne? Something about trouble at home."

Jeanne's body followed her head into the cubicle. She loomed larger in that cramped space, looking down at Sandy slouched at his desk. "Rumors, mostly," she said. "I went ahead and looked up his records. Nothing there, only that he transferred schools."

"No therapy? Guidance counselor notes?"

"Nothing."

"Strange…" He tugged on his tie and dodged Jeanne's attempts to make eye contact.

Still, she pressed him, "Be careful, Coop. You've got enough on your plate already."

He waited for Jeanne to leave. Then, after licking the tips first of one set of fingers then the other, he reached for the phone.

Information listed only one number for that name and now it was scrawled on his pad. He stared at it for several seconds, listening to his breath and rehearsing some lines he knew sounded ludicrous. The school had to yet to install touchtone phones and the turning dial tsk-tsked in his ear.

Twice it rang, four times, while Sandy recalled the story of how Howard had received a single karate-chop on the back from Arthur, spun, and pounced on him. How Arthur, pinned under that weight, was pummeled by fat fists until some passing kids pulled Howard off.

The phone, meanwhile, kept ringing. Sandy muttered "What was I thinking?" and moved to hang up. But somebody answered.

"Yes."

"Am I speaking with Mrs. Warhaftig?"

"Depends. Who's calling?"

The voice was smoky. He struggled to keep his own from trembling. "Mister Cooper. The guidance counselor."

"You mean the man who instructed one of his students to mug my son?"

"Yes." He chewed an inner cheek. "How is he?"

"At home, healing. Physically, at least."

"Good. I'm sorry…"

"Sorry, are you, Mister Cooper? I'm sorry I'll soon be demanding your dismissal. I'm sorry my lawyer's preparing to sue."

"I understand." Sandy choked, he hoped not audibly. "But can we meet first? Can I invite you for a chat at the school?"

"A chat? Why of course! How lovely."

He nearly punched himself. "Sorry. Wrong word. Can I ask you to come in for meeting? At the school."

"No," she said flatly and paused for what sounded like a cigarette drag. "Not at the school. You come here. Monday night, ten thirty. Arthur'll be asleep."

"To your *house?*"

Exasperatedly, she exhaled, "I see, deaf as well as stupid."

"Okay. Fine. Where?"

"Really, Mister Cooper. Anyone diabolical enough to incite children to violence can surely find an address."

For a long time after the closing click in his ear, Sandy sat listening as the receiver first hummed and then bleeped in his ear. He tried telling himself that the hardest part was over. But then, depressing the hook with his finger, he dialed the Appleton Police Station and asked for Sergeant Saperstein.

*   *   *   *   *

Sunday seemed like months away and, by the time it arrived, the tension was too much for Sandy. He sat in the rear of Sobotnik's, before a tongue sandwich so untouched it could have served as a display, waiting for Saps to speak.

"Great game yesterday," he finally mentioned. "Your Pressman kid shone."

Sparkled was more accurate, passing ninety yards, running 140, for a victory over Harrison Heights. But Sandy merely went through the coaching motions. Nor did he care about handball, losing points even when granted to him. He needed information.

"Enough, Saps. What do you got?"

The policeman's own sandwich was already mauled to a crust, which he used to sop up the mustard. "Eat that," he nodded at Sandy's plate. "This'll be tough on an empty stomach."

Though the file was thin and sketchy, with a single report from a force several counties over, it said that Arthur Warhaftig transferred from not one but a number of schools, some out-of-state. And yes, there was trouble at home. "We're not talking marital trouble in the usual sense or even divorce.

We're talking…" Saps's voice dropped so low it was drowned out by fat Bernie's call for more herring behind the counter. "Murder."

For the second time in just one week, Sandy's face betrayed his astonishment—mouth drooped, eyes popping—as he swallowed. "Who?"

"Her husband," Saps continued. "A rich bastard, real estate businesses here and there, investments. And some women, too, I guess—the file's mum about that—and a brutal streak. Seems he beat the kid pretty regular. Sometimes using tools."

"Tools?"

"Things he brought back from the war. You know, Jap souvenirs. And karate stuff. The guy was obsessed."

Sandy looked perplexed. "But the son's into it, too. Weird. Why, when it was used against him?"

"Typical abuse syndrome," Saps explained. "The victim falls in love with his torturer. We see it a lot."

"And so she killed him. How?"

"That's the best part," Sap sniggered. "With a sword."

"You mean…?" Sandy's knife sliced the air.

"According to the report. The asshole husband gave the kid one too many chops and the mom went ga-ga. Took his Jap sword off the wall and split his skull."

"And she was arrested…."

"Tried and found not guilty. Justifiable homicide. Hushed up pretty quick, too. A few newspaper articles, back page stuff, and then…nada."

The ceiling fan that hadn't spun since they were children cast an X across the table. Sandy stared at it and then at the Manischewitz calendar that, he noticed, was already one year old. He looked everywhere except at his best friend's face as he said, "I've made a date to see her."

"A date? Like, with shakes at Wexler's, a kiss at the door if you're lucky?"

Sandy made a face. "No, a meeting. A conversation. At her house."

"Are you serious? Listen, Coop, you don't know anything about this person. She may be nuts, maybe dangerous."

"Whatever." He pushed his sandwich away. "I need to straighten things out."

"Yeah, like your head," Sandy thought Saps said as he snatched up the sandwich and chomped. "And you might want to wear a helmet."

* * * * *

He didn't know why, not yet, but Sandy never told Esta about the meeting. Was he afraid that she wouldn't understand and dismiss the idea as *narish-keit*? Or, on the contrary, did he fear that she would be supportive and trust him thoroughly? He had this inkling that, if somehow successful, the conversation with Mrs. Warhaftig might require some twisting of the truth that his wife would find unpalatable. He needed Saps to cover for him.

"You want me to lie."

Saps stated this dryly on the floor of the Y's handball court. So poorly had Sandy been playing that his friend could not even throw him the last game.

"I want you to give me an excuse to go out at that hour and not make Esta crazy with worry." Sandy massaged his sore thigh. "You know how she gets." He didn't, in fact, and Sandy knew it. He raised wrapped hands in the air. "Yes, goddamn you. If she asks, yes, I want you to lie."

* * * * *

Celebrating a patrolman's birthday at some swanky bar was the ideal pretext for dressing fancier than Sandy's usual. The khakis were replaced by darker trousers and the white button-down with a black turtleneck. He even combed his hair, though it was too short for any comb. Esta joined him at the mirror. "Careful that some policewoman doesn't fall in love with you like I did," she joked, and made him miserable.

The working-class neighborhood was quiet as he snuck into the Impala—so quiet that the engine turned with a roar. Gingerly as he could, he rolled out of the driveway and accelerated to the end of the block before swinging onto Union Street with its delis, drug stores, bakeries, and school. Well before reaching the temple, at the intersection, he signaled left and climbed.

So, too, did the houses—up the social ladder from the clapboard dwellings below to the colonial manors near the top and, on the summit, castles. A Jewish area but Jews of German descent, contemptuous of those of Russian and Polish stock, like Sandy, whom they considered little better than peasants. Uneasily he drove on, past the Hartmont Country Club, the flagstone gates guarded by lions and gas lamps. The shrubbery shook under raindrops.

A slight drizzle Sandy could handle but not the deluge that followed. He switched on the wipers and then the radio, surfing for something sedate. No Perry Como, no Nat King Cole, only some rock band ranting about brown sugar—hardly soothing. He killed the volume and squinted at the numbers outside.

From the school's timid secretary, Mrs. Tannenbaum, he managed to pry an address, but it was none he recognized. The road reached a crest from which, during daylight, one could see the nearest city, now obscured in darkness. He followed the asphalt to the edge of some woods. "Damn," Sandy palmed the wheel. He must have missed it. No choice but to k-turn and double back more carefully.

Just then, while reversing, he saw it: an opening in the trees, a gravel-lined path just wide enough for a driveway. Though there was no signpost, he surmised that this was the place. The tires crunched loudly as he entered, no doubt announcing his arrival.

The path snaked farther up to a crescent-shaped driveway notably empty of cars. Through the rain and mist, a single bulb struggled to define a door. It took another bolt of lightning to reveal what he would call a mansion and the row of statues outside. Cupids, nymphs, satyrs—all naked, all glistening in the flash. *Esta would hate this*, he thought.

The door was equipped with an intercom, which Sandy pressed once and then waited. He pressed again, worrying if perhaps he had made a mistake and whether some nervous old couple were right now phoning the police. Raindrops coursed down his face, through his clothes and into his heels. He bit his lower lip, cursed, and rang a final time.

The intercom crackled with a woman's voice. "Yes?"

Yes? Maybe this was the wrong house. "It's Mister Cooper, ma'am. From the junior high."

A silence followed, probably to make Sandy wait in the downpour. "It's open," she said finally. "Come in and sit in the library. And for God's sake, wipe your feet."

The door was heavy and made of materials unknown in Sandy's neighborhood. And the smell inside was resinous, as if he'd just entered the woods. Through his gummy soles he could feel the floor's great expense and sensed the presence of a ultra-modern chandelier overhead. There was artwork on the walls, vast abstract splashes, but their colors were muted in the dark. The only light came from a faint glow at the end of the hallway, and Sandy followed it. Down three stairs and into a room the size of his den and crammed with books and keepsakes.

Lowering himself into an armchair, under a single reading lamp, Sandy studied the walls. One displayed an elaborate kimono and another held prints of Asian women, half-clad and showing their thighs. There were rice paper proclamations and some evil spirit masks. A pair of what looked like legs from an old colonial chair—amulets, perhaps, or bludgeons. Yet, because of the sparse light, the souvenir he noticed last was the one slung over the sofa in front of him. Mounted lengthwise, glossy in its sheath, a curved ceremonial sword.

Sandy blinked at it, astonished. Why, if she'd used this very weapon to chop her husband's head in half, would she hang it on a wall? Was the woman sane? Was she dangerous?

Lightning glazed the room, thunder reverberated. Sandy thought, "How hokey can you get?" Still, his arm hairs stiffened. It was almost a relief to smell her, or rather her cigarette, on the stairs behind him.

"Sit," she snapped as he tried to rise. Sandy sank back and watched as parts of her came into the light. Silken robe, brocaded slippers, a necklace carved from jade. With one hand supporting an elbow and the other swinging a cigarette to her lips, she hovered over him. Though not a tall woman, seated, Sandy felt dwarfed. And judged, a high, intense gaze looking both down and through him

"Misses Warhaftig…"

She pointed her cigarette at him. "Quiet. I get to do the talking."

He sunk deeper.

"You understand how serious it is, how spectacularly dumb, to tell one child to beat up another? You understand the mountain of shit that puts you in?"

Sandy's eyes lowered. "Dumb… Spectacularly…"

"I could sue you for every penny and more. Though I suspect that wouldn't be much."

"Not much…No."

"I could take away your job. Your standing in the community."

Sandy lowered his head. "I know."

"I'm sure you do." She said this with a huff of smoke and, with her eyes still pinned on him, took a seat on the opposite sofa. Sandy lifted his gaze to the tray of accordioned butts on the coffee table, and from there, to a single alabaster knee.

"I'm curious, Mister Cooper, what qualifications does one have to have to be a guidance counselor?"

"Qualifications?"

"A psychology degree? Clinical experience?"

Sandy shrugged. "I like kids, if that's what you mean. My advice is usually solid." He paused. "Usually."

A clap of thunder, so loud it seemed to originate inside the den, cut short her laugh. "I'm curious, Mister Cooper—they call you Coop, correct?"

"My friends, yes. Coop."

"Tell me, Coop, what is it exactly do you like about kids?"

Though he knew she was staring at him, he could only study his shoes. "Junior high school kids, you mean, adolescents? I like them because they *are* kids. Children, really. And children are never more childish than just before they become adults."

"Interesting." The cigarette winked at him. "You can still shape them, then."

"The last chance. After that, they're finished products."

"And you, Coop? Is your product finished?"

Sandy looked up into the woman's face leaning toward the lamp. The short, sharp nose and tapered cheeks, the aristocratic forehead framed in sable hair. Her complexion even whiter than her knee. Most startling, though, was the mouth, pulpy red and wide. Sandy could imagine it devouring him.

"So, are you?"

"Am I what?" He realized that he'd been staring.

"Finished. Product-wise?"

The question eluded him. "I guess so," was the best he could muster. "Yes."

"Too bad." She stabbed out one cigarette and started to light another. The flame revealed sculpted brows, hazel eyes to match her jewelry. "Though I don't believe you. You seem far from finished."

He wanted to ask her how she knew so much about him—his nickname, his sense of incompleteness—but never got the chance. She stood again and wafted past him to one of the library's corners. Behind the thunder's boom, he discerned another sound, a tinkling.

"Would you like a drink?"

She didn't wait for an answer but glided back with two glasses. "Here. I think you need this," she said, handing him one. A one-beer man unaccustomed to strong liquor, the whiskey burned but also becalmed him, melting him into the chair.

"You grew up in this town, didn't you?" she resumed after returning to the sofa. "Worked here all your life, married." Into his glass, Sandy nodded. "Saw class after class of young people come and go. No doubt you preferred those who were the most like you. Popular, athletic. Kids with a future."

Where was she going with this? Leading him somewhere, he suspected, though the destination remained unclear. Yet he put up no resistance, still afraid of losing his job. Or was it something else?

"I'm sorry..."

"Kids, I mean, like you. Or like you were."

"How do you know how I was?"

"Small town. Doesn't take much. Your nickname, for instance, or the fact you were once a star."

He tried to shrug her off with a chortle, but the woman would not be deterred.

"It must be lonely living with a past like that. Surrounded by everyone else's future."

Flummoxed, he squinted at her—at the lipstick wreath on her cigarette butt and the scarlet dragons on her robe. "I'm not sure I get you."

"Oh, don't sell yourself short."

She was shifting forward now, toward him. Her hand twisted the jade. "I think..."

He was going to say that he thought it best to be leaving, that their conversation had gone off-course. But in daring to raise his eyes above her kneecaps, he caught sight of the wall behind her head. The sword smiled back.

"You like the decor, I see." She puffed and fiercely exhaled. "Belonged to my late husband. He fought in the Pacific and got himself captured. He always said this was his revenge. Like stuffed heads."

"Heads..." *I must sound like an idiot*, he thought.

"Did you serve?"

Sandy blushed. "Too young for World War II, and for Korea, too..."

"Lame."

"An old football injury."

"Yes," she said. "That," and chugging the remainder of her drink, she rose. "Well, this has been instructive, don't you think?"

He leapt to his feet as well, as fast as his thigh allowed, and followed her out of the den. The thunder had faded only to be replaced by her slippers' rustle. Neither abstract art nor the chandelier could now overcome the dark. She turned before escorting him out.

"There's something you have to know about me, Mister Cooper. I am a widow and Arthur is all that I have. I will do anything to protect him. And as for your dismissal and lawsuit, we shall have to see."

She said this so suddenly he could barely internalize the words. And he was too overpowered by her smoky breath and that resinous scent which, he realized, rose not from the house but her skin. She opened the door to a night that was silent and wet. Sandy began to thank her, "Misses Warhaftig…"

"Elizabeth," she corrected him. Her hand brushed the top of her hair, as though to smooth it. Her nails, he noticed, matched her lipstick, which accentuated the white of her teeth. "But friends call me Liz."

And then he was outside. Like a man who knows he's been shot but not sure where, he stood for a few moments shivering. He recalled that they had only talked about him, not her, and scarcely mentioned Arthur. And though it seemed she no longer wanted to ruin him, how could he totally be sure?

On his gum-soled shoes that felt strangely aerated, he floated toward his car. That's when the lightning flickered. A final silent bolt, it was weaker than those before it but still luminous enough to reveal those nymphs and cupids. They appeared to judge him dispassionately. Yet that same flash also afforded him another glimpse of the man he saw on the football field that night. Unchained and dashing, hellbent on his goal.

The memory of that man, of the kimono and the sword, hounded him as he climbed into his car. Only when the Impala skidded off the gravel drive and plunged through the trees did he slam on the brakes and clutch the steering wheel. "Holy shit," he gasped. "Liz."

*   *   *   *   *

Three nights later, he was back in Beth El supervising the youth group with Esta. Or rather, she was supervising and he was wandering more aimlessly than usual. Through the hallways and the kitchen, past the library, to find himself alone in the sanctuary.

Sandy didn't think of praying but only reliving his conversation with Liz. The humiliation, the fear, but also the sense that here was a woman who knew him or at least thought him worth knowing. Who made him feel frail, at first, then manly. A dangerous woman, possibly even unhinged, but clearly smarter than he was, and alluring.

He remembered returning from her house to his own. The objects in the den—the vase, the clock, the darkened family photos—seemed alien to him suddenly. The creak in the staircase sounded accusatory. Only Esta, snoring in their bed, appeared familiar. "You smell like booze," was all she said when he slipped under the covers next to her, and Sandy felt ashamed.

But why? Nothing had happened, not even nearly. Nothing to report to Esta or even to Saps, who probably wouldn't ask. Still, standing all by himself in the sanctuary, Sandy was prickled by guilt. For the first time in his life, perhaps, he was a man with a secret. And a secret so obscure that not even he understood it.

Slipping into a pew, Sandy surveyed the memorial plaques, the Eternal Flame, the pulpit. The trappings that were supposed to supply answers. "*The Lord is Near to All Who Call on Him*," declared the golden quote on the wall, "*To All Who Call on Him in Truth*." But would he recognize the truth even if it tackled him, Sandy wondered? Would he even know how to call?

Sandy sat, inhaling the fumes of Rabbi Isaacson's Scotch, steeped in silence. He barely heard the great pine doors opening behind him but sensed a presence there. He swiveled in the pew to find Louis hovering in the aisle.

"Give me a heart attack, why don't you."

"Deal. And you give me a raise."

The big man came forward. Minus his apron and rubber gloves, in a blue Oxford shirt and chinos, Louis, if white, would pass for an upscale congregant. Unlike bare-headed Sandy, he always wore a white *yarmulke* in the sanctuary—out of respect, he said. And now he held out an offering. "You look like you could use this."

The wedge of cake bore fragmented icing: "Stevie. Happy. Mitzvah."

"Thanks, I might," Sandy said, accepting the plate.

The janitor handed him a fork. "We could all use a *simcha* now and then," he smiled. "A little *mazal tov*."

"*Mazal tov* to you, too, Louis," he mumbled through frosted lips. "*Mazal tov* to us all," he repeated after he was by himself again, talking to the pulpit. Admitting finally what he knew the instant he'd left the Warhaftig house. Somehow and as soon as possible, Sandy had to see her.

5.

Ringing in his ear, her phone sounded strange to him. Ominous. Siren-like. Once, twice, it rang, and a part of him urged him to hang up. But another part realized it was too late already, and that this was her way of testing him, of seeing how long he'd wait. Fourth ring, fifth. And still he stayed on the line.

Someone finally answered. He could hear the breath, punctuated by a cigarette puff. Clearly, he had to speak first. "It's me."

"Yes?"

"It's me, Liz. Sandy."

A too-long silence, followed by a near whisper. "Yes."

The rendezvous this time was set not at night but at midday, and not at her house but in a movie theater. Laying the phone delicately on the receiver, he remained motionless in his cubicle. The thank-you notes reminded him of how dutifully he'd once performed his job, but now, feeling unworthy, he considered taking them down. He might have, too, if a student's silhouette had not then appeared on his frosted glass door. A seventh-grader, a girl, shaken by some pubescent passage. Sandy smiled at her, tugged on his tie, and said, "Come in."

The bulk of a week separated that moment from the one at which he'd walk into that theater—a vast track of time, it seemed. How would he transverse it? One way was to put it as far as possible out of his mind, to concentrate on the team, on Russel Pressman, and Saturday's game against

Scottsville. The other was to avoid the teacher's lounge and the questions of whether he really told Howard Weintraub to beat up Arthur Warhaftig and if he'd managed to hire a lawyer. The last thing he needed was another peace sign from Charlotte Fox or Wendell Barr cursing kikes under his breath. Most of all he had to avoid Jeanne Pagonis, whose empathy for him only made Sandy feel guiltier.

"You hang in there, Coop." Her bob-haired head poked inside to his cubicle. "We're all with you. Well," she simpered, "I am."

"You're very kind, Jeanne, thanks," he said, and could have punched himself. But, at the same time, there was something about this young woman's attraction to him—for that's what it was, not merely deference—that awakened a power he had long thought extinguished. Not since his glory days on the gridiron, when Esta practically had to shove the other girls away, had Sandy so sensed his potency. "I can handle anything," he said, and flushed when he saw her smile.

That virility accompanied him home and helped him get through the weekend. Beyond that, it endowed the Coopers' bi-monthly sex with an eroticism so lacking neither of them ever noticed it was missing.

"What do you call that play, Coach?" Esta panted into the pillow.

Sandy, spread over her back, trumpeted, "Quarterback sneak."

"I'll say." She strained her chin over her shoulder and winked at him. "How 'bout a replay?"

He gave her one—a record unmatched since their honeymoon—anything to avoid talking to her at length and lying to her straight-faced. For he was indeed lying to her, he knew, if only by omission. He was lying to himself, too, about the impending need to lie even more.

* * * * *

His dread of dishonesty, though deep, still could not match the misery he felt driving up the serpentine entrance. Passing through the pines and the gardens that stubbornly defied the season, his stomach clenched. From the outside, at least, the Daughters of Jacob Home looked benevolent enough. Inside, he knew, seethed hell.

With a fullback's determination, he plowed through hallways, the formations of uniformed nurses, the implacable smells. To door number 35 where, knocking, he was stopped by a simple, "Go away."

Sandy nevertheless entered and as usual saw a very old man in a wheel-chair. Positioned next to a window, he appeared to be gazing out. He ignored the "Hiya," responding only with a rise and fall of his chest. Taking off his jacket, Sandy pulled up a seat next to him, leaned on his kneecaps, and tried it again. "Hiya."

He considered saying how good he looked, how nice his hair, a few strands of which remained, meticulously plastered, and handsome his suit, a three-piece gabardine that went out of fashion decades ago. He wore a floral tie with mother-of-pearl pin, a silken handkerchief in his breast, and in his flared lapel, an emblem of the Order of Elks. "A salesman must always look as smart as the customer wants to be," his father always said. Sandy was even going to call him that, "smart," but instead merely commented, "Nice day."

Another rise and fall, this time of the shoulders, accompanied by a har-rumph. "I wouldn't know."

"Well, I could take you outside for a stroll."

Maurice Cooper glowered at his son. Everything he'd done in life, said the look, from early childhood to this visit, was a disappointment.

"Or we could walk down to the cafeteria." His father took meals solely in his room, insisting that the other residents lacked manners. A rolling table waited at the foot of the bed, beneath framed pictures of his older sister who married as soon as she could and moved out to Oregon, and of his mother, who died before Sandy turned thirty. "I could bring you lunch if you'd like."

The suggestion earned him the back of a mottled hand and a surly order, "The Victrola."

Sandy quietly obliged. From a bookshelf that contained no books but many dog-eared albums, he selected a record and placed it on the pad. Scratchy seconds followed until the room filled with the only kind of music the old man listened to: show tunes.

A fed-up woman was washing a man right out of her hair, but the song seemed to soften him. But only momentarily. Even in his youth, Maurice Kuperberg—so he was then known—elevated disgruntlement to a precept. Dismay was carved into his cheeks and stamped into his flinty eyes. The stroke five years ago had softened some of his features while freezing others in umbrage. Still, his face was unmistakably Sandy's, right down to the bridgeless nose, only withered by years of spite.

"Team's doing okay," Sandy said without being asked. "Two for one. My quarterback looks like a future champion if only he…" He halted. Along with finances and the youth rebellion, talk of football injuries was verboten. "Esta's fine, too."

His father serenaded an imaginary woman, younger than springtime. In a warbled voice, he sang with eyes half-shut. "Yes, Esta."

So the litany began. It opened with Sandy in high school, naïve and frisky and taken in by the first pair of sweatered tits to bounce in his face, and progressed to the missed opportunities, the tragedy, the childless home. All were attributed to Esta, a woman who nonetheless put up with her father-in-law's bitterness, showing him nothing but warmth. Today, fortunately, he spared Sandy the list and cut to the maxim.

"Once tailored, a suit can never be altered," his father stated. "Lengthen the sleeves, let out the seat, no matter what, it'll never fit."

Meaning, of course, Esta. The wrong girl for his all-star son, the one who pushed him off fortune's path and head-on into failure. Who couldn't bear him a single living son.

"Esta's not a suit, Dad. And she never had to be altered. Not for me." Sandy routinely stood up for her. "She thinks the world of you."

The only response was a snort, immediately followed by humming. The next song praised a mystical Pacific island with Maurice mimicking the hand motions of its faux-Polynesian performer. Sandy watched him and wondered what it'd be like to have a parent he could confide in, who'd console rather than fault him and listen to his fears.

"God, they don't make music like that anymore." Maurice Cooper looked enraptured. "You never liked Rogers and Hammerstein, did you? Cole Porter."

"No, Dad, sorry. Sinatra's more my speed."

"Some speed."

That remark hung in the air while sailors sang Bloody Mary's praises. Sandy's eyes again wandered the room, landing on the photo of the sister he often forgot he had and the mother so retiring she hardly left a memory. A card or two from last Christmas. Golden chrysanthemums arranged by some ultra-patient nurse. All coated in stale window light, awash in loss.

But Sandy's mind roiled with different images. Vermillion lips folding over a cigarette, porcelain knees parting—all illuminated by sword slash. He pictured them and almost forgot where he was and what record was playing.

Ezio Pinza was bellowing about crowded rooms, again and again belting out the word "strangers" where the recording skipped.

Sandy said, "Sorry, Dad," and hurried to adjust the needle. It screeched to the word "enchanted," and on that lyric, Sandy sighed. "Until next time, then."

His father nodded but he appeared to be elsewhere. On islands and beaches where romance prevailed, on stages for happier dramas. Pinza mourned nearly having it all but losing it as Sandy stepped toward the door. "I'll give Esta your best," he remembered to add before leaving.

* * * * *

The movie theater was several towns away, far enough to minimalize the danger of being recognized. And at noon, most adults would be at work and not at some artsy matinee. Apart from a few retirees and loafers, the place would likely be empty. That would give them two hours at least to sit and whisper, sit and maybe touch. The mere thought of those knees close to his, that mouth, unnerved him as he drove.

And yet, a segment of his mind still argued that this was not about Liz, really, but her son. About making sure she'd never go to court or demand his job. Earlier that day, he had peeked through the narrow window into Jeanne's homeroom class. At first Sandy didn't see him and his heart clenched. But then, craning his neck to glimpse the furthest rows, he spied Arthur slumping down in his chair. He was staring at his teacher but not seeing her, simultaneously daydreaming and doodling on his desk. His expensive clothes were baggier than usual, and his stringy hair long. Apart from a scab at the base of one ear, his injuries appeared to have healed.

He mentioned that fact to Dr. Steinseifer in passing outside his office and asked whether the mother had since called. She hadn't. Sandy let it drop to Jeanne, as well, while crossing through the lounge. She seemed earnestly happy to hear that incident might be behind him but concerned to see him rushing off to the doctor's.

"Oh, it's nothing. A pain here and there. But better to check it."

The moles on her face converged on her pout. "You've been under a lot of strain lately."

"No need to worry about me, young lady," he assured her. "I'm a tough old bear."

"No, seriously, if you feel you need to talk to somebody, a cup of coffee outside of here, let me know."

The offer made him blush and not only with its warmth. He had just lied to Jeanne, he realized, and had to admit that his need to see Liz had nothing to do with school. Flattered and thrilled, he rushed to his Impala in the lot.

The theater was a relic from the thirties, ornate and rundown and seemingly deserted. Only the presence of a snoozing granny in the ticket booth told him that the place was still showing films. Not blockbusters, but the foreign productions favored by English majors and housewives with domestic help. Tapping on the window, Sandy aroused the old woman, diverted his gaze as he passed her the money and bought a single ticket.

The lights, dim when he entered, suddenly went out, reducing the sparse audience to shadows. Still, he could see the walls thick with rococo and, above him, a mezzanine, balcony, and boxes. As the brocaded curtain lifted, Sandy climbed.

On moldy carpets he ascended through dust motes and a miasma of popcorn. Reaching the top floor, he made out three or four entrances and chose the furthest. The mantel was so low he had to duck, and only when straightening inside did he discern the outline of a slender back and high-cheeked face turned away from him. He smelled her cigarette well before he saw smoke entwining in the projector light. He inhaled that woodsy scent.

"Hi," he whispered.

She tittered "Hi" back, possibly making fun.

The box had real chairs, rickety but plush, set at oblique angles. He sat on one and twisted it toward her. "I found the theater, I found you," he boasted and instantly regretted it.

Liz tapped his knee. "Well done."

On the screen, dapper men were speaking in Italian while clowns played macabre tricks. She watched them while he studied her in flicker—the clothes less flamboyant now, almost business-like. No big jewelry this time, no dragoned robe. Instead, a tight lavender tunic that accentuated petite breasts and an elongated neck. A sudden pulse of light—a clown-shooting cannon—revealed the hair again piled on top of her head, her knees encased in pants but nearly touching his own. Her profile—the short, upturned nose and that enveloping mouth—looked sharkish.

Then, without looking at him, she asked, "Do you like Fellini?"

A food? Some sex act? Stymied, he tried a diversion. "I saw Arthur today." It was the first time he'd ever mentioned the name. "He looked much better," he stammered, and, "Another week, he'll be fine."

"Outwardly, maybe." Her eyes never left the screen.

He was going to tell her that all boys get into fistfights—part of growing up. How many had he been in as a kid? That in a time of wars, race riots, and radical bombings, the Kennedys, Martin Luther King, and Kent State, a few landed punches were meaningless. It's a violent world, he wanted to say, but instead waited for Liz to continue.

And she did. "I've thought about your future, Sandy, and here's the deal." And this was the first time she'd ever used *his* name, though she seemed to be addressing the clowns. "I'm prepared to forget everything, but I expect you to keep an eye on Arthur. He's a sensitive boy, vulnerable. I need you to protect him."

Sandy said nothing but something inside him—an emotional scaffold—collapsed. This clandestine meeting at the movie theater was not about him at all, it seemed, but Liz's son. How ironic, after first telling himself that the tryst was necessary to save his job, here she was confirming it.

But then, while harlequins paraded on horseback, he felt a grip on his injured thigh. Pain shot up its length, but Sandy surrendered to it as she pulled his body closer. He might have toppled out of the chair and on top of her, but his flight was stopped by a kiss. It caught him in the corner of his mouth, but the heat, that encompassing wetness, made another internal piece of him crumble.

Shifting forward, he pressed his face into hers. Not since high school had he been kissed by another woman and certainly not one so refined, so exotic and, yes, beautiful. Powerful, too, though the extent of that strength he couldn't begin to gauge. Sandy tried to kiss her back only to find himself blocked. A varnished fingernail pressed to his lips.

"Not here. We're not teenagers."

"What are we, then? And where?"

The final credits scrolled across her cheeks. "We are adults, consenting and independent," she declared, stood up, and brushed imaginary lint from her pants. "As for the place," she said before exiting the box, "wait for my call."

*　*　*　*　*

Sandy waited for a week, and then another. The temperature meanwhile dropped, and the students went from wearing sweaters to jackets to coats. Leaves changed color and proceeded to die. Pumpkins appeared on doorsteps, even on Sandy's—a rare concession from Esta. The Appleton Rams were three and two, losing by a single point to Chesterfield but trouncing Harrison Lakes. Miraculously, Tony Metallo, the center, remembered all the counts, and receiving his hikes, quarterback Russel Pressman broke all mid-season records.

But when not on the field or counseling freshmen, Sandy hid in his cubicle and anxiously watched the phone. He checked the level of its tone, raised the receiver and hung up, just to make sure it worked. And when, on the third week after their theater meeting, the ringing started, Sandy leapt.

"Hello," he nearly shouted, sounding like a rescued child.

"Hello and how. Just who were you expecting?"

His heart constricted. Esta. "Nobody...I was outside, down the hall, and ran for the phone."

"Ran damn fast. It only rang once."

He didn't like the sound of her voice, had never heard it like this before. "Well...the important thing is I got you. What's up?"

A request to pick up a rye at Hershkey's and, from Wexler's, the latest issue of *McCall*'s. "No problem, sweetie pie," Sandy chimed.

Sweetie pie, the pet name he called her in high school, and Esta was touched. "I'm sorry I snapped at you, sweetie," she sighed. "You don't deserve it."

"Snap? What snap? Don't be silly."

"You're the best, Sandy." Her voice went husky. "Remember the other night? I do. What's say you come home quick."

Long after she hung up, Sandy remained staring at the phone. It was not too late to turn back, he realized, to tell Liz that his marriage was more important to him than any job and certainly any affair. He could phone her, not wait, and speak calmly. Time remained to return to the man he knew— the coach, the guide, a truthful husband.

But there'd be no breakup with Liz, he admitted. Lying to Esta would soon become second nature—*that* was the truth. If he felt unshackled and sprinting again, he ran with a churning stomach. And the nausea only worsened with the image of his wife innocently cheering on the sidelines.

* * * * *

Sandy did not go home quickly that night or many nights after. Pointing to the bedroom mirror, he complained to Esta that his paunch refused to be reduced by an hour of weekly handball. He needed to exercise every evening after football practice. Yet more lies. Behind them lay his desire to look his best whenever the moment came and gain some accounted-for time.

He worked hard—sit-ups and deep-knee bends—muscling through the soreness. Throughout, he imagined what it would be like to see Liz without her fine clothing, her hair unwound. Her mouth on his mouth, his body. The thoughts were so potent that, afterward, his shower had to be cold.

Then, emerging from the locker room one night, toweling his hair, he distinctly heard a cry: "Help me." He glanced frantically around the gym, but it was empty. "Help me," the voice again pleaded. "Help me, Mister Cooper."

It occurred to him that someone was playing a trick. Fourteen-year-olds were certainly that cruel. "Joke's over," he chuckled. "Come out before you get in trouble."

"I can't come out, Mister Cooper. I'm here."

That's when Sandy looked up, breathlessly cursed, and dropped his towel. Suspended from the top of one of the thick climbing ropes, near the girdered ceiling, was a boy. A fat boy, dangling.

"Howard?" Sandy had not seen him since his suspension from school, but the girth and the grating voice were giveaways. "Howard Weintraub? What are you doing up there?"

"Climbing, Mister Cooper. And I don't know how to get down."

"Scissor the rope between your thighs, shimmy slow," he advised and watched as the pudgy legs punted the air above him.

"I can't...I can't hold on anymore. I'm going to fall!"

From that height, at his weight, the kid could break both ankles. Sandy saw himself confronting yet another mother, another threatened lawsuit. "There's no choice, then, Howard. Hold on and slide."

The rope, searing through his hands as he fell, made a crescendoing whiz. Howard hit the parquet hard, his legs buckling but remaining intact. "I made it! I made it, Mister Cooper!" In triumph, he held up his palms. Both were weeping pulps.

"Jesus, Howard, what did you do?" He clutched the boy's hands and turned them upward. Sandy winced, "Why?"

"Because I could never climb rope. Ever. They always made fun of me in gym class, always laughing." Howard was rambling, not yet in pain. "But I'll show them."

"Hold on. Don't move." He ran for the first aid kit in his office, scrambled back, and placed gauze pads on the open burns, taping the dressings as delicately as he could as Howard finally sobbed.

"I'll show them, Mister Cooper. I will," he snorted up his tears. "I'm going to lose weight, get in shape. Fight them all, just like I did Arthur Warhaftig."

The mere sound of that name sickened Sandy. "I told you, Howard. No more fighting."

His streaming face suddenly beamed, the eyes behind his glasses burgeoned. "Fighting? With these mitts, how can I?" Braces, zits flashed as he laughed. "At least for another month!"

Howard's laughter pursued him out of the gym and into the empty lot. Huddled against the cold as he headed to the Impala, Sandy had an impulse to turn. What he saw shocked but didn't surprise him, as if he always knew it could happen. Only the color was weird. In a blue so glaring it obscured the Appleton sign, the words seemed to glow. "Blacks Out."

6.

Unlike the previous graffiti, scrawled on the rear wall where the students would see it only at recess, this new one accosted everyone at the front entrance. The incident could not be hushed. Saps explained, "Hating Jews is old hat. Hating Negroes is headlines." Which was why Captain Rizzo himself showed up to witness the outrage and make a statement. Sandy, for once, merely watched from the side while the custodians tried to scrub.

"I need to take some drastic action," Dr. Steinseifer, coming up beside him, said. "Drastic."

Sandy nodded but he was trying to study the script. Was this an adolescent's handwriting or an adult's forging an adolescent's? "We will not permit this type of bigotry in Appleton," Rizzo, dark and burly with a deeply pitted face, announced while Sandy peered around the onlookers. In gusts of breath smoke, the captain vowed, "We will root it out and punish it." The guidance counselor caught sight of Wendell Barr.

The vice principal looked more uncomfortable than guilty, as if vandalism gave prejudice a bad name. He stood in the frigid moments before first period, motionless among the shivering faculty. The look he shot at Sandy said, "Don't even think it."

Yet how could he not, what with the comments Wendell often let loose in the lounge? He waited for Saps to pass by, still scribbling in his pad.

"Now can you investigate?"

"You heard what Rizzo said. We're going to root it out. *The Appleton Gazette* will print it tomorrow. And you want an investigation, too?" He licked the tip of his pencil. "Don't think so, Coop."

"Why not?"

"Shortage of detectives. Budget cuts." He ceased speaking to his pad, tipped up his cap, and inserted the pencil under it. "But don't let this brotherhood stuff fool you, nobody really cares. Just the opposite. Secretly, a lot of folks agree."

Steam rose from the scalding water the janitors splashed on the Appleton sign. The paint had turned the orange brick a garish brown almost impermeable to soap. Sandy considered what Saps said about people's private racism and concluded, *Can't be*. But then then he thought about how his own working-class neighbors would react to a Black family moving in. Even the rich people up the hill would quietly resist, citing property values. But what Blacks? The school had only one so far, Rae Henderson, distinctive in so many ways, only one of which was color. Who could possibly object?

"Drastic," Steinseifer repeated yet again, this time for himself. Jeanne Pagonis swept by. Bundled in her trench coat, with her dark cropped-short hair, she could have passed for a spy.

"What are we coming to?" she asked and seemed to expect an answer.

Sandy didn't have one or need to. With the force of what sounded like a five-alarm fire, the bell rang for homeroom.

* * * * *

Inside, the halls teemed with demands for more precipitate action. Several students, self-styled radicals sad to have missed the sixties, their army jackets studded with Mao and Che buttons, demonstrated outside the principal's office. Word spread that a schoolwide assembly would be held, and the students would be addressed by inspirational speakers: clergymen, veterans, a science fiction writer rumored to be living near town. And tasked with explaining the importance of love, Appleton's own Rae Henderson.

"No way! It's not fair. You have to stop them." In a single sentence, she went from protesting to complaining to begging, all too quickly for Sandy. All he managed was, "Okay, okay, calm down."

Dressed in a tartan skirt and mauve crewneck sweater, with her hair braided back, Rae looked ladylike, especially when she cried. "I mean, do they have any idea what that feels like, people coming up and apologizing to you in the hall?" Tears shellacked her cheeks. "As if I represented every Black person on earth. Some symbol."

He did, in fact, know how she felt, remembering the time Jeanne asked his forgiveness for anti-Semitism. But to be begged by an entire school was a different matter, Sandy understood, especially at an age when kids just wanted to fit in. Reaching into his desk, Sandy handed her a tissue.

"You won't have to speak, I promise."

"And no assembly, either."

"I'll do my best."

Rae blew her nose and when she looked up again, the tears were gone. So was the hurt and the fear, replaced by anger. "Still want me to 'go with it,' Mister Cooper? Still want me to embrace my identity and say 'no sweat, whitey, we're cool."

Sandy's response was lamer than his leg. "Go with whatever makes you feel comfortable, Rae," he sputtered.

"What makes me feel comfortable is catching the fucker who painted that shit and beating the living crap out of him." She stood to her full height, regal again, and looked down at him with imperious eyes. "Happy?" she asked.

Sandy thought about following her out of his cubicle, accompanying her to class, but remained seated. Only the sound of chanting lured him into the hall to find the radical pupils still demanding action and Wendell threatening them with detentions. Again, their eyes met and Sandy's narrowed. "I know," they said. "You can't keep it secret from me."

Wendell just ignored him. He completed the task of shooing the students away, kicking their posters into a corner for the custodians. Only then, while watching the fatigues escape down the hall, he stated, "None of 'em would have lasted a day in Inchon. An hour."

"And that's what you fought for?" Sandy's head motioned toward the entrance and the hatred that might take months to fade. "In Inchon?"

Wendell's head finally turned, turret-like. "What we fought for, four F's like you will never understand."

"Freedom? Equality?"

Wendell snorted. "Survival. Yours and the guy's next to you. Kill the gook or the gook'll kill you. And no chance of surrender."

"Really?" Sandy's hands floated palms-out in front of chest. "Can't ever say, Wendell, I give up?"

"Higher," the vice principal said to those hands. "Higher so they can see." He marched toward Sandy with a piercing gaze. The buzzcut looked razored. "Higher, so the gooks can get a bead on you and put a bullet"—a calloused fingertip poked his brow—"right here."

Sandy still felt that finger between his eyes as he returned to his cubicle. A few feet away, though, he heard the telephone ring and bumbled forward. Pitching across his desk, he strained for the receiver and panted, "Hi, sweetie pie, what's up?"

"Sugar plum, I could understand. Honey bunch. But sweetie pie?" That same gritty voice, the same puff of cigarette.

"Oh, Jesus…"

"Now *that's* affectionate."

"I'm sorry."

"Don't be sorry. Just be where and when I tell you."

Balancing the receiver between his shoulder and chin, giving one last tug to his tie, Sandy scribbled.

*   *   *   *   *

The head, bald and bony where not crested in fat, presented its crown in the darkness. It hovered while the screams amplified. Wails so high-pitched they were hardly human. Sandy saw and heard this, though he, himself, was not present. He observed the glint of something metallic, something oiled, but it took a full second to perceive the blade. Curved, chisel-tipped, it rose high above the head. Then it plunged. Skin and bone all parted before geysers of blood and brains. The wailing ceased and only the sword remained, dangling and gory up to its handle. So, too, were the manicured fingers clutching it.

Sandy jerked upright in his bed. This was no dream but a recurring vision. The head belonged to Arthur's father who was once again beating him and the Japanese sword was removed from the wall. The fingers were Liz's. This was how he pictured the moment when the woman he would soon meet secretly took another man's life. "I'll do anything to protect my son"—the words resounded in his mind. *Anything.*

Sandy looked down at Esta slumbering heavily beside him. She didn't shift much, didn't dream either, she claimed, except for occasionally about

Joey, but even then wouldn't talk about it. In the ghostly light of their radio, he studied her, envied her ability to seal off emotional chambers. That's how Esta survived.

His own strategy—so he learned—was simpler. Not to compartmentalize but merely divide in half. One half worked to help young people slalom adolescence, strove to be a productive community member and devoted spouse. But the other snuck off to strange houses and made assignations at hotels. He limped in the first and sprinted in the second, appeased and horrified, apologized and galled. The trick was to keep them separate.

One half of him climbed out of bed, showered, dressed, and came down to a breakfast of runny eggs over blackened toast. That same half kissed his wife's still-puffy cheeks as he pushed his arms into his coat and hurried out of the front door, trailing "Love you, sweetie pie" behind. The other half, though, turned on the ignition and sat enveloped by fumes while the car heated up; his mind dashed through the workday up to the instant when he entered another door and a radically different reality.

Yet even that would be bifurcated. With Liz, Sandy would have to distinguish between a lover and the mother of one of his students, a woman able to bring him to sensual heights and another capable of murder. And who knew how many chambers he would still have to seal, Sandy pondered as he taped the notice to the gymnasium door. One could get lost in the maze. He reread the message—"Practice cancelled today due to illness"—and hustled out to his car.

* * * * *

The hotel, located not far from town but on the far side of the nature reserve, might have been built for liaisons. The rooms stood apart from the main lodge, each encased in trees. Sandy squinted through the twilight, searching for the right number, and suddenly thought, "She's done this before." An entirely new feeling—envy—pierced him and for a moment drove out all his fears of getting caught or not performing. The fears returned soon enough, though, as he approached the door and knocked.

She didn't ask, "Who's there?" or even invite him in, only stated, "It's open."

And it was. He smelled her first—the cigarettes, the woods, and something else, something savory. The room was dark but speckled with enough light to reveal that she was barefoot and shorter than he expected. Slighter, too, clothed only in a sashless robe that exposed most of her breasts, a remarkably flat belly, and tuft.

"This is where you say 'Hello, Liz,'" she recommended, and Sandy complied. "This is where you take me in your arms."

She felt so tiny, birdlike, though he was the one trembling as his hands delved inside the robe. Her skin was burning, the hairs on her nape so soft. He kissed her neck, her cheeks, and finally her mouth, and the sensation was more enveloping than any he'd ever imagined.

Between kisses, Liz undid her hair, his tie, buttons, zipper. Somehow he found himself standing in his white Fruit of the Loom underwear, strangely embarrassed by their bulge, and feeling silly until she said, "You might want to take those off."

Whether he tackled her or allowed himself to be tackled he would never remember, only the spectrum of tastes from tobacco-tinged to zesty and the need not only to be inside her but blanketed by her entirely. He remembered the end table rocking as he plunged, the shame he felt when it stopped rattling too early, and then the pride when it started rattling again. Though he tried not to, the image of Esta kept appearing to him: Esta just lying there, demure. But here was Liz writhing beneath him, rising up to engulf him, cursing in his ear. Here were Liz's lips sucking the life out of him—or so he felt—like a lamb in a lion's jaws.

After, there was little time to talk. With her butt pressed into his midsection, she drew his arms around herself and sighed. "You are the experienced one, aren't you, Mister Cooper?"

His sigh was more of a whimper. "No, not really. Truth is, I've never…" His chin traced the scoop of her neck. "The sixties kind of washed over me, I guess."

"No free love, huh?"

"Not much love, no. And certainly not free."

He studied her ears. They were small and delicately formed. Ornamental. "You make me want to make up for lost time."

"I have all the time in the world. You're the one with the schedule."

He was, and the awareness of it was suddenly acute. "I have to go," he said, and she replied snappishly, "Of course you do."

Sandy dreaded leaving her and the universe of that room for all that awaited him outside. Guilt, horror, the sheer shittiness of his act. Yet none of those feelings delayed him as he washed her smell from his skin, climbed back into his standard khakis and button-down, and even remembered his tie. Kissing her one long, final time, he catapulted toward the door, pausing only to say, "I want to see you again. I need to. Soon."

"I know," said Elizabeth Warhaftig.

* * * * *

Driving home in the darkness, he felt like a pilot, his Impala transformed into a jet. The trees, the lampposts, the Deer Xing signs that lined the nature reserve and gave way to Children Crossing signs when he exited—all zoomed past. The familiar storefronts of Wexler's Drugs, Hershkey's Bakery, and Sobotnik's seemed toy-like. Temple Beth El, with its pentagonal sanctuary and plexiglass dome, could have passed for a spaceship.

Only when he steered downhill, into his working-class neighborhood, did Sandy return earthward. And what he found astonished him. The mostly barren trees were draped again, not with leaves but toilet paper. Streamers of it dangled off the boughs and encircled trunks. Broken glass studded the street. Had there been a riot, Sandy wondered, a clash with gangs from the city?

Only when he turned into his one-car driveway did he recall this was Mischief Night. Not a tradition when he was a kid, it had recently become one when, on Halloween eve, youngsters rampaged for an hour or so before their parents or the police showed up. Further proof of the world gone rotten.

Yet what were a few rolls of Charmin, even some busted lightbulbs, compared to what he had just done? One was merely pranks and the other deeply wrong, maybe evil. And yet both were fun, he had to admit, reckless and contemptuous of norms. Both found freedom in darkness. And the mess could be left for morning.

He locked the Impala and followed the flagstone path to his door and its smashed pumpkin. There, perhaps for the first time ever, he rang the doorbell. He rang again until finally Esta answered, looking scared. The hazy light of their living room haloed her and smoke from something torched in the background. Sandy smiled at her—mischievously—and pointed to the orange viscera. "Trick or treat," he said.

7.

"Testing, one, two. Testing."

Outside of Sandy's cubicle, workmen connected the last of the wires and prepared to seal them in the wall. For nearly a week now he had been unable to hold a decent conversation with a student, much less a *sotto voce* phone call with Liz. The hammering and drilling could barely be shouted over, and the soldering chased most guidance-seekers away. And now that the project was complete, he had to contend with Dr. Steinseifer droning, "Testing, one, two."

This was the principal's idea of drastic measures: a PA system. Installed in the classes and at strategic junctures along the halls, it would communicate vital updates such as the first meetings of the chess and debating teams or the lineup for vaccinations in the gym. Mornings, it would play "The Star-Spangled Banner," wish everyone a pleasant day, and, most crucially, convey a thought. These could be drawn from the Bible or the Constitution or even Eastern philosophy, as long as the message was tolerance. Students and teachers alike would choose and read them, and discussions would be held in class. People would pause and think while their minds expanded and the world became more embracing, explained Dr. Steinseifer.

He tested, cleared his throat into the mic on his desk, and began. "Good morning, Appleton Junior High. Welcome to everyone." He spoke in his usual monotone, haltingly, as if each word was a hurdle. "I have something I want to share with you. Something important. But first, please rise for our national anthem."

Sandy stood at his desk as a recorded band boomed through the round aluminum grills. "By the dawn's early light," he sang, and, "by the twilight's last gleaming," but with his focus entirely elsewhere. In the hotel rooms Liz rented for them—never her house where Arthur might somehow barge in—and for which he had to invent endless excuses. Another doctor's appointment. Servicing the car. A condolence call. Not since he dodged defenders on the field had he sidestepped so many threats.

But the elation at the end of each meeting was greater than any touchdown. Each time yielded wondrous revelations: the taste of her toes, the slightly gurgling, dirge-like sound she made while lovemaking. And no less gratifying than the sexual stages were the spoken intervals, when most of the whispers were his.

He told her about growing up with a father who, disappointed in himself, expected only excellence in his son. How he rushed from practice to practice—football, baseball, wrestling—and competed under his father's glare. He was never a stellar student—Sandy struggled through remedial math—but at sports he proved ingenious. There wasn't a ball he couldn't master, a play beyond his skill. League champion, captain of every team, Super Coop, they called him, our star.

Jostled into the present, standing in his cubicle, Sandy remembered to sing, "And the home of the brave," before retaking his seat. The announcements were far from completed, though, as Dr. Steinseifer began reciting Eleanor Roosevelt. "Freedom makes a huge requirement of every human being," he stammered. "With freedom comes responsibility. For the person who is unwilling to grow up, this is a frightening prospect."

But Sandy was still elsewhere. Hunched over his desk and studying his phone, he was thinking about his last conversation with Liz. The hardest and most intimate ever.

"So you have no children?"

"You probably found out I didn't."

"Probably. But did you ever?"

"I don't want to talk about it."

Cupping his shoulder, she hugged his head tighter to her breast. "Don't you?"

Outside of a single conversation with Saps long ago, he'd never discussed it with anyone. But there he was, his legs entangled with Liz's and relating how proud he felt, how completed, at the birth of his first son. A beautiful boy, the doctors said, and the nurses purled, "An angel." Blonde like Esta and boxer-faced like Sandy. "My little all-American," he cooed.

They called him Joe after Uncle Yossele, dead of heartbreak in the thirties, Joey. Evenings, Sandy rushed home to see him, barely pausing to brush Esta's cheek at the door before clomping up the stairs to the baby's room. Those itsy fingers clutching one of his, the blue-gray sequins of eyes. Sandy sang to him, in a voice like migrating cranes, and tickled every one of his chins. And he bought him the embroidered bear, or whatever it was. Weekends, Sandy strolled with him around the neighborhood, accosting passers-by with a near-threatening, "Hey, meet my son, Joey. A knockout, isn't he?"

But then, at six months, suddenly a red dot in one pupil. Suddenly, a sensitivity to noise and light and an inability to turn. The name the doctor gave it sounded innocent enough: Tay-Sachs, almost playful. Until the seizures began, followed by feeding tubes. Hospitalized, institutionalized, Joey would never ask for another bedtime story, never once call him Dad.

Still, he kept vigil by his hospital crib, consulted with doctors, and spent every dime of their meager savings. Not much of a crier, he held Esta and listened to her sobs. Often, he felt himself going mad with agony. Sometimes, sitting alone in Beth El's sanctuary, Sandy almost prayed.

"It happened when I was out on the field coaching. They called to tell me it was over. For an hour or so I just stood there, the wind knocked out of me. My only son Joey—the boy I was going to teach football to, baseball, life—was gone."

Sandy, his face buried in Liz's chest, imparted this directly to her heart. She held him as he convulsed. "Alright," she murmured, "everything's alright," and kissed his bristly crown.

Back in his cubicle, he heard but didn't listen as Dr. Steinseifer recited Frederick Douglass. "The white man's happiness cannot be purchased by the Black man's misery," the principal averred through the speaker. "It is easier to build strong children than to repair broken men."

* * * * *

The announcements ended at some point, but he remained gazing at his phone. That is, until Rae Henderson's ginghamed torso appeared in his doorway.

"Eleanor Roosevelt? Frederick Douglass?" Her hands slapped over her ears. "Can't you get him to stop?"

Sandy weighed his palms. "Frederick Douglas or that assembly—which is worse?"

"Some idiot spray-paints something on the front of the school and I've got to pay for it. Every morning. Kids looking at me as if I made them listen to this crap." Her finger stabbed the air in front of Sandy's face. "You people aren't fair."

Later, entering the lounge, he wondered what she meant by "you people." Faculty members? Adults? Or was it, as he suspected, about race? He didn't have time to ponder it, though, as he stumbled into another rancorous debate.

The algebra teacher, Earl Bronowski, a man of negligible depth, was ranting against the new intrusion on his privacy. "I don't think it's right, damn it, not in school, not nowhere—in church, maybe—being preached to."

Cranky as he was, Bronowski's counterpart in geometry, Tom McGonnigle, was grumpier. "It's about time someone brought some love into this school," said the man who, with the sixties behind him and well into his thirties, still dressed like a teenager at Woodstock. "Not just math and history all the time. Love."

Charlotte Fox of course agreed—"Ditch the math, *just* love," she suggested—while Ronald Stephens, the portly science teacher who'd been rejected by Rensselaer, countered that love was entirely subjective, unquantifiable, and therefore inappropriate for the curriculum.

Other teachers sauntered in: Brooks, fresh out of shop class, sullen and sawdusted, and geography's Miriam Loftus, with maps rolled under her arm. They entered just as D'Angelis declared, "Screw the curriculum." Bulging through his skin-tight t-shirt, curling an empty coffee cup like a weight, the PE teacher proclaimed: "Soccer scores, good. Pledge of Allegiance, great. But keep that mushy-wushy stuff out of my gym."

And Charlotte protested, "You think love's mushy—there's your problem, Vinny." She rolled her emerald eyes. "Another threatened male."

"You want a problem, Foxy? I'll show you a problem!"

D'Angelis cocked the coffee cup back as if to hurl it, but Stephens stepped in front. "Let's take it down a notch."

"Stay out of it, fatso," Bronowski warned. "It's about time that bimbo got slammed."

McGonnigle's long hair and bell bottoms flared as he stomped toward Bronowski who lowered his anvil-shaped head in defense.

"Cool it, all of you!" Charlotte commanded them, but D'Angelis only laughed and countered, "Cool it, hell. Let's see 'em fight!"

"Keep it down!" Peering anxiously down the corridor as if the principal might hear, Jeanne Pagonis pleaded with her colleagues. Then Sandy Cooper sauntered in. "They've gone nuts," Jeanne whispered to him. "Do something."

Sandy shrugged. "Me?" He crossed the room to the counter and its pot of charred coffee. He poured, sipped, and scowled while Charlotte asked, "And what do *you* think?"

The guidance counselor seemed clueless.

"The PA system," Stephens prodded. "The sermonettes."

They were all looking at him, searching for support or another reason to protest. Sandy, typically, gave them neither. "If it doesn't offend anybody, fine. If it does, then not fine."

The entire lounge moaned. Even Jeanne looked disappointed. He lifted his mug and heard, "We should've known better than to ask Coop."

"Ask *me*."

Their heads simultaneously turned—Sandy's too—toward Wendell, entering from the hallway outside.

"Ask me and I'll tell you exactly what I think."

A brief silence followed, broken by someone conceding, "Okay, we're asking."

Wendell grinned. A hand drew across his buzzcut while his eyes, like twin muzzles, swept the lounge. They centered on Sandy. "I'm all in favor. And when it comes my turn to read, better believe it won't be any of that hippie pinko shit. No way. I'm going to tell these kids what nobody else will. That this country belongs to us. Not to the long-hairs, not to the druggies and the Commies and the colored of all stripes. To us. And not to your type, either."

The silence now was permanent. The teachers' heads toggled between Wendell and Sandy, waiting for a response. They didn't get one—yet. Only after he laid his cup on the counter, tugged on his tie and pushed up his sleeves, when he was already making his exit, did Sandy say, "No you won't."

"I won't?"

At the door, he paused and turned. "No, you won't. 'Cause if you do, that speaker"—he pointed to the stainless steel grill in the wall—"will be announcing out of your throat."

"I'm so proud," Jeanne exclaimed as she caught up with him in the hallway, but Sandy didn't respond. His only care at this point was to get back into his cubicle, close its frosted door, and dwell on images of Liz.

*   *   *   *   *

There weren't many. Liz insisted on meeting him in the near-dark, and even when rising from bed, carefully covered herself. Still, he cherished the few features he discerned—the flat tummy nestled between pelvic bones, the contoured back, nipples both supple and hard. More than how she looked, though, he remembered their conversations.

Amazing the truths she drew out of him. How his relationship with Esta changed after Joey's death. Reeling with grief and told she could never again bear children, she withdrew inside her cheerleader's façade and beamed as if winning. But Sandy was less adept at disguises and unable to simulate intimacy. His life, mostly loveless since then, was redeemed by counseling and coaching.

Amazing that he told Liz so much but also frustrating, as the confessions were all one-sided. He longed to ask her about herself—about her marriage and the abuse that Arthur suffered. He wanted to ask what drove her to reach for that sword. And was Sandy special to her or just one of a procession? Did Liz feel herself, as he did, falling?

8.

The day, he remembered, was spanking cold, the sunlight searing. The bleachers erupted when he and the team took to the field. He heard his name being chanted—"Give me a D! Give me a Y! What's that spell? Sandy!"—and discerned Esta's voice cheering loudest. Only his parents stayed silent. His mother's face embedded in a knitted scarf and his father rigid in a houndstooth coat and feathered fedora, presiding over the gridiron like a courtroom.

He strained not to look at him, to keep his eyes on the defense and his mind on the play throughout the first quarter when he aimed for an early lead. And he got one, when everything—handoffs, the laterals—gained yardage. One touchdown, two, and a third that he, himself, ran in from a draw. The crowd exploded. Esta raved and even his mother might have rooted, quietly into her muff. There was a reason that his classmates called him Super Coop, even the *Appleton Gazette*. Only his father remained unruffled. He watched and he judged. The drums, to Sandy, sounded like gavels.

Halftime brought a premature celebration that he, as quarterback and captain, was duty-bound to suppress. Instead, wobbling in his cleats, he climbed onto one of the locker room's narrow benches and exhorted his teammates to stay focused. Half an hour was an eternity out there and just about anything could happen.

Anything did. In fewer minutes, the visitors racked up twenty-four points while their hosts remained scoreless. Suddenly, with time nearly expired, he found himself with his back to his own goal and the opponent's impossibly distant. Yet this, he realized, was his moment. Scouts were reportedly observing from the stands, armed with full college rides. Annapolis had also expressed interest, and he imagined himself bedecked in midshipman white with a stunning date on his sleeve. Yet his paramount concern was still the man in the houndstooth coat. No scholarship, no uniform could rival the glory of a single dip of that feathered fedora.

The snap went off crisply and he fell back for a bomb. That's when the unexpected happened. A gap yawned in the defensive line and revealed, between it and the endzone, nobody. The ball looped from behind his head to under his armpit. Helmet lowered, he charged.

He bolted. He shot. Never before, not even out of uniform, had he sprinted so fast. The wind whistled through the single bar of his facemask and whirred around his ears. He could hear his own frantic breathing and, beyond that, the frenzy of the crowd. Thundering drums, a confetti of autumn leaves. Past his own thirty, forty, and into enemy turf he churned, a goal post rising before him. He already saw himself kneeling beneath it and planting the ball to score. He saw Esta launching her pom-poms and scampering out to embrace him, the scouts racing forward with deals. He imagined his father still staid in his Thanksgiving best but beaming.

Looking back, he would wonder why he hadn't performed the basic open-field maneuver, zigzagging to avoid pursuers. Perhaps because he was so damn certain, the absence of any defenders in front of him meaning none were closing in from behind. After all, this was the most ecstatic moment of his life—who could've pictured its end?

He would not remember that end. Only a dull crack like that of tree about to fall, which he not only heard but felt. He no longer saw the goal-post but only the sky and worried faces peering down at him. Someone asked questions but his only answer was pain. A crazy pain that erupted after they lifted him. Then he noticed his leg trailing behind him, listless and twisted. He heard a scream—Esta's—and but there was no sign of her, of his mother, or anybody else in the crowd. Only his father's face, sealed in disappointment.

* * * * *

The bitterness of that look still chilled him, especially today, on a Thanksgiving every bit as blustery as that one twenty-five years ago. Though his father was no longer in the stands and Esta rooted with fake rabbit fur mittens rather than pom-poms, standing on the sidelines, he experienced that same trepidation. Maybe it was the memory of lying in a hospital bed and realizing that there would be no scholarships for him, no dress whites or statuesque dates, but only a local teachers' college, khakis and half-knotted ties, and the local girl who carried his books while he hobbled to class on crutches. A limp that later stiffened with age. Perhaps he knew even then that his future was to remain in school and his job to nurture other athletes' dreams. Knew that when he next took to the field it would be not as Coop, but as Coach. His duty would be to his players, especially Russel Pressman, who showed all of Sandy's promise and more.

And he displayed it today, lavishly, passing for major gains, nimbly evading tacklers. If prep school scouts were indeed note-taking, Russel filled up their pads. Sandy had never seen a better performance, and against rival Mount Tabor, the favorite. But Appleton jumped to an early lead and widened it. No penalties, no fumbles. Tony Metallo, at center, remembered the calls.

Yet still Sandy struggled. It wasn't so much the marching band blasting, the cheerleaders' rants, or even the cold. His mind was a rip tide of thoughts—memories of his injury colliding with concerns for Russel's safety every time he ran with the ball. And coursing through them all, Liz. He tried his best to appear riveted by the game, sending out plays and adjusting the line with hand motions. He even remembered to turn occasionally and wave at Esta. She waved back vivaciously, even when he was clearly gazing elsewhere in the stands. There, in the furthermost section, he spotted them.

Arthur had his usual absent look, disconnected and bored. But not Liz. In a real fur coat made from some spotted animal and her matching hat, she smugly peered at Sandy. Only at him, disinterested in the rest of the spectacle. Her expression seemed severe, eyes narrowed and capacious mouth pursed, and he wondered if this sight of him in a varsity jacket and woolen cap stamped with a black-and-gold 'A' might have wakened her to reality. Maybe she was experiencing regret.

That worry consumed him well into the fourth quarter, along with the fear that Esta would see her eyeing him and somehow know. Anxiety fused with guilt.

Preoccupied, Sandy would barely recall how, with the game now almost tied and only minutes remaining, his team lined up on its own two-yard line. Metallo managed the snap and Russel dropped into the endzone preparing to pass. But then his front four opened a hole and the quarterback, with no more than a glance downfield, galloped.

The crowd went wild as Russel passed the fifty with nothing but emptiness in front. Only Sandy remained frozen. He kept waiting for that sole defenseman to catch up and pounce on his player with a tibia-snapping tackle. It was like watching an old newsreel of himself, only high-speed and in color. And with a different ending. Linebackers and safeties chased him, but Russel outran them all. Spiking rather than kneeling with the ball, he pranced around the goalpost.

The stands seemed to come apart and even Sandy found himself clapping. In the stands, Wendell and Jeanne and other faculty members rose applauding. Saps tossed his cap skyward. Students howled.

But Arthur appeared unaffected, and his mother austere. Only when her eyes met Sandy's did her sternness give way to a grin. He beamed and waved to her adoringly while Esta waved back, unaware for several moments that the gesture wasn't for her.

*　*　*　*　*

Marjorie's bird looked enormous this year, almost prehistoric, taking up half the table. If strict at bookkeeping, Saps's wife was extravagant when it came to food. All of her portions were large, even the cranberries. She, herself, was a big woman, wider than her husband and heavier. The outfit she wore— dun skirt, pink acrylic sweater—didn't help, nor did the Annette Funicello hairstyle. Still, nothing could detract from Marjorie's face, a confection of dimples and sparkly green eyes, a baby doll's nose and mouth. Her nature was sugary as well, prone to laugh while her two sons, Mark and Gerald, raced model cars around the table, and to giggle at her incompetent carving.

"Here, let me do that, honey," Esta offered and relieved her of the knife that was more weapon than cutlery.

"Amazing!" Saps slapped his peaky forehead. "Freakin' incredible!"

Marjorie chided him, "Language," and motioned toward the boys. "And Esta doesn't need cheerleading."

But Saps went on, "Passing, screening—you name it. And that run! Holy shit!"

"Arnold." A plea, not a protest, it went equally unheeded by the children, whose toys were lapping the condiments. Both boys were towheaded and rangy for their ages—eleven and ten, slightly younger than Joey would have been.

"Harroom. Harroommm," they grunted, and "Screeech!" as their father persisted. "Damn it, Coop, that Pressman's gold."

Sandy agreed, but absently. Thanksgiving meals often found him silent, beset by memories and, in more recent years, by the need to deliver leftovers to his father at the home. Another hour of Rogers, Hammerstein, and bile, but now he only thought of Esta. He watched her leaning onto the blade handle and sawing through the breast. He fought to keep his eyes on her, appearing as if nothing had happened. Nothing did, after all, merely an exchange of salutes with a fan. What could be suspicious about that?

And yet he sensed that she did suspect, and he felt awful. Watching her separating chest from thighs with both her hands on the knife made him think of Liz with a similar grip on a sword. Only Esta's hands were bloodless.

This was Sandy's frame of mind when, just before digging in, Esta asked him about that finely dressed woman he was waving to. "That coat must've cost a fortune."

Spearing some meat and stuffing, Sandy chewed carefully before answering. Even then, "Which woman?" was all he said.

Esta didn't respond. She just let Sandy have another bite, another chew, before he conceded, "Oh, her. The mother of one of the players. Yeah, she's a wealthy one alright. And concerned about her baby's safety."

"Well, I hope you kept that baby safe," Marjorie said, but Saps just laughed. "That baby just scored four touchdowns. That baby just handed Coop here a five-and-two season."

"Of course he did," Esta, herding peas to the outskirts of her plate, said, with a sarcasm so sharp it cut only Sandy.

"Harrooom!" Mark and Gerald roared as their tiny Ferraris rounded the gravy. "Eeeek!"

"Enough, boys," their mother scolded them softly. "This is family time. We don't misbehave."

On his third mouthful, Sandy allowed himself a glance at Esta, who didn't return his look but was staring longingly at the boys. *Idiot*, he inwardly berated himself while asking to pass the cranberries. *Bastard, what were you thinking?*

Yes, Liz made him feel special—more than that, alive—and free for the first time since high school. And with all his many disappointments, his dutifulness, didn't he deserve this one indulgence? But the affair also sullied him, Sandy now admitted, degraded him from faithful husband to philanderer. The counselor responsible for turning adolescents into adults had, himself, committed adultery.

Suddenly, he knew. Come Monday, he'd call up Liz and break it off with her. Swift and decisive. He could never see her again, Sandy would insist, not even to say goodbye.

* * * * *

Only Liz saw and spoke to him first. Later Monday afternoon, Sandy would wonder what would have happened if he hadn't procrastinated all morning, hadn't found the need to rearrange his files and schedule seventh-grade tutorials. The phone loomed enormously on his desk—too large, it seemed, to lift. He was still shifting through paperwork when Jeanne burst into his cubicle.

"Quick, Coop," she gasped, "Come…"

Their eyes met—hers urgent, his utterly confused—but before he could ask for clarification, she began pulling on his rolled-up sleeve. "Hurry!"

She tugged him through the lounge, Sandy amazed by the power of her tiny frame, half-embarrassed and entertained by it, until he heard the noise. Grunting, growling, a series of hyperventilated snorts. Until he saw Arthur Warhaftig again performing his karate moves, chopping the air and kicking, not outside or alone this time, but in the intersection of two hallways where Wendell Barr usually stood in ambush. And, sure enough, the vice principal for discipline was there, for the moment hanging back. Then, after ducking one more roundhouse, he grabbed Arthur beneath his clavicle-length hair and hauled up him by the scruff.

"Try that gook crap on me, little man, and I'll fry you."

Without thinking, Sandy wrenched his sleeve free of Jeanne and lunged. "Put him down right now!"

With an expression as contemptuous as the one he'd shown Arthur, Wendell turned to him. Though shorter by a head, he had a way of looking down at the counselor and threatening him. Arthur remained hoisted.

"Let him go or so help me." The same sleeve was now pushed above his elbow, unsheathing forearm and fist.

"Oh, so that's what you want." Released, Arthur fell listlessly to the floor as Wendell squared off opposite Sandy. "You first."

Sandy took a step, as did Wendell, until their faces were as close as linemen's.

"No, you two! No!" Jeanne implored, though neither of them really heard. Nor did they notice the students. They now filled the halls and gathered at the intersection to gawk. To Sandy, they were just a swath of faces, even Rae's, the most agitated. He was only aware of Wendell's puss and an irrepressible need to punch it.

"Go 'head, hero. Take your best shot," Wendell hissed.

Sandy shifted back and forth on his heels, shoulders pumping, as if bouncers were holding him back.

"Course you won't. Hebes can't fight for shit."

The flat of Sandy's palm smacked Wendell's shoulder hard enough to make him flinch, though he didn't. "Like I said...."

The second strike, with knuckles bared, nearly landed, when a stentorian voice ordered them, "Stop!"

They both looked up at the wall, but the words came not through the PA grate but from Dr. Steinseifer himself, summoned no doubt by Jeanne. He stood in the intersection, bland and furious, demanding explanations.

Wendell, suddenly obsequious, offered his. "I was just handing out a detention to...to..." He searched the crowd. "This girl. She was chewing gum in the hall."

"But I wasn't," Rae protested. "I swore to Mister Barr, I wasn't."

She said this to the principal, but his deputy answered. "Quiet you," he snapped, then turned back to Steinseifer. "I caught her and the next thing I knew this, this nutjob comes at me swinging."

For a single instant, the adults' attention turned to Arthur still sitting, head lowered and hunched on the floor.

Sandy protested, "He can't talk to a child that way."

"That's no child and, yes, I can talk to him any way I want when he tries to assault me. I can expel his ass."

Sandy again lurched forward, fingers furled, but Dr. Steinseifer inserted his bulk between them. "You two should be ashamed. We're supposed to be teaching tolerance."

"Sorry, sir." Sandy did his best to sound penitent. "But this boy is under my personal care."

"Yes, and under your care he was nearly hospitalized. And you were almost...."

"I said I'm handling it." Sandy's face was now in Dr. Steinseifer's but then he contritely pulled back. "I know I screwed up then, but we've come a long way, Arthur and me, and I'm asking you, please, let me deal with this. The boy has...difficulties."

The principal waited a beat before consenting. "Alright. He's yours. But to be safe, my office will inform his mother."

That said, Steinseifer retired to his office. The students scattered, including Rae, hugging a breastplate of books. Only Jeanne remained, pinching her golden cross and shooting Sandy a disappointed look he knew too well, and Wendell Barr, glaring.

He turned his back on both of them and retrieved Arthur from the floor. Steering toward the cubicle, though, Sandy heard a sneer. "You think you can gang up against us. All of you." By 'you,' Sandy understood, he again meant people of his and Arthur's religion as well as those of Rae's color. "Well, think again," warned Wendell.

*   *   *   *   *

He could scarcely remember a longer hour, as talking with Arthur proved excruciating. Asked about his classes, his relationships with his peers, he recoiled behind his bangs and buried his chin in his throat. A shoulder jerked up and down, indicating yes or no. His stone-gray eyes darted.

If only he could ask the boy about the torture he'd endured from his father, the trauma of his violent death. But a guidance counselor is not a psychiatrist, Sandy realized. Nor could he reveal all he'd heard from Saps. All he could do was ask about Rae Henderson, whether she and Arthur were friends.

Adolescents have strange ways of expressing their crushes—sometimes with cruelty, others with smothering love, sometimes both. Arthur merely said, "I won't let them hurt her. I won't," but wouldn't identify the "them." Nor would he offer another word, flattering or even factual, about Rae. It was almost a relief when his mother rushed into the cubicle and slammed its frosted glass door.

Flew was more like it, in a single high-heeled stride covering the distance between door and desk and then, in a fluid hoop, sweeping Arthur into her arms. She pushed the hair from his face and flattened his cheek with kisses. "Are you okay? Are you okay?" Liz pressed him, only to receive some mumblings. Finally, she looked up. "Is he okay?"

Sandy wondered who had almost gotten into a fistfight, Arthur or him, but nevertheless managed to smile. "Don't worry. He's fine."

"Poor you...."

She meant Arthur, of course, and Sandy immediately saw that, with her son in the room, serious conversation was impossible.

"Maybe we could have just a few minutes alone?" he asked the boy. "Just me and your mom?"

This finally elicited a reaction—a glare of startling intensity aimed first at Liz and then at him, but which only Sandy noticed. Liz was too busy stroking Arthur's hair. "Go back to class now, love. Mommy'll see you at home."

He shrank into the corridor, leaving them to face to querulous face. An instance's silence ended with Sandy blurting, "I was meaning to call you this morning...."

"How dare you talk about us!" she flashed. "This is about Arthur. *Only* Arthur."

Reflexively, Sandy shrank behind his desk. The ferocity of her expression astonished him, made him forget the long weekend with Esta, the alternating looks of suspicion and hurt. It reminded him, once again, of the extremes this woman could reach whenever defending her son.

"Arthur will be fine, I promised you. No student's going to touch him. No teacher, either."

"They better not. For your sake."

"Are you threatening me, Liz?" Sandy's voice dropped to a rasp. "Threatening *me?*"

She sat in the chair opposite his desk and stretched across it, close enough to kiss. "I'll threaten anybody I have to. That and more."

He gaped at her. This was the first time he'd seen her face in full light, the wrinkles around her mouth, a patch beside her right eye that might or might not be a scar. But the same fluorescence that diluted her beauty also highlighted her rage. It seemed like a living thing to him, more powerful than any passion.

Liz straightened in her chair and reached into her purse. "I don't have to remind you, Sandy," she said, wincing into a pocket mirror. "You have a lot more to lose than your job."

Was she going to tell Esta? Send a memo to the school? He was going to ask her straight out, but she suddenly changed the subject.

"Do you remember what I did to you last time in the hotel?" She showed him an open-lipped smile with the tips of teeth and tongue. "And the time before that?"

The questions hit Sandy physically and made his injured thigh twitch. Dressed in a periwinkle business suit, hair lashed back, her formality both excited and diminished him. That woodsy, cigarettey smell. He suddenly felt as helpless as any student in the hall—too weak to beg her to leave.

"Will you remember what we did in your office?"

The question befuddled him just long enough for her to stretch her hand underneath the desk. "Are you crazy? In school?" He frantically searched for shadows behind the glass door and saw none.

"Shh," was all Liz said.

"But Arthur...."

Her head and mouth followed her hand beneath. So much for phoning her, for ending it and returning to honesty with Esta.

"Arthur's in class," Liz whispered.

* * * * *

That evening he waited until well after the last bell, after the clubs and sports teams had practiced and left the school, to escape. The last thing he wanted was to run into some teacher prying into his near brawl with Wendell. Or Jeanne Pagonis with some questions about that rich-looking woman who entered his cubicle to talk about her son, only to emerge thirty minutes later with smeared lipstick. Bad enough he recalled the quick, scorching glance from Arthur when he and Liz finally came out into the corridor, where Arthur had in fact been waiting.

Like a convict on the lam, he scurried, pulling on his ski jacket as he fled. The temperature outside had fallen below freezing, unseasonable for these last days of fall. Sandy cursed himself for not bringing gloves; he would have to scrape his windshield barehanded.

He was already blowing on his knuckles as he approached the Impala, the last car in the lot. Its off-white exterior, though faded, refracted the school's security lights and the bulbs of its Christmas decorations. Likely that was the source of the red he saw playing on the hood. Only when he took out his scraper did he notice that the color was frozen.

"Shit," Sandy thought, "Spray paint."

But paint wasn't laced with fur. And red looked different when accompanied by a tail of some animal—a squirrel or rabbit—speared on the antenna with its head skewered on the grill. Numb and retching, Sandy scraped the frigid puddle of blood.

Winter

1.

"Now, everybody, together! Sing a song of peace!"

The smack of clapping hands reverberated around the sanctuary, rattled the stained-glass windows, and ricocheted off the pews. The Eternal Flame wobbled in its sconce—or so Sandy imagined—dappling the memorial plaques in light.

The bearded man sang, "*O-se shalom bimromav, hu ya'aseh shalom aleynu,*" and shouted, "Come on now, everybody!" He jumped up and down, heavyset and gray but cherubic, a kosher Santa pounding a guitar. He leapt, sidelocks and fringes flouncing, and the pulpit rolled like a prow.

"Sing!" Sandy was ordered, not by the performer but by Esta, punctuated with an elbow in his ribs. He didn't know the words, but he mouthed some anyway and did his best to clap—anything to spare himself another jab. Anything to get through the temple's version of a hootenanny that his wife insisted he attend.

"*Ve'al kol Yisrael*—sing, sing for love!—*Ve'imru, ve'imru* amen."

Not only did the old Orthodox hippie bounce but also the younger man beside him. Far younger—a teenager, Sandy thought, his chin as smooth as it was receding. Longer haired than one might expect from a clergyman, with aviator glasses and a beaked, bumpy nose and eyes too closely set, his appearance was far from impressive. Yet for all his physical shortcomings, Stanley Rosencranz more than compensated with fervor. A "Save Soviet Jewry" button on his collar, peace symbol on his *yarmulke*, he was a person of causes, all of them burning. Bursting out of seminary school, the assistant rabbi was determined to fix a world that God had somehow left broken.

Beginning with Beth El, where the previous rabbi preferred Chivas Regal to ministering, Stanley set to work. A month after the assistant's arrival, lapis Israeli jewelry was on sale in the lobby's gift shop and "Save Bangladesh" posters lined the halls. There were the sermons comparing Abraham to the late Reverend Dr. Martin Luther King, to Moshe Dayan, and even Eugene McCarthy, and the inexhaustible effort to render everything—brises, Sunday's Bagel Brunch—relevant. The results were instant. Synagogue attendance was up thirty percent, along with Hebrew School enrolment. Membership for the first time in memory climbed. Old Isaacson could stay locked up with a Scotch bottle in his study. Nobody cared anymore. They only wanted Stan.

Esta wanted him, too. Saturday mornings, often his only time to sleep in, Sandy awoke to find the bed next to him empty. His wife had gone to services. She joined the Women's Club, Hadassah, and scoured the garage for the Rummage Sale. Even her cooking changed. In place of bacon and cheeseburgers came matzo balls and gefilte fish, indistinguishable in density and appearance. "Really, sweetie, you have to see him," she urged while serving her husband. "Talk to him. Confide in him. Just once."

That made Sandy feel even worse. It seemed to him that Esta's spiritual turn was spurred by a need to grasp something—anything—as her world split further apart. She needed to believe that the man she had lived with and loved most of her life was not drifting but merely experiencing a phase which, with a little rabbinic assistance, would pass. "You can trust him, I promise," she stressed, failing to add, he felt, "because I can no longer trust you."

His wife was desperate. He sensed it in the way she'd kissed him that New Year's Eve, hard on the lips, pleading in his ear, "Let's have a loving '72." He saw it in the argyle tie she stuffed in his Hanukkah stocking. Sandy hated argyle. Still, he appreciated her out-of-the-box attempts to please him and felt sorry for her, almost, fixing him up with Rabbi Stan.

But confiding in anyone, even his best friend, was alien to Sandy, a man who kept his feelings to himself and considered solitude manly. Meanwhile, he tried inching closer to Esta, dispelling her suspicions. Taking her to movies, asking more about her day. He listened to her complaints about cancelling Home Ec. "Sewing, knitting, how are young ladies ever to learn?" she worried. He heard her frustration with teaching about sex and drugs when many of the fifteen-year-olds were richly exposed to both.

But, for all his attempts to remain close to her, Sandy could not resist the greater pull. He was already spinning off into another woman's orbit, leaving his wife in emotional space. Sexually, too, the initial ardor he'd experienced with her had given way to an aversion increasingly difficult to disguise. More than sleeping alone, sleeping together made Sandy feel isolated. Increasingly in the night, when he felt Esta's hand reaching out to him, his own hand recoiled.

"Everybody, get up and dance!" Unslinging his guitar, the paunchy folksinger leapt from the pulpit and began waddling along the pews. "Everybody, let's *hora!*" Behind him, Rabbi Stan sweated and sang, "*Am Yisrael Chai!*"

The congregants fell in. A serrated line of them vivisected the sanctuary from the wrought-iron doors to the ark. Sandy could almost imagine the scrolls inside rocking. Yet he remained seated, rubbing his bad thigh, while Esta treated him to a smirk.

The circle whirled, the floor trembled. "*Od Avinu chai!*" the people ranted, though none of them understood the words. Yet still they rejoiced, laughing and crying both. Esta, too, her beehive unraveled, her face turned up to the plexiglass bubble with a glow.

He tried to clap, tried to hum, but nothing moved him. Not even when the singer halted in front of him and gave his cheek a wet, whiskery kiss. Minutes after the congregation danced out of the sanctuary and snaked toward the gym, Sandy still sat inert.

"Not into all that love and peace?" Louis asked as he entered.

"Old fashioned, I guess," Sandy shrugged. "Happy with '*Hava Nagila.*'"

The big man bent, gathering up discarded song sheets and tissues. "A 'Mighty Fortress' man myself. Can you believe they actually brought a rock band into my church?"

Ignoring the question, Sandy posed one of his own. "What do you make of this new junior rabbi?"

Now Louis shrugged. "Nice kid, he seems. Upbeat." He stuffed the paper into the back pocket of his khakis. "Let him get a few funerals and divorces under his belt. Let's see how joyous he is then."

"Children with horrible diseases. A suicide or two."

"You said it, brother."

"Broken hearts. Broken dreams."

"Amen."

He bowed again, this time to retrieve a prayer book knocked to the floor. Straightening, returning the *yarmulke* to the back of his head, he gave Sandy at penetrating look. "But you should go see him sometime."

"Me? What for?"

Shouting and applause infiltrated the sanctuary. Louis went to the wall with the gold-lettered quote. "Can't hurt. From Isaacson you'd only get booze and from this guy, who knows?" he asked, adjusting the first letter, T. "Maybe some peace and love?"

2.

Daily he determined to break it off and then, just as frequently, he relented. He lived from one assignation to another, from one sensual thrill to the next. Though the fear of getting caught forced him to plan meticulously, it also heightened his sense of freedom. Irrespective of the bed, lying beside Liz was sweeter than ever, more liberating, and addictive.

And therapeutic—oddly so for a man unaccustomed to opening up. From his fraught relationship with his father to his injury on the football field and even the death of his only son, no memory was too intimate for Liz. Not just carnally but emotionally, he emptied himself into her. Their sessions left him drained.

"First was the way she took care of me in the hospital. Never leaving my side, sleeping there. Even emptying my bedpan. Could you beat that?"

"No," Liz admitted. "I couldn't."

This bed belonged to a motel off the interstate, with chirping springs that seemed to communicate with those in adjacent rooms. The furniture was sparse, the lighting less so, to camouflage the carpet stains. Yet this, for Sandy, was heaven.

"That means something to a seventeen-year-old kid, especially one with a no-show mother and father too mad to even talk to him. It creates—what can I say?—an obligation?"

"So you married her because you felt obliged?"

"Partially, yeah." His finger traced the saddle from her shoulder to her hip as Liz lay on her side facing him. "The other part I suppose you could call expectation. That was just what young couples did in those days. You went out in high school, went steady, danced at the prom, and got married. Simple as pie."

"My mother made Linzer torte," Liz chortled, "And it was anything *but* simple."

Though only several years older, he spoke to Liz as though they came from different eras. From separate universes, almost. Sandy's working-class, be-tough-or-get-clobbered neighborhood, with its mid-street stickball games and summer's cool-off under hydrants, versus the world Liz deigned to describe, of boarding schools, soirees, exclusive camps, and college at one of the Seven Sisters. Unlike his father, who anglicized his last name and called his son Sanford, Liz's parents were German-Jewish and proud of it, looking down at everyone, even the WASPs.

Liz was still laughing when Sandy went on. "Then Joey, and that created another obligation. How can you leave the mother of your dead child?"

"How indeed. But you never cheated on her?"

"Not before..." He shifted his body closer. "Now you tell me something for a change. About your husband."

He could have strangled himself. He had never before asked about Liz's marriage or hinted that he knew about the abuse. About the sword. Perhaps *not* knowing excited him more.

"My husband?" Even in the low wattage, Sandy could make out her sardonic smile. "He died. I'm a widow. End of story." She rolled away from him, abruptly, onto her stomach.

"You don't want to talk about it, I understand. But what *do* you want?"

"You know." The small of her back rose and fell.

"You want me to leave Esta?"

"God, no."

"Then *what*?"

Sandy ran his hand along her spine and downward until it disappeared.

"Yes," Liz cooed. "That. And something else." She reached back and grabbed a piece of his flank. "Something you have to swear to me." Her fingernails dug into skin as she pulled him toward her and whispered, "I need you to take better care of Arthur."

"But I'm already keeping an out for him. Hell, I almost punched a guy."

"I need you to do more. To guard him whenever you can. However. With your life, if you have to."

The nails sunk deeper. "Okay, okay, I swear," Sandy cried, yet still she squeezed. "I swear," he vowed as she finally pulled him on top of her. "I swear," he repeated several times, to the accelerating twang of springs.

* * * * *

Fulfilling that promise required him to venture out of his cubicle more frequently than he liked, and conspicuously. Guidance counselors were not accustomed to prowling the halls and peeking into classrooms and cafeterias. They did not often question teachers about their students and especially about one student in particular. But there he was slipping out at third period and scaling staircases to Bronowski's Algebra I, cracking its door just enough to reveal the last rows where Arthur habitually sat. Disheveled, distracted, he was at least safe, Sandy noted, and for the moment out of trouble.

And yet trouble seemed drawn to Arthur. As if his cavalier manner, the eyes vibrating behind his spindly hair, the clothes that said at once "I'm rich" and "Fuck it," were all intended to provoke. Junior highs always had their unpopular kids, the nerds and the pizza-faces, who generally clung together. But though clear-skinned and smart, Arthur remained friendless. He was too weird, even for the hippie types, and thoroughly disinterested in art. Karate was his only passion, along with—Sandy suspected—Rae Henderson.

While Sandy was trailing Arthur, the boy often stalked Rae. Lunchtime found him at a table not far from hers, seated alone but always within view, and during assemblies, positioned strategically behind her row. He had yet to approach her in any serious way that Sandy could see, or frighten her, but he sensed that she resented this attention. Grappling with her own differentness, Rae had zero patience for oddballs.

Still, Sandy worried. The run-in with Wendell revealed an all-new threat: whether she wanted him to or not, Arthur might rush to Rae's defense and end up getting walloped. Last time it was with the vice principal but the next could be with toughies incensed by the presence of this brilliant Black girl in their school, who'd bloody Arthur even worse than Howard Weintraub did.

So far, though, such hazards had been averted. Arthur remained quirky and obsessive but otherwise unharmed. And though doubtful whether credit for this went to his quiet supervision or just dumb luck, Sandy claimed it with Liz. "I keep my promises," he reported, and she rewarded him to ensure he still would.

*   *   *   *   *

Returning from one of his scouting missions, Sandy was surprised to find his cubicle occupied and not by a student. The identity of the slump-shoulder figure seated with his back to him escaped Sandy at first. Only the apron strings crossing his neck hairs and the ripe smell of sawdust tipped him off. "Brooks?" he ventured. "What are you doing here?"

The shop teacher looked up long enough to acknowledge Sandy's entrance before returning his gaze to his lap. His hands, scarred from his shop's many tools, revolved. "I thought…maybe…you had a second."

"Take two. They're free." Sandy sat behind his desk. "Some kid giving you guff?"

His always-sad face nodded slowly, straining under its weight. "A kid, yeah. Guff."

Pushing up his sleeves, Sandy leaned back in his chair. "Shoot."

"A year ago, he escaped. An entire year. And I used to see him every week, every day sometimes." Brooks gazed not at Sandy but behind him, as though at a ghost. His features—a blob of a nose, chubby cheeks—appeared unfinished, all except for the eyes, wide and glassy. "I can't stand it anymore."

"Did you file an RTR?" It was the best response Sandy could conjure. Pupil plays hooky, the teacher submits a Repeated Truancy Report, preferably to the vice principal.

"They drafted him—his number was low," Brooks, ignoring the question, croaked on. "They're were going to send him off to their fucking war. What choice did I have?"

Sandy fidgeted with his tie. "We're talking here about…"

"My son. Robert. He's a criminal in his own country now and can't come home. Can't visit me."

Some details came back to the counselor. The wife who died young and left her husband with a baby to dote on, to cling to raft-like throughout a white-water childhood. Experiments with LSD, with the SDS and other radicals, before going AWOL to Canada. "I'm sorry, Brooks," Sandy said. He remembered all that, but not the teacher's first name. Nobody did. "Really. But this is a bit out of my field.…"

"I told him I'd come to him but he said no. Afraid they wouldn't let me back into the States."

"Cheer up. Not even this war can go on forever. Someday it'll be over and everything will be forgotten. Soon. And you'll be reunited with Robert."

"No. It's just going to go on and on and the one thing I have in life, the one thing that means everything to me, will be torn from me. Again."

That last word gave his eyes a glossier coat from which a single droplet seeped. Sandy rummaged his desk for a tissue and thought about the endless spectrum of suffering in the world, the staggering variety. But then he thought about Joey and felt an anger rise. What was this idiot blubbering about? At least his son was alive.

"I'm sorry, Brooks, but this is the wrong place to be having this conversation. And the wrong conversation."

"I just thought you could direct me somehow. You're good at that. At listening."

"Why don't you talk to Miriam?" Sandy almost suggested, referring to the marmish geography teacher, Miriam Loftus. She and Brooks were known as good friends and rumored to be lovers. He nearly mentioned her, but in the end suggested a social service, scribbling out a phone number and pushing it across the desk. "They're great at this stuff."

The shop teacher sniffed deeply and drew a forearm under his nose. "Thank you," he said, which might have meant "Thanks for nothing," and folded the note into his apron. "This stays between us, yeah?"

"You have my word."

And then Sandy was alone again in his cubicle with its pinned-up letters. He wondered whether they, too, said "Thanks for nothing," for what help could a guidance counselor really give? What relief from anyone's anguish? And what, apart from a wanton hour with Liz Warhaftig, might ever lighten his own?

"You look almost as sad as Brooks."

Her tiny upper half bobbing puppet-like around his doorway, golden cross dangling, Jeanne Pagonis waved. Sandy faintly returned the gesture. "Don't ask...."

"I wasn't going to. Doctor-patient privilege and all that."

"He's no patient of mine," Sandy protested. "And I'm no doctor."

But Jeanne merely smiled. "Still, you're a person that people like talking to, tell their problems. I know I'd like to."

Ever since Howard beat up on Arthur, when it seemed likely he'd lose his job, Jeanne had been extra gentle with him. Too gentle, making him feel even frailer. The last thing he needed now was a confession of the emotions he suspected she felt.

He returned her smile, saccharinely. "Some other time."

"Sure," Jeanne pouted. "And if you ever need someone to talk to, you know where my office is—that stained Formica table in the lounge." She laughed at this as she sauntered down the corridor, halting only to ask herself loud enough for him to hear, "But why would the Coop need to talk?"

*   *   *   *   *

"Talk to me," Saps said, though Sandy wasn't sure if it was to him or to Sobotnik's Sunday Club Special. Like a cross-section of the earth's crust it rose in layers from the policeman's plate, alongside a prism-shaped pickle. "You're holding something back."

"Me? You're the one who's sitting on your butt when I asked you to do something. One thing. While your buddy's getting attacked."

In twin fists, Sap lifted the sandwich and calibrated whether it was too wide for his mouth. It nearly was, but he managed a bite and, at the same time, the question, "Attacked?"

"What else would you call it? You've got any idea how long it took me to clean my car?"

"A rat smeared on your windshield," Saps audibly swallowed, "hardly constitutes assault."

Sandy contemplated his pastrami. "Squirrel."

"Huh?"

"It was a squirrel. I think. But that's not the point."

"What is?" Saps fingered the pickle, thought again, and went back to the sandwich.

"That I asked you to do a background check and you did squat."

Another chomp, another sentence nearly lost in a hash of turkey, roast beef, and tongue. "There's nothing there, I told you. No priors. No bad associations. Nothing."

"No Birchers? No Klan?"

"An honorable discharge and a silver star from Korea. Sorry."

"Sorry?"

"The Weathermen are bombing courthouses. Nixon's in China." The pickle spear leveled at Sandy's chest. "Nobody cares about your car."

Sandy sank into his bench. He found it hard to believe that Wendell Barr's record was that clean, that there wasn't some splinter of evidence pinning him to the vandalism on the school, the spray paint, and, yes, the squirrel. His eyes wandered around the deli—at the ceiling fan still frozen at two o'clock and last year's calendar on the wall. Behind the counter, Bernie's belly had grown so fat that his hands now barely reached the slicer. A world on the brink of disappearing, not unlike his own.

"You going to eat that?"

"What?"

"That." Saps's almost conical head pointed at Sandy's plate. The vermillion meat, the gristle. Everything but fur.

"It's all yours."

Outside, shivering on the ice-coated gravel, they paused to say goodbye. Normally, "See ya" was the most Sandy ever got and gave, so Saps's parting words surprised him.

"I meant what I said in there. Talk to me."

"About what?"

"I don't know about what, but you do."

With hands in his PAL jacket and a lumberjack hat covering most of his face, Saps rocked impatiently on his heels. "The way you played those last few games, I couldn't even *let* you win. You're distracted, angry about something, or nervous. Or both."

Sandy looked at the barren branches, at the smoke clouds barreling behind cars—anywhere but at Saps. "I'm fine. It's nothing. Some issues at work."

"Bullshit. I'm the guy you've known all your life. Who knows you maybe better than you do."

Sandy made a face, half-grin, half-grimace, to show that Sap was off-mark. "Like I said, nothing."

"Nothing," Saps repeated, "Just like Wendell Barr's file."

Sandy turned toward the Impala. Starting it in this weather would be bitch, he thought, as his fingers stuck to the handle. "Go home to your wife, Coop," Saps called out to him as the engine sputtered again, growled, and turned.

* * * * *

"Turn, goddamit!" Sandy shouted as the ball sailed past the back of the center's head. "Can't catch it if you don't turn!" Yanking up the sleeves of his ratty sweatshirt, licking his fingertips, he stomped onto the court, and took hold of the boy, Falcone, a ninth-grader. "There! There!" he spat into the befuddled young face. "Now maybe we can win."

Football, baseball, Sandy loved them both, but basketball bored him. Maybe it was the absence of weather, of the fields that give balls bad hops or of just about any equipment. Sure, the pace was fast, with few huddle breaks and scores in the double-digits, but much of the drama was missing. No crack of helmets on helmets or of horsehide on wood, just that constant dribble, like some leaky faucet, and the occasional backboard bong. Yes, there was speed, there was agility and motion, and for an all-star like Russel Pressman, a chance to break Appleton's records. But in the end the game left him emotionally if not physically numb, much like winter itself.

"Mobility!" Sandy hollered as his five starters scrambled back and forth across the court. "Passing!" By which he meant move and throw the ball to Russel who, from just about any position, could score.

"Pivot!" He was just too old for this game, a product of an era when foul shots were pumped from the chest and lay-ups never underhanded. And what the hell was a dunk? So much change, Sandy marveled, too fast for aging man with one bum leg in the past. Yet, as with any sport, he loved the smell of athletes' sweat and the sound of the word "teamwork." And he appreciated the time that practices gave him to be free of student problems and teachers' gripes, to be out of his own smoked-filled house and, when he could, slip off to some motel.

An afterburn of hair and freckly sparks was all he caught of Russel as he whooshed by. Point guard, shooting guard, forward—there was no position at which he didn't excel and none that Sandy could improve. Sure, he could yell at Falcone or Schacter, hound them to pick up the pace. But the show was essentially Pressman, with the rest, himself included, as props. "Sure, Coach," the captain would say, "Gotcha," but with the faintest smirk that said, "You know and I know this is bullshit."

"Pick and roll!" Sandy hollered. "Full-court press!" to no real effect. He didn't mind. He was going through the motions and not only in basketball. At school, in his counseling, and especially with Esta. But that veneer, too, was thinning. Arriving late, eating in silence without even the bogus compliment about her cooking, he retired to the den, watched television and dozed in his chair before going up to a bed that might well have been empty. A glancing touch of elbow or knee might remind him of Esta, but only for a second before both of them pulled away.

Increasingly, his only reality lay in those rooms off the interstate, in the stuffy darkness scored by light from faulty blinds and the shadows of TV rabbit ears. There, enfolded, he felt completed as never before since his youth, removed from time and yet restored to it. With Liz he was vigorous again, light of foot and charging. An entire field stretched before him and not a single tackler in sight.

*   *   *   *   *

He had just replaced his sweatshirt with a ski jacket and emerged from the coaches' room when he sensed that he wasn't alone. He peered around the gym, at the wooden stands and the arsenal of pommel horses, balance beams, and springboards. Empty. Only when reaching for the light switch did he hear a gasp. Sandy looked up and gulped. High above him, near the ceiling, a boy clung to a rope.

"Howard," Sandy thought, remembering the last time this happened, back in the fall when the kid managed to climb all the way to the top before realizing that he couldn't get down. The memory of those flayed hands, and Howard's creepy pride in them, made him squeamish. But then again, this boy didn't look like Howard. If chunky in his gym clothes, he was far from fat, and limber. To the top of the rope he scooted with seemingly less effort—or, for Sandy, less pain than mounting stairs.

He watched, impressed, as the boy descended using only his arms from which several muscles rippled. The parquet barely sighed when he landed. "Good work," Sandy applauded, twice, before his palms froze in mid-clap. Though narrower, clear-skinned, and freed of glasses, the face was unmistakable, as was the voice.

"Hiya, Coach."

Sandy waited for his mouth to close and his eyes to resettle in their sockets. "What happened to you?"

As if out of modesty, Howard shrugged. "Worked out, I guess."

"And these?" Sandy swirled a finger around his eyes.

"Contacts, Coach," Howard laughed. "They're the newest thing." He bared his teeth to show that the braces, too, were gone.

"Well, I'm very happy for you, Howard. And proud."

He tried to sound sincere as he always did with problematic students, yet the words rang disingenuous. Though radically altered, Howard's appearance still unsettled him. Behind the prize-winning smile, he suspected, lurked an angry nerd still in search of pain. The need to punish and be punished. "Maybe now you should go out for sports," Sandy suggested. "Track and field? The shot put?"

"Nah, thanks Coach, but I've got bigger things in mind. Better things."

A chill spidered up his spine. "Remember what I said, Howard, no more fighting."

"Jeez, Coach," Howard laughed. "I know exactly what I want. You'll see." Only his voice remained annoyingly shrill. "I'm way beyond that now." And he laughed again, deliciously.

*　*　*　*　*

That laughter rebounded around Sandy's mind as he negotiated the iced-over flagstones to his porch. Six feet from the door, he could already smell the over-fried latkes and thought, "Oh, God, just let me sleep."

His prayer—if that what it was—went unanswered as, entering, Sandy scarcely had time to wipe his feet.

"Sweetie! The best news! Guess what?" Esta's hands flew down her apron and up to her husband's cheek. "I made you an appointment."

With a psychiatrist? A marriage counselor? Sandy was fazed.

"Next Tuesday night, sweetie, while I'm with the youth group." She brought that cheek to her lips and smacked it. "You're seeing Rabbi Stan."

3.

Though yet unmarked, the small office wasn't difficult to find. He had only to follow the eighty-proof smell escaping from Rabbi Isaacson's study and count another two doors. Nor did he need to knock. A voice on the other side sang to him, "Come in, Mister Cooper. Come in."

An unexpectedly gentle voice, Sandy for a moment saw himself in the strange position of seeking advice from a fourteen-year-old. And the scene inside did little to change it. Not much larger than a walk-in closet, the office was lined with books stacked on books, autographed baseballs, posters of the Grateful Dead and Golda Meir, a panoply of menorahs, mezuzahs, Kiddush cups, and other silvery objects unknown to Sandy. Distracted by this clutter, he almost overlooked the small wooden table that served as a desk and the thin, floppy-haired man behind it.

"So good to see you, Mister Cooper. Coop, Coach. Sorry, you seem to have a lot of names." He was dressed like an adolescent as well, in a wrinkled plaid shirt with buttons missing and a *yarmulke* cut, it seemed, from carpets.

"Sandy will do."

"Sandy, then." Flourishing as if at a throne, he motioned to a metal folding chair. "Please."

Sandy sat and gazed around. "I think you need a bigger space."

"No, it's fine. Perfectly fine." He threw out his arms to the side and stretched to his full five-foot-eight. Aviator glasses glimmered in the bulb light, skin barely post-pimple. His accent, rooted in some New York borough, tortured "fine" into "foin."

"Space is what we make it," Rabbi Stan declared.

"Well, yeah, I only get a cubicle myself."

"But look at the massive good you do in there. You're a guidance counselor, I'm told."

Sandy wondered how much else about him Esta had revealed and how
she explained the urgency of this meeting. His only objective now was to
satisfy her and get this over with as painlessly as possible. "Massive? Really? I
mean, who even *remembers* junior high school? Better we forget."

"Not true!" Behind the glasses, his eyes, closely-set and carob-colored,
gleamed. "As Rabbi Nachman of Breslov said, 'Never underestimate the suffering in any man's heart or the mitzvah of making him laugh.' And what's
true of men is true of children. Helping, humoring—it's all true."

"True, not true. Now I wouldn't know. Once, maybe…" Sandy wished
he were in the kitchen with Louis, snacking on lox and *bialies*, or on his own
in the sanctuary. Even the gym with Esta and her group was preferable to
this nook with its fusty air and pop philosophy. "Once, for me, true meant
scoring a touchdown with five seconds left to play. Homering with runners
on first and second."

The rabbi, laughing, pointed at his outcrop nose. "Getting through a
school day without getting this sucker socked, that was my goal."

"But isn't your God supposed to know what's true or not?" Sandy closed
one eye at him. "Seems to me, God shouldn't even have to ask."

Rabbi Stan's chin, what little of it existed, thrust outward. "You've got
to meet Him halfway. It's what it's about—life, the universe, the reunion
with God. Marriage, man and woman completing one another, it's all a
metaphor. The old I and Thou." Rapid-talking, arms mimicking wings, he
lifted in his chair. "Truth is what holds it together, Sandy. Truth is the glue."

"The glue…."

"And even then, it's not easy. Facing that truth. Hell, it's terrifying."

"Tell me about it."

"More frightening then the league's fastest fastball." The rabbi stretched
over his desk, face pressed close to Sandy's. His voice sunk to a whisper.
"More than a tackler from behind."

Sandy flinched. Which of his secrets didn't this weirdo know? "I've got
to go back to the gym," he muttered, knocking over his chair as he stood.
"Esta needs help."

"Hey, don't we all?"

Crablike, he exited, knocking over an anti-war placard and a Middle
Eastern drum. "Sorry…Sorry…" he muttered, over the crack and boom.

"No sweat, Sandy," Rabbi Stan assured him, and called to him as he left, "Just remember, all the world's a bridge—that's what Nachman said. Just don't be afraid to cross it."

Shaking but uncertain from what, Sandy filed through the cinderblock halls toward the gym. Already he could hear the clangor of musical chairs played without music, only Esta's voice counting off numbers and halting with a cheer. She was a good-hearted woman—too good for him—giving more than she possessed. Pausing before the double wooden doors, he experienced a flash of affection for her, and sadness.

"Look who's here!" she clapped when he entered. "Moses, himself, entering the Promised Land!" Her face went through the usual succession of smirks, smiles, and frowns, culminating in one Sandy hadn't seen before. Hope.

Sandy's own face was self-deprecating. "Moses is the principal here. I'm merely on staff."

With this, the participants in the youth group giggled at him, though none of them understood why. Only one of them remained quiet, glaring and motionless. He hung back from the others, observing their game through bar-like bangs. Sandy barely noticed him at first, but then, despite a sudden loss of breath, managed to utter his name: "Arthur."

*　*　*　*　*

"Are you crazy?"

Liz sat on the far edge of the bed, her robed back to him. Her arm, pinned at the elbow to her flank, pivoted mechanically as it brought the cigarette back and forth to her mouth. "Don't call me that."

"What do you expect me to call you?" Sandy stood in the middle of the room, still wearing his coat and gloves, railing at her. "How could you put him in the youth group? With my wife? At the temple?" He was shouting, he realized, losing his temper in the way he hated but unable to stop himself. "Christ, you're not even a member."

"Wasn't." Half-turning, she pursed her lips. "Let's say I found religion."

"You *are* crazy."

The pout disappeared, supplanted by an expression so fierce it almost looked deranged. "I told you, don't call me that. Ever. Understand?"

He nodded, feeling boyish suddenly and scolded. "I won't say that again. Promise." He sloughed off his coat and gloves and the rest of his clothes while crawling toward her on the bed. "I tried calling you. Two whole days. Why didn't you answer?"

She lit another cigarette and puffed as he hugged her from behind. "Because I knew you'd be angry. I knew and wanted to talk to you about it in person."

"So here I am. Right here. Listening." He spoke between kisses on her throat, hands penetrating the terrycloth, but Liz remained stiff.

"I need you to keep an eye on him, even after school. It's a cruel age— you know that—and he's different from the others. He's liable to get hurt."

"Everybody's different at that age."

"Perhaps. But not like Arthur."

He nodded again while biting her shoulder. "Okay."

"And anyway, it's perfect." She stamped out the cigarette, faced him, and vised his head between her hands. "You and your wife supervising him in the youth group. Who'd ever suspect?" She kissed him hard on the mouth, infused with sourness and sugar, and poked a fingertip painfully between his ribs. Sandy groaned but not so loudly that he failed to hear her whispering, "And don't you ever call me crazy."

* * * * *

In the dark and misty parking lot, Sandy fished for his keys and tried to start the Impala. But the engine wouldn't turn. "Shit!" he said as he smacked the steering wheel. "Shitshitshit!" He pounded it with both fists. He was late enough already and down to his last excuses. What could he possibly tell Esta?

He pumped the pedal, hoping not to flood, and twisted the ignition repeatedly, letting it growl. Still nothing. "Please," he pleaded, not to the dashboard but to the roof, his eyes aimed skyward. "Please, I'm asking. Just this once."

Another three "pleases" left him nearly sobbing and no longer thinking of his wrist as it rotated. The roar of combustion startled him. He hooted and laughed and wiped away a tear before backing out of the lot.

Sandy swung onto the interstate so fast he failed to see an oncoming car yet managed to swerve in time to avoid it. "Thank you," he said, again to the roof. "Thank you," mindless of the buff gray station wagon following at a distance behind.

* * * * *

Snow encrusted Appleton. From Sobotnik's Deli and Wexler's Drugs to the Starbright Pizzeria where perennial Christmas decorations glowed through the frost—all were equally glazed. The row houses down the hill, the Cooper residence among them, and the stately homes above, were united in whiteness. Stillness reigned, as if the town had awakened blanketed but had yet to shake itself free. Only the junior high showed signs of movement as janitors shoveled off paths and parking spaces. Students shuffled in dejectedly. Not yet cold enough outside, there wasn't enough accumulation for a snow day. Classes convened, slush-bound but insulated, as usual.

"Darkness cannot drive out darkness. Only light can do that." Charlotte Fox's voice poured out of the PA system. It had a succulent quality, brandy smooth. Many of the boys found themselves curiously stimulated and even some of the teachers squirmed. But this was Dr. Steinseifer's order, that faculty members take turns reciting the daily quote, and today was Charlotte's. "Injustice anywhere is a threat to justice everywhere," she read, sounding more like Carly Simon than Martin Luther King. "A lie cannot live."

Sandy half-listened while peering begrudgingly through one of his corridor's windows. The snow outside had turned to rain with a lugubrious fog swirling off the pavement. Through the mist emerged the memory of a dream he had the previous night, or thought he had; the image had been so fleeting. Esta was walking with him, to two of them laughing and holding hands with a boy swinging between them. Though asleep, he realized that this was a scene from what might have been, which made it even more hurtful. The light around the three of them so blinding that Sandy, even in the dream, had to look away. He opened his eyes to a darkness that persisted as he dressed and left the house early, before Esta.

The dream deepened his wistfulness. A day like this, lightless and freezing, was precisely the time to spend with Liz. Pellets rattling the windowpane, their bodies the only source of heat. The two feelings—sadness and want—competed with one another in his mind, making him ask, "How could you?" one moment, and answering in the next, "How could I not?" Had he ever felt so soul-dead, he wondered, and yet more dazzlingly alive?

The two halves of him were still clashing in his cubicle when sobs stirred in the corridor outside. He emerged find Rae Henderson sniffling and holding a mittened hand to her head.

"What, Rae? *What?*"

"Nothing."

"It's obviously not nothing. Somebody hurt you. Who?"

"Nobody," she wept.

Sandy approached her carefully, peeling the glove away. Beneath the ridge of hail-studded hair was a bright red welt.

"Who did this to you?"

She looked up at him with those paisley-shaped eyes, through tears that suddenly turned indignant. "Does it really matter, Mister Cooper? To you or anybody?"

He could only insist that it did, though he knew it was useless. "Guidance counselor," he thought, "my ass." All he could recommend that she get the thing checked by Nurse O'Shanassy.

"Thing, Mister Cooper? A thing like the school's only Black girl getting pelted outside the main entrance, and no one sees, not even the vice principal?"

Over her protests, Sandy escorted her most of the way to class, before backtracking as fast as his leg could churn. The floor was slippery and the air sluiced by gusts from the double metal doors that opened and closed as students stomped in late. Unaffected by the cold, positioned sentry-like, Wendell Barr scrutinized the stragglers. He was interrogating one of them—Suskind, a short, curly haired smartass—when Sandy charged.

"You saw it. What they did to Rae. You saw it and did nothing." Accusations, not questions, he hurled them with a force that made Wendell step back but only long enough to shove Suskind off to class. Then he, too, sprung, meeting Sandy face-to-gritted-face in front of the doors.

"Fuck off, Cooper. If you know what's good."

"What's good for me is to beat the shit out of a two-bit racist."

"Well, if that's what you people call patriots, I proudly wear the badge."

As if decorated, Wendell's chest expanded toward Sandy and made him conclude that the vice principal himself had thrown the iceball. After all, hadn't he pitched a season in the minors? Placing a strike over a seventeen-inch home plate was certainly harder than hitting a fifteen-year-old's temple.

Onto that inflated chest, Sandy placed both his palms and pushed. Wendell responded with a startled face that instantly turned murderous. He lunged at Sandy with a punch clearly learned in the Marines, straight for the chin. The blow just missed, but the next one, a jab to the gut, wouldn't, even if Sandy got off a haymaker. And he nearly did, just as the double doors burst open.

"I'm so sorry!" The apology blew in, sleet barbed. "So sorry! My car got stuck."

Wendell and Sandy remained pinioned with less than a foot between them, but that was space enough for Jeanne to insinuate herself, even when swaddled in wool. "How much of homeroom did I miss?"

They mumbled inaudibly and awkwardly stood apart. Jeanne, her face ruddied by the cold, smiled coyly at Sandy. "Will you walk me, please? My shoes are wet and I'm afraid of slipping."

She grabbed his forearm and yanked him hard toward the hall. There was no time to hurl a final threat at Wendell or even to look back.

"Are you insane?" Jeanne hissed at him when out of earshot. "With the trouble you've been in already this year, you still want to fight that creep?"

Sandy was going to explain about Rae Henderson, about the bigoted remarks in the lounge. He was about to share with her his suspicion that Wendell was behind the vandalism in the school, even to his car, but Jeanne's hand closed on his forearm. "Not that I should give *you* advice," she whispered in a way that let him know she would. "The next time you sneak off to that doctor of yours, have him give you a Valium."

* * * * *

So this is what it feels like. The words occurred to him as he refilled his styrofoam cup with hot chocolate and grabbed another cookie. The cocoa burned his tongue and the peanut butter chips turned his stomach, but still he sipped and ate, slurped and devoured.

"Sandy, really. You're supposed to be *selling* those things, not guzzling them."

Esta excoriated him, but if he heard her at all it was distantly. Though standing next to him at the booth, in her outsized faux-fur hat and coat, he barely sensed her presence. He hardly felt anything, not even the cold front that descended that week and froze most of Appleton solid. Walking outside became painful, the air almost unbreathable, with teachers and students scurrying half-bent into school as if under shellfire. The only benefit was the icing over of Dennison Lake—a pond, actually, and a small one at that—and its official designation as a rink.

A local tradition, Night Skate brought together students from all the surrounding schools and mobilized their faculties for safety and refreshments. Through the steamy beams of arc lights, Sandy could make out Jeanne Pagonis tying some seventh-grader's laces and Wendell Barr joylessly supervising from a bank. Charlotte Fox in Tibetan sheepskin and Dr. Steinseifer dressed for a wintry funeral helped the fallen to their feet. But Sandy remained fixed behind this booth, fast beside Esta, alternatively selling and gobbling snacks. Before him passed a dizzying circumambulation of scarves and knitted hats, parkas and peacoats, their quickened colors melding. The moon on the ice like a fisherman's hole. *So this is what it feels like*, he marveled, *being stoned*.

For that's what he was, hours after smoking a joint with Liz. His first—he had not only missed the sixties' sex scene but the drug scene, too—and when held out to him, he glared at it as if it were a gun. "What am I supposed to do with that?" he'd asked.

"I don't know, talk to it. Reason with it. Give *it* advice."

Liz was making fun of him, he knew, but he couldn't help himself. "And what about the smell in here?"

"In here?" She glanced around the hotel room with its nondescript furniture, stained carpet, and manila lampshades that captured more light than they transmitted. "Poor, sweet Coop," she pouted and inserted the J between his fingers. "In here, people make worse stinks than this."

Inhaling, he thought his lungs might burst. His cough sounded tubercular. "I feel nothing," Sandy kept insisting, right up to the sixth puff. That's when the room started wobbling and items—the TV, the end tables—took on inflated dimensions. Making love was different as well, intensely detached. He couldn't remember dressing afterward, kissing her goodbye, or miraculously finding his keys. He had enough difficulty steering the Impala straight, much less noticing that same gray station wagon trailing it.

Now, hugging Dennison's slippery shore, he struggled to remember the afternoon's encounter with Liz. All that remained was a thrumming headache and an indomitable need to snack—that and the fear that someone would notice his rosewater eyes. Esta might not, even though she taught

Drug Ed, but not so their students. Around and around the lake they whirled and skittered and with an abandon that convinced him that they, too, were high.

"Hi, Coach," someone called to him and almost made him jump.

Sandy squinted into the light. He made out two figures, one unusually tall and the other stunted. He saluted and stretched over the booth but couldn't make out who they were.

"It's me, Coach," the tall one announced and scudded forward.

"Russel! And...."

The diminutive shadow also advanced and took Russel's hand. The pixyish Chrissie Esposito who, in that horrid autumn play, had aroused Howard Weintraub in public. The event that pitched Sandy onto the convoluted path leading here, wasted and hungry, sated and scared. Stiffly, he extended his hand.

"Sandy!" Esta scolded him and scowled at his gloves. Sandy removed them and started again.

"Russel. Chrissie. Glad to see you...together." He wasn't, really. Though aware of Russel's many girlfriends, none of them lasted more than a few days, which was fine by Sandy. Nothing should interfere with the young man's concentration or drain his will. But now, strangely, he found himself indifferent. It wasn't just his disinterest in basketball or his reaction to the pot. Sandy didn't care about most things these days, and the few that he did—his cravings, his fears—didn't include Russel.

"Tonight's our one-month anniversary," Chrissie announced in a voice as precious as her looks. She held up Russel's hand, trophy-like.

"How wonderful," Sandy lied. Chrissie, he realized, rubbed him the wrong way. Too much intensity packed into a pint-sized frame, with too big a hairdo and a fully developed body dressed to flaunt it. "It *is* wonderful, isn't it, Esta?"

"Fantastic."

Perhaps she was remembering that their relationship had also begun this young, when one-month anniversaries were milestones. Or maybe she was thinking only of the chill penetrating her phony fur. Or maybe Sandy was just imagining all of this as the marijuana still clouded his brain. "Here, let's celebrate," he said and handed the couple Styrofoam cups and cookies, free. He toasted them with cocoa, "To love!"

Russel and Chrissie gaped at him, at the cups, and finally at each other, giggling. "To love," they chimed. Through the lusty breaths, he could see their expressions—half-infatuated, half-confused as to what to do next. Finally, with flurry of "Bye, Coach. Bye, Misses Cooper," the two of them skimmed off, holding hands.

Sandy watched as they disappeared into the steam but not before another skater swooped down on them. He circled them once, twice, clipping Chrissie's shoulder and nearly knocking her down. Russel tried to react but—for once—too slowly. The attacker whisked off with only Sandy shouting after him, "Hey! Hey, you!"

"For God's sake, keep your voice down," Esta scolded him.

"Did you see that? Did you see what he did?"

"I see a man who I thought I knew. Or used to."

He was going to say that he got a glimpse of hotdogger's face but couldn't place it. He was going to apologize for raising his voice. But instead, Sandy cowered into his ski jacket while Esta badgered him, "You're acting like something out of my Drug Ed class. It's embarrassing."

He didn't respond to her but rather let his eyes glide across the ice. There was Rae Henderson, alone in the center, inscribing figure eights. And Charlotte Fox sailing alongside another person who he eventually realized was Jeanne. He remembered her parting words to him, "The next time you sneak off…." Clearly, she knew something, but what? How had she found out?

He searched for any sign of Arthur, a tell-tale flailing of hair and limbs, and was happy to find neither. He was also relieved to see the Night Skate winding down, with teachers and students on enervated legs faltering toward the shore. But one figure lingered, staring at him.

Sandy, stuffing the last of the cookies into his mouth, tried not to notice. He cleaned up the booth, made a show of helping Esta, and only occasionally looked up. There he was again, the last man on the ice. His features were lost in the darkness as the arc lights went out, though from the tapered shape of his head, his rangy stance, his identity wasn't a riddle. Just the reason why he wouldn't come over to him, not even say hello. What horrible thing had he done, Sandy worried, what crime, to anger his very best friend?

* * * * *

He worried still through the next day, Thursday, and that evening's opener against Merrick. The gym was a dynamo of sound and action: balls slamming against backboards, fans screaming, players crisscrossing the court. With his tie unfastened and shirtsleeves crimped, Sandy paced in front of the bench and shouted orders. Not that anybody listened, least of all Russel, whose only purpose was to receive passes from the other four and take shots from wherever he could. He made most of them, to Appleton's delight and rapture of Chrissie Esposito, hopping in her cheerleader's skirt with pom-poms half her height. The buzzers blasted like fog horns.

So much commotion might have distracted him from any considerations other than the game. Yet he couldn't help notice that neither Esta nor Saps had come. But while basketball bored his wife, his friend was an addict, rooting for any team. Perhaps some emergency had come up at the station, an issue with Marjorie and the kids, or was it Saps's anger at him—for what, exactly, Sandy was uncertain. Fear of finding out led him to spend more time with students, go over old records, linger over his coffee in the lounge—anything but pick up the phone. But tomorrow he would do it, he promised himself. Tomorrow he'd get up the guts.

Russel dodged one Merrick defender and dribbled around another before launching a full foot into the air and, from well outside the key, swishing. The home side of the gym sprung to its feet. Only one student remained, chin in his hands, stewing. Sandy squinted at him for an instant but long enough for the cheers to turn to groans and shouts. He turned back to see Russel doubled over with a hand over his nose. Blood dripped through the fingers.

"Hey! Hey! Ref!" Sandy stormed onto the court. "What the hell?" He hollered without knowing what had happened but figuring Russel had been fouled, perhaps intentionally, with only seconds left to play. But no penalty was called. Seemed Appleton's star had stopped a Merrick jump shot with his face. Sandy pressed a towel to stop the bleeding and escorted Russel out-of-bounds. Chrissie, teary-eyed, ran out to hug him and the fans once again cheered. All but that one boy who still sat brooding.

The sight of Russel's blood on the parquet unnerved Sandy but not as much as the boy who he now recognized as Howard Weintraub. Something in his expression, a coldness, triggered alarms in his counselor. He would have to call him in for a session and as early as possible. But the sight of Howard's face was quickly obscured by Dr. Steinseifer's as it loomed over the bench. "Family emergency," he stiffly informed Sandy. "Call your wife at once."

With the final buzzer and the crowd's applause roiling behind him, he rushed out of the gym. Hobbling down to his office took too much time so he just ducked into a phone booth, searched his pockets for a dime and bumbled trying to dial. Already, he could hear Esta sobbing, "Don't even think of coming back." But then, when she answered with "Bad news, sweetie, something's happened at the home," he almost laughed with relief.

* * * * *

Gunning the Impala, he reached the Daughters of Jacob in record time. He pitched past the reception desk, ignoring the duty nurse's calls to stop. As fast as a gimpy man could, he hurled into room 35.

The scene inside showed nothing unordinary. His father in a wide-lapeled, double-breasted suit last popular in the forties, pomaded and Elks-pinned and marinated in rage. Standing over his wheelchair was a white-uniformed orderly holding a plate of institutional food. She was a large-bodied woman with a kindly aura. In the tepid light, her broad black features glowed.

"What?" was all Sandy asked, but it more than sufficed for his father.

"The fat bitch won't let me have my music."

The nurse gave him a look that said, *Now you see why we called you.* Still, she explained, "He won't eat and he's abusive to the staff. We can't have that, you understand?"

Only then did Sandy notice the Christmas cards tiling the floor, the tipped-over vase and chrysanthemums spilled on the table. The family photographs upended. As dutifully as a seventh-grader, he nodded, embarrassed, saddened, and mad. Yet the first question that emerged from him was, "But why won't you eat?"

"The food here isn't fit for human consumption," Maurice Cooper declared.

To the orderly, Sandy shrugged. "I guess he's not hungry."

"But he still can't talk to us like that."

"I'll talk to you anyway I like!" the old man hollered, then hissed at his son, "Don't listen to the *shvartze.*"

"He thinks we don't know what that means. We're not stupid, Mister Cooper." The last words were hollered into Maurice's ear, making him cringe.

"I'm not deaf, you know!"

"Yeah, just dumb!"

Sandy finally stepped forward, tapping five fingers into his palm. "Time-out!" He strained to read the name on the nurse's tag, "Thank you, Misses Biggs, and I apologize for my father's rudeness, but could you let us have a minute alone?"

She handed him the plate and gave her patient an acerbic look. The door behind her snapped. Only then Sandy hissed, "Do you want to get thrown out of here?"

"Not that you'd care. Or anybody."

"*I* care. *I* care. But how can you expect anybody else to when you mistreat them this way?"

"Them? They mistreat *me*!" A craggily finger pounded on one of the lapels then pointed at Sandy. "The way you mistreated me. Always."

"You mean the guy you've never given anything to but crap? The guy who stayed with you even when you hated my wife? Even when everybody else—Mom, my sister—left?"

"Your mother died...."

"Ask me and she couldn't wait to. Anything to get far away from you." Sandy checked himself. "Sorry..." But it was too late. His father seemed to deflate in his chair.

"You can't imagine it."

"What, Dad? Imagine what?"

"The disappointment."

Please, Sandy thought and felt a familiar anger welling. "For Chrissakes, it wasn't my fault. The tackler came out of nowhere. Clipped me from behind. Today it's illegal, a fifteen-yard penalty."

But his father wasn't listening. He was gazing at the nightscape framed by the window. "Disappointment," he said too softly for Sandy, still rambling, to hear. "Not in you."

"And you'll be penalized, too, if you don't eat."

"Okay," Maurice grumbled.

"No privileges. No music."

"I said okay."

Sandy shut up finally and gawked at him. "You mean it?"

"Just how lame are you? Give me some."

Scooping a spoonful of whatever-it-was, Sandy presented it to the turned-down mouth. It couldn't open very wide since the stroke, and much of the food dribbled onto his chin and checkered tie. Sandy dabbled at the stains with a napkin until his father pushed him away.

"Enough! You can't even do that right." He snatched the spoon from Sandy and trawled it across the plate. Chewing bitterly, he snarled. "Now do it."

Sandy halted momentarily, unsure of what he meant. But in that instant, he recognized his own face in his father's: the frustrated hopes in the furrows, the vulnerability behind the flint. Without a word, he went to the bookcase, randomly selected a disk, and laid it on the turntable. A few scratches later, the dim room in the Daughters of Jacob was filled with the golden haze of an Oklahoma morning, with corn and meadows and cows. He watched the album spin while the old man sang along. He had this beautiful feeling, Maurice Cooper crooned, everything was going his way.

*   *   *   *   *

Though he told himself more than once not to, and was already turning downhill toward his home, Sandy stalled at the intersection. He knew the urge was a bad one, but still he dallied. Finally, with a groan, he spun the wheel sharply to the right and drove up the hill to Liz's.

Entering the crescent-shaped drive, he killed the Impala's engine and glided. He hadn't been back since that first rainy night in the fall. This evening, though, was starry, clear, and cold. Sandy stepped out onto the gravel.

Parked in front was a Thunderbird. It might have belonged to Liz if not for its macho appearance, the waxed bronze exterior and leather seats. If not for the California plates. On the tips of his gum-soled shoes, Sandy drew closer.

The mansion was illuminated this time, the light from its windows placing faces on the cupids and satyrs outside. They watched, smiling, while he strained to hear the conversation within. Only one side of it was audible.

"I can't seem to satisfy you," Liz protested. "Ever."

He barely recognized the voice. This was not the unflappable Liz he knew but a frazzled woman pleading.

"When you ask me to do something, I do it. Right away, no questions. I even kept that…."

Whatever "that" was, Sandy could only guess, perhaps one of the mementos in the den. Liz, meanwhile, cried on.

"I've always done everything for you. Things I can't even say. And all you do is torture me."

Seesawing on his heels, Sandy debated whether to break into the house, barge down the hallway and the steps to where Liz was being accosted. Already, he saw himself lifting the creep up by his collars and smacking him one. But then other words reached him. Softer, impassioned.

"Because you know that whatever you do, I will always be here. I will always love you."

His anger dissolved into envy. He saw it all: the cruel West Coast lover, the wounded woman seeking comfort in a stand-in. He felt weak, suddenly, and nauseous. Shuffling back to his car, Sandy collapsed inside and feebly switched the ignition. The house and the T-bird, the garish lights and smirking statues, retreated in his rearview mirror.

At home, in bed, he curled into a ball on the sheets. Hands on his ears, mouth opened, he tried to channel the words out of him. Still they kept repeating—*I will always love you*—like his father's scratched-up records.

"It's okay, sweetie," another voice beside him whispered. "He'll be fine."

On his bare shoulder, her touch made him flinch. "He?" he asked in all cluelessness. The lover?

"Your father, of course. He goes through stretches like this."

Sandy said to the wall, "Yeah. Stretches."

Esta switched off the light and tried to fit her curvature in his. "He'll be fine, you'll see," she said, "and so will we."

* * * * *

The eighth-grader opposite him, whose name he thought was Kimberly though he wasn't entirely sure, was complaining to him about her homeroom class, rife with bullies, and the need for adult supervision in the girls' room. She griped, this plain, frizzy-haired crank, about everything—classmates, teachers—except for her real grievance, which Sandy knew well after all these years. Puberty had fashioned her unevenly, contouring her lower body while leaving the upper part planed. He understood her anguish, even when conveyed in codes, yet failed to register it. Her lips moved but seemingly made no sound. All he heard was *I will always love you*, over and over, with a needle gouging his heart.

The torment continued in the teachers' lounge. Bronowski and McGonnigle were at it again, arguing over whether Nixon's trip to China was a sell-out of America or a breakthrough to peace.

"Surrendering to the Commies, that's what he's doing. Simply giving up," Bronowski groused. His Navy-gray flattop bristled.

McGonnigle's hair, coppery and neck-length, flounced. He pointed a finger between the dimes of Bronowski's eyes. "Another war, that's what *you* want," he shouted. "Another war with the yellow man, just to prove you're white."

"You're the yellow one. With stripes."

"White makes right, that's you, Earl. If you can't beat 'em, bomb 'em."

Others joined in the fracas. Stephens, who held that all terms were relative, said, "One man's peace is another man's war and vice-versa," and D'Angelis snickering, "Fighting for peace is like fucking for virginity." Brooks nearly wept, "Doesn't anybody care that the talks broke down?" while wringing his tool-scarred hands. "We're never getting out of Vietnam!"

Alone on the sofa, gazing into his cup, Sandy stared at his murky reflection. Even when Jeanne Pagonis sat next to him and touched his telescoped sleeve, his eyes remained sunk in coffee.

"Did you hear about the new Mafia movie coming out? With Marlon Brando? Supposed to be amazing."

"I'm sure…"

"I so much want to ask someone to see it with me, but, you know…"

"I know?"

"How shy I am." She anxiously massaged her cross. "Besides, the person's not exactly—how can I say this?—available."

Here she was flirting with him again. It made Sandy uneasy and not a little annoyed. He wanted to seek solace in his coffee, to nurse his hurt, not deal with a twenty-something's crush. "Then find somebody else," he snapped.

"Yes," she sighed, surprisingly agreeing with him, "I suppose you're right," as, on the other side of the lounge, Charlotte Fox insisted that all this talk of peace and war would be meaningless if only we had love.

"Love is for the weak," Wendell, entering the lounge, announced. His face, as creased as a catcher's mitt, was pierced—incongruously—by a lollipop. The stick circled menacingly as he explained that love was what "they" wanted to weaken the country and give it to "undesirables." Love, he said, "puts real Americans to sleep while certain types take over."

Protests rattled the lounge. "You're paranoid," Charlotte charged him and McGonnigle agreed. D'Angelis snorted, "Oh, please," and even Bronowski registered an objection. Softness on Communism was abhorrent enough without hostility to love, he declared. The voices rose to hollering pitch and nearly drowned out Sandy's.

"What do you mean by 'certain types?'"

The teachers turned to find the counselor standing beside the sofa and handing his cup to Jeanne. His freed hands were fisted, his mind clenched with an anger so dark it eclipsed the memory of Liz's conversation.

With a pop, Wendell plucked the candy from his mouth. "You know exactly who I mean,"

"Spell it out, then."

"Oh, no. Not again," Jeanne groaned, no longer touching but tugging his sleeve. "Let it go, Coop."

"I'll give you a hint," Wendell grinned and licked his sucker. "A five-letter word that rhymes with yikes."

Suddenly the lounge was in motion. Sandy lunged at Wendell who sprung back at him while the others rushed to intercede. They nearly converged at the Formica table, which wouldn't have survived the clash. But then, just short of collision, a single word froze them in place.

"Please."

Not the word so much as the person who spoke it. Mrs. Tannenbaum, the school secretary, a slight woman of indeterminate age and consciousness. With her cat-eye glasses and bramble of steely wool hair, she sat outside of the principal's office with a presence so dismissible that teachers often forget she existed. Her sole job, they believed, was to keep her boss caffeinated and isolated from the troublemakers outside. The clack of her typewriter like gunfire scattered them.

"Please," she repeated in a surprisingly stringent tone. "Doctor Steinseifer is working on the mid-year report for the Board of Ed. So, please, shut the hell up."

The lounge went silent long enough for the secretary to leave and then erupted in laughter. They roared—McGonnigle and Bronowski, D'Angelis and Wendell Barr. Even Jeanne and Charlotte chuckled. If not by love, all were united by hilarity. Only Sandy remained mad.

Before Jeanne could stop him, he tottered out of the lounge and into the halls. The period bell had just sounded, and a surge of students parted as he passed. If some of them called out his name, if others hooted "Coach Roach" or even "Coop the poop," he didn't notice. Stiff in his khaki pants and button-down, Sandy was a monument to fury. He raged at Wendell, at Liz, at life, but especially at the object of those words, "I will always love you." He could almost imagine himself reaching for a sword and cleaving that person's head.

4.

The next three days were some of the worst in his life. More depressing than when his mother died suddenly and left him to deal with her husband. And almost as devastating as when, at seventeen, the doctor told him he would never play football again—in essence, never escape Appleton. Even now, hesitating outside the motel with snow flurries tipping his lashes, he wondered how he would grapple with it. A depth of jealousy unknown to a man whose wife had never slept with another. The images of Liz penetrated by her lover, more lacerating than any blade.

How would he handle it? Sandy silently wrestled outside her door. Could he possibly act naturally, as if nothing had happened or would he drop to his knees and weep? Or, God forbid, strike her? He knocked three times—two fast, one short—as agreed. Maybe she wasn't there at all? Maybe she was, at that very moment, with him?

Finally, through door hinges, a sultry voice seeped. "Waiting for an invitation?"

He entered and everything changed. Liz in her silk dragon robe, with her hair piled up and hazel eyes turned forest green in the twilight. Fruity lips, enveloping mouth. The mere sight of her expelled all strands of anger and replaced them with a passion surprising even to him. He embraced her—too hard, "Easy, easy, Mister Cooper," she inveighed—and tore off his layers of clothing even as he easily pealed hers. He would have ravished her there, in the center of the room, if she hadn't giggled in his ear, "There are beds for these things, you know."

Later, after lighting a cigarette, Liz poked his cheek and puffed, "I brought you a present."

Sandy was struggling to collect his thoughts, spilled around him like a bumbled card trick.

"Don't get too excited now," she teased him. "It's not a Rolls Royce." It was, rather, a purse-sized object in waxed paper that she laid on his chest and expectantly watched him unwrap.

"A sandwich?"

She girlishly nodded. "Go 'head."

The bread was darker and thicker than any he'd ever tasted and whatever it was between the slices nearly choked him. "What is this, Astroturf?"

"No, silly. Sprouts."

"And this green stuff?"

"Avocado."

Sitting up in bed, Sandy struggled to swallow. "I've never had one of those."

"That's because you've never lived in L.A."

Now he did choke, remembering the Thunderbird. The images of the other man, bigger, richer, and pounding harder into Liz, consumed him. He reeled between asking her outright just who else she was seeing and realizing he couldn't bear to hear the answer. At most, he managed, "I've never lived anywhere but Appleton."

"*Tant pis,*" she said. "There's a world out there. A life."

Sandy looked hurt. "This, for me, *is* life."

"And a fuller life," Liz teased him, "thanks to avocados."

They made love again, more cautiously now for Sandy. As though recovering from some on-field injury, he feared his bones would break. He considered asking her why she traveled with a service when a sportscar was right outside her house, but that meant admitting he'd spied. Instead he said nothing.

Emerging from the hotel, staggering as much from physical as emotional depletion, he wanted to throttle himself. More accurately, he longed to kill Liz's other lover and *then* throttle himself. What had begun as an indulgence had decayed into an obsession and then descended into something darker. Had he gone too far to reverse himself? Crossing the parking lot, he thought, *Can I ever turn back?*

He yearned to leap into this Impala and speed through the gloom, to swerve into his driveway and march into his home with its reek of overcooked latkes and kugel. "Esta, I'm home," he'd holler. "I'm back, sweetie pie," he'd cry.

In the parking lot, though, he paused. At the far end, beneath the barren trees, a single vehicle idled. Not the Thunderbird, thank God, or his wife's beat-up Corolla, but a dull gray station wagon that he instantly recognized but nevertheless failed to place. Only when its owner emerged from the front seat and stood starkly, pinhead pricking the low-hanging sky, did Sandy gasp. Pop-eyed, open-mouthed, his expression never looked more astonished.

"Hiya, Coop," Sergeant Arnold Saperstein greeted him. "Asshole."

* * * * *

They drove back to town but not to Sobotnik's, their usual haunt, but to the pizzeria where they would not be disturbed. "Like always, Dom," Saps said to the short bald man who took their order. "With extra cheese for my friend."

"Gotcha, Sarge," Dominic replied. Everything about him was stubby—from his aproned waist to the unlit stogie in his teeth, even the pencil in his stout fingers. With one of these, he pointed at the front window. Along with the perennial Christmas lights, the leaning towers and gondoliers, was a new embellishment. Crosswise over the silvery letters of Starbright, the word "Wop" was spray painted raggedly in green.

"We tried everything—terp, gasoline—but it won't come off," the proprietor sighed. "We'll have to replace the whole damn thing."

"Sorry to hear that."

Removing the stogie, Dominic bit into a knuckle. "*Va fongul*," he spat and trundled back to the kitchen.

Alone, finally, Saps's expression changed from neighborly to vicious. "Care to make a statement?"

"What can I say? Things happen." Sandy played with the oregano dispenser, kneading it between his hands.

Saps nearly yelled. "Things, sure. But not cheating on your wife of twenty years. Not lying to me!"

"Keep it down." Sandy glanced around as if someone could hear them. But except for Dominic, trilling in the kitchen, the restaurant was empty. Still, he whispered, "How did you find out?"

"You have any idea how weird you've been acting? Everybody's seen it. Esta. It didn't take a detective to track you down."

He gazed at the jar, his face refracted by bevels. "So what do you want me to say?"

"Say? Say!" Saps was yelling again. "I told you about this woman. The murder. The sword. Are you out of your fucking mind?"

"I saw it."

Now Saps looked nonplussed. "Saw what?"

"The sword."

"You saw the sword."

"On the wall. She keeps it there. Hanging."

"The sword she used to slice her husband's head in two and she displays it like some trophy? Doesn't strike you as strange?"

"At first. But then…" Sandy shrugged both shoulders.

"Then what?" Sandy answered with silence and his best friend groaned, "Don't tell me…."

He released the dispenser and placed both palms on the checkered tablecloth. What he was about to say he had never confessed to anyone, not even himself. "God help me, Saps, I never expected to feel this way."

"Jeez."

The cook came back with their order. "Extra, *extra* cheese."

Saps inhaled. "Love it already, Dom. Thanks." Then, leaning forward, chin on fists, he rasped. "So what are we going to do?"

"We?"

"You have no idea who this woman really is. A killer, we know, but did you ever question her about it?"

Sandy reddened. How could he tell him that, for all their intimacy, they never once discussed Liz's husband? Not in any depth.

"Jeez," Saps repeated. "I'm going to have to check her out."

"But you already read her file."

"In Appleton, yeah. But what about before she moved here?" The slice that Saps held up sagged under its own topping. "Her story just might not hold up."

He thought of mentioning the Thunderbird, the California plates, and berated himself for not memorizing the number. He thought of all the things he didn't know about her: where she spent her days, the way she spoke with Arthur, even whether Elizabeth Warhaftig was in fact her real name. He stared at the vacant triangle in the pie.

"Eat some," Saps commanded him. "Eat or I'll finish the whole damn thing." He pushed a wedge toward Sandy's mouth, but paused and replaced it with a napkin. "First, for Chrissakes, clean that snot from your nose."

Sandy wiped and inspected. "Not snot. Avocado."

"No shit," Saps grunted through a mouthful of cheese. "I heard of those."

Dominic opened the door, and into the remorseless cold, they left. "Please, Sarge, find the bastard that did this."

He was referring to the indelible "Wop" on the window, but Saps could only shrug. The writing resembled that sprayed on the school and the color was similarly psychedelic. A teenager's doing, perhaps, but the distance between there and the pizzeria suggested a more mobile hand. Someone with wheels.

"World's full of bad people, Dom," the policeman explained, and slapping Sandy's back added, "Just ask the Coop."

* * * * *

The world was indeed crammed with bad people, many of them, like Wendell Barr, with automobiles. Those words dominated his thoughts even as the Appleton five took to the court. With layups and foul shots they warmed up while waiting for South Central to arrive. Russel Pressman performed deep knee bends and tried not to notice Chrissie's pretty face wedged between black-and-gold pom-poms, ogling him. But Sandy was thinking of graffiti on walls and windows, of a car with California plates—everything but the fracas that was about to erupt.

And it exploded the moment the opposing team's buses arrived. Their passengers marched into the gym jiving, "Bing-bing, bang-bang, ungawa, Hawk powa," while the home side merely gawked. It wasn't just that their players towered above the tallest of Appleton's, were leaner and looser limbed, but the way they swaggered in lockstep with their fans and taunted the home side in unison sent the entire gym into a frenzy. The jeers seemed aimed directly at their hosts, provoking them and increasing the chances for violence after the game. Fearing that possibility, Sandy had asked South Central's coach to refill those buses right after the final buzzers and drive home before someone got hurt.

But tensions intensified well before then, in the first quarter when the Hawks took a ten-point lead and shut out Russel from scoring. The chanting, the teasing escalated to the pitch that even Chrissie fell silent, pompoms limp at her feet. Scanning his subdued stands, Sandy was relieved not to see Esta or Jeanne there, and even more so Wendell. Not satisfied with spray-painting his hatred, that racist could easily spark a riot. Catching the eye of his South Central counterpart, Sandy tapped the air with both hands, motioning, *Let's keep a lid on it.* A slim, mocha-skinned man in a bowtie and cardigan, the opposing coach anxiously tapped back, *Okay.*

Nothing could cap what happened next, though. The visitors' catcalls, formerly aimed at all of Appleton, suddenly concentrated on one student. Most of the slurs seemed to be foods—Wonder Bread, marshmallow, Oreo—harmless enough, but then some, like pasty face and bird shit, weren't. Sandy strained to find the object of that scorn and found it as Rae Henderson ran weeping from the gym. That was bad enough, but then several students pursued her out, all but one from South Central. The oversized clothes and string-like hair told Sandy more than he wanted to know.

Or could ignore. Frantically signaling time-out, he left his team and their fans gaping as he bustled through the double metal doors and into the night. Cold punched the breath from his lungs and tears nearly blinded him. Only the sound of more cursing and Rae's cries told him where to head, and another sound—out of place, sibilant. He stumbled toward it.

There, shivering under a streetlight, sobbed Rae Henderson, frozen not by winter but shame. A few feet separated her from a mob of girls mostly but also two or three boys. They were dressed differently than Rae—no bellbottoms or pullovers but faded jeans and hooded sweatshirts. Each with a thick nimbus of hair crested with lamplight. They hooted and sneered while a slight figure in bulking clothes confronted them.

Hissing, he sluiced the air with his hands and feet. But this did not prevent the biggest of the boys from striding forward and clownishly chopping back while his friends goaded him on. The laughs grew hysterical until the young man's head violently snapped back and he tottered.

Arthur had hit him but he still wouldn't stop. Again and again he struck with blows that could have felled much older men. But then the rest of the crowd, girls and boys, converged on him swinging. "Stop!" Sandy shouted and lurched.

Such agility was long beyond him, he would've thought. But there was no time for thought or even to remember his bum leg as he swooped in front of the South Central kids and wrapped his arms around Arthur. He struggled and jabbed Sandy's sides but the coach held fast while barking, "All of you, back to the gym! Now!"

The visitors glared at him, uncertain whether to take him on, too, and for a second it seemed they would. Sandy could not have done both—protect himself *and* Arthur. "You heard what I said!" he hollered, still clutching Liz's son. "Go!"

A gelid second passed when nobody moved. But then, with a flick of his sore jaw, the boy who mocked Arthur waved to the others to follow. Only when it was clear they were alone did Sandy loosen his grip.

"You trying to get yourself killed?"

"Let go," Arthur writhed. "Who the fuck asked for your help?"

"Hey, watch your language."

Sandy tried to hold him again, but Arthur spun free. "Leave me alone," he hollered, his little boy's voice heightened by anger. "I can take care of myself. *And* her."

Arthur gestured toward the space behind Sandy, who only then remembered Rae. He turned to see her no longer weepy but livid. "Tell me, Mister Cooper, would you have come out if he weren't here?" She practically spat at him. "Would you have just come out for me?"

Sandy blubbered a response, but Rae didn't wait to hear it. She pivoted and vanished into the night while Sandy watched on helplessly.

"You did, didn't you?" Arthur asked.

"Did what?"

"Come out here just for me."

"No...."

"You can't lie to me, Mister Cooper. Not like the others. You did it for her."

"For who? What are you talking about?" Clearly it wasn't Rae.

With this, Arthur backed off, turned and followed Rae into the darkness. Only Sandy remained, embarrassed and miffed but above all stricken. How much did the boy really know? He tormented himself wondering. And who did he mean by *the others*?

5.

The others meant there were more than the owner of the T-bird, more than the Californian. *The others* meant he was one of a long line of naked men he envisioned waiting at Liz's bed.

"They need some more pretzels out there."

This was the third time Esta asked and still Sandy didn't respond. It took another tug of his argyle tie to yank him back to consciousness. She repeated loud enough for some partiers to hear, "Pretzels!"

"Sure," he said, half-registering. The other half was stunned by the surreal scene in front of him. This Sunday morning saw the temple's gym festooned with game booths and balloons. The Purim carnival celebrated yet another failed attempt to kill all the Jews, this by an ancient anti-Semite named Haman. Parents with kids in hand, youth group members, congregants—many in costume—guzzling snacks and competing for prizes such as plastic dog whistles and Chinese handcuffs. And presiding over it all, slung from one of the hoops, a papier-mâché effigy of the would-be butcher himself, hanging.

"Pretzels, right."

This was his chance to escape the gym for a while, to flee the noise and the people dressed as kings and clowns and rock stars, all desperate to be someone else. Even Esta wore a pair of psychedelic glasses, a flower in her platinum hair. But Sandy didn't need a costume. The khakis and button-down sufficed, along with his usual gum-soled shoes. The only concession was the argyle tie that Esta had given him and guilted him into wearing. Sandy tugged hard on its knot, loosening it, as he cut across the parquet to the kitchen.

"Let me guess, Mordechai?" Louis looked him up and down, laughing. The reference was to the hero of the Purim story, but Sandy hardly felt heroic.

"No," he said. "Just his pretzel bearer."

The custodian produced a foot-deep cylindrical box. "Well, bear him these. We've got a kingdom's worth."

Louis himself was dressed as a pirate—minimally, with an eyepatch and bandana stretched around his scalp. Sandy marveled at the man's multiple identities: the handyman, the cook, Beth El's resident prophet. "You play this noble game?" the custodian asked.

Sandy was unsure which game—the penny-pitching or beanbag toss—and took a second to notice the chess board. It sat on one of the bare aluminum tables, a wooden square arrayed with black and white figures.

"No," he said again, ruefully. "Maybe you could teach me sometime."

Louis's laughter, deeper this time, sounded like it was amplified by the freezers. "Sometime, yeah, when you're not hanging out in the sanctuary or bearing pretzels to the fair." Lifting his eye-patch, he winked at Sandy and then looked wistfully at the board. "Truth is, I'm sick of playing myself."

"Truth is," Sandy said as he cradled the box football-like under his arm, "so am I."

Back out in the gym, after delivering the pretzels to Esta and being scolded for taking so long, Sandy ran into Russel Pressman. Predictably dressed like a prince, he was accompanied by a gowned and tiaraed Chrissie Esposito. "My first time in a temple," she twittered. "Cool."

Russel held up a fistful of prizes. "Super cool. Look what I won, Coach."

"Good for you," Sandy said blandly. The prizes, he knew, were from foul shots on the second hoop, the one without the effigy. Chrissie's hands also brimmed with plastic charms and candy-button paper. "I'm rich!" she trumpeted, just as the tiara flew from her head.

"Hey!" Russel managed to shout before he, too, was struck. He pivoted around, looking for someone to punch, but Sandy calmed him. "It's just a joke, Russel," he said, holding up what looked like a withered potato. "Beanbags."

He helped Chrissie restore her tiara while quietly scouring the crowd. Who among those Spidermen and astronauts had it out for Russel? Which of these devils? And could beanbags ever become rocks?

His forebodings were interrupted, though, by two towheaded boys who ran to him and hugged his waist. Both were dressed as race car drivers and by that he identified them well before their parents caught up. In black jackets, woolen caps, and greasepaint moustaches—burglars, one broad-hipped, the other reedy. Saps and Marjorie peeled their children from Sandy.

"We're going as the bad guys," Saps explained. "Get it?"

Marjorie rolled her eyes. "He was too cheap to buy real costumes."

Sandy smiled but the disguise wasn't effective. He needed to get Saps alone and ask him what, if anything, he'd dug up. Fortunately, the boys provided a diversion, tearing off toward the water pistol range and trawling Marjorie after them.

"Let's have it."

"It's not much. From a friend of a friend in that township I told you about. The one who read the file."

"Skip the introduction. Just show me."

"It's this…" Saps reached inside his jacket and extracted a photo. A mugshot, more precisely, dated two years earlier. He might not have recognized the subject if not for the name card she held.

"Yeah, so, you said she was arrested. Tried and cleared. So what?"

"Nothing strange about this picture?"

Sandy gaped, clueless.

"The face, Coop. Look at it."

He did and winced. No wonder he scarcely recognized her. The swollen lips and cheeks, the bruise that almost closed her right eye.

"Horrible."

"Inconsistent."

"What?"

Saps returned the photo to his jacket, placed a hand on his best friend's shoulder, and whispered in his ear. "The file said the kid was the one beat up, Sandy. Not her."

Sandy's eyes began to bulge and his mouth widened, but he did not have time to react. A commotion had broken out in the center of the gym. A crowd had gathered and was egging on someone who was swinging what looked like broom handles.

"Saps…."

"Don't look at me," he replied with a twirl of his painted-on mustache. "I'm off duty."

With a parting frown, Sandy pushed through the throng and froze. Whirling ferociously, hair whipping, Arthur was putting on a show. He was wrapped in the kimono and spinning the thick wooden chair legs that Sandy remembered from Liz's den.

"Why don't you put those whatchamacallits down, Arthur. Somebody's liable to get hurt."

"Not whatchamacallits," Arthur, still hurling, corrected him. "Tonfa. Like Bruce Lee uses. Like my Dad."

Sandy didn't know who Bruce Lee was but had a clear enough image of Arthur's father. Leave it to him to teach his son how to swing those clubs and then turn them on him—perhaps on Liz as well.

"Really, Arthur, I'm going to have to insist you stop."

Sandy stepped forward and found himself ducking as one of the sticks whizzed over his head. Tugging on his tie so hard it unknotted, he lurched again only to be halted by a familiar voice behind him.

"I wouldn't do that," it said.

He turned to find himself faced with horns, fangs, and a demon's ember eyes. Sandy recognized the voice through the mask as it added, "Just let him be."

Sandy wheezed, "You *are* crazy."

"I told you never to say that. Now leave us. Go play chess or whatever with the janitor."

Crazy and spying on him. Had she seen him speaking with Saps as well, sharing that mugshot? "Leave now, please," he whispered. "Esta's here."

In its red satin robe, the evil spirit shrugged. "Arthur asked that I come and I couldn't say no. So go back to your wife. Enjoy the fair."

With the Tonfa still smacking behind him, Sandy turned away. His own face was now the façade of confusion and fear that he wore limping back to Esta.

"Who's that person you were talking to?" An accusation, not a question. "I hope you said something. Imagine wearing a costume like that to a Purim carnival, scaring all the kids."

He gazed around the booths, at the balloons and the hanging effigy of Haman. The colors merged and whorled. As if for a rescue rope, he reached for his tie but found it had fallen off. No loss, he thought. He hated argyle.

"I need a break," Sandy mumbled and earned a querulous look from his wife.

"Go off, that's all you ever do." She adjusted her psychedelic glasses and re-pinned the plastic flower in her hair. "Weatherman says there's a storm coming," Esta warned. "I won't wait."

* * * * *

He fled to where the bells and honks of the carnival no longer reached him. Beyond the wrought-iron doors, he retreated, sliding into a pinewood pew. He hardly remembered a time when he reveled in minor pleasures: the pep talks in mildewed locker rooms, Sobotnik's pastrami, his wife's incinerated roast. The times when all he had to grapple with was his father's disappointment in him and the loss of his only son. Now there was Wendell and Rae, Russel and Saps, and even creepy Harold Weintraub. And there was Arthur and Liz, Thunderbirds and station wagons, and murder by Japanese sword.

As if looking for an escape route, his eyes scanned the sanctuary. They alit on the Eternal Flame and memorial plaques, the pulpit and the ark. The stained glass looked just that, stained, the air besmirched by Rabbi Issacson's Scotch. Only the psalmist's words seemed golden. *"The Lord is Near to All Who Call on Him, To All Who Call on Him in…"*

"Truth," Sandy said out loud, and his own voice sounded alien. How was anybody to approach anything when the truth was impossible to attain? Who really spray-painted the walls of the school and the window of the Starbright Pizzeria? Who smeared a dead squirrel on his car? Who, in truth, was Liz Warhaftig and who, beside him, were her lovers? And who—counselor, cheater, coach—was Sanford Cooper, a man he no longer knew?

Looking up through the plexiglass bubble, he saw the low-hanging sky and felt leaden. His head fell back, jaw slackening. If he began snoring, Sandy was unaware. His sleep was bereft of dreams.

He awoke not with a start but a scream. Gazing down at him was the President of the United States. Fully conscious, Sandy might have laughed at the notion that Richard Nixon might visit this or any suburban synagogue, but all he could do was gasp. That is, until a shrill voice told him to chill out and a delicate hand lifted the mask to reveal Rabbi Stan.

"Sorry to scare you like that," he chortled. "I was just locking up."

"Oh, Jesus." Sandy had a hand over his heart. "Jesus Christ."

"Now *that* would've been a costume!"

With the mask raised visor-like on his forehead, the young rabbi sat next to him. "I come here at lot myself. Not to sleep, maybe, but to think."

"And pray?" The question sounded snarky but Stan merely grinned.

"Sometimes. More often not. God can't solve all of our problems, you know. Dollars to doughnuts"—dollars, in his mouth, sounded like Dallas— "He wants *us* to take responsibility."

"Like a guidance counselor."

Another smile and a glint of aviator glasses. "Take the Purim story. Did you know that God's name isn't mentioned even once? Here are the Jews threatened with genocide and what does He do?" His chin jutted the little it could. "Nothing."

"Big of him."

"God made *us* big." The rabbi slapped him hard on the knee. "He made us into adults."

"Oh, Jesus," Sandy moaned again, not out of befuddlement but dread. "What time is it? My wife's been waiting."

"She's gone, Sandy. They all are." He pointed up at the bubble, the plexiglass now encrusted with snow.

"I gotta run...."

He pushed passed his rabbi's knees and tumbled out of the pew. On his one good leg, he vaulted out of the sanctuary and down the cinderblock halls to the gym. He arrived to the echoes of his own panting and a mess of carnival debris.

"Esta?" he called out. "Esta...."

Only the effigy remained. Haman, with his popped-out eyes and malicious grin, his ears of tri-colored cookies, appeared to look down at Sandy. "You see?" he seemed to ask. "You see how it can all end up?" Meaning, Sandy imagined, alone and dangling from a basketball hoop. And hanging by an argyle tie.

Spring

1.

More than the crash of helmets, perhaps, he loved the sound—half-smack, half-pop—of ball in pocket. Especially when the ball was one of Russel Pressman's deadly curves and the pocket hovered over home plate. Not even the sigh of batters too dumbfounded to swing or the umpire's "steer-rike!" were sweeter. Supervising the practice from the third-base line, Sandy would have happily stayed silent. But a sudden, "For fuck's sake" from Russel spoiled the revelry, along with the catcher crying through his mask, "Sorry, Coach. I'm sorry."

Tony Metallo, the sweet-natured but slight-minded center who could not remember when to hike footballs could not recall pitching signals, either. Was it three fingers for a slider or two? Thumb down or up for fastballs? Sandy tried drilling him, even writing them on the back of his mitt. Hopeless. Sandy might have replaced him if another player could catch those curves as faultlessly or tag a stealing runner. But Tony's confusion was causing Russel to lose focus on the mound, kicking up clouds of lime.

"Time-out," Sandy announced and took to the diamond one more time to drum on Tony's chest guard. He knew it was futile but relished the opportunity anyway. The smell of fresh spring dirt and reborn turf. The April sun chipping away winter's layers. For a moment he almost forgot about the fact that, instead of Tony Metallo, he might have been coaching Joey.

He would nearly be old enough, entering seventh grade. More than football or basketball, baseball was a father-son game. And Sandy could have taught him all the techniques: fielding grounders on one knee, shagging flyballs. He'd be a strawberry blonde like Russel, maybe, but with the

Coopers' squared-off features. Joey leaping to snare an outfield fly or doubling with bases loaded. Or just playing catch with his dad. Joey.

The fantasy distracted him from Tony's assurances of "I've got it this time, Coach. Promise," but only for a moment. Soon, the images of his son were replaced by others—of Thunderbirds and demon masks and, most indelibly, that mugshot of Liz. The memory of her swollen features, that nearly shuttered eye, filled him with sorrow and hate. Sorrow for her, of course, and for Arthur, and hate for Allan Warhaftig, her late husband.

*   *   *   *   *

Sandy learned his name finally not from Liz or even from Saps, but on his own, in the Appleton Library. It didn't take much sleuthing, only taking out microfilms of another town's newspaper, allegedly searching for a competing team's stats. Nor did it take him long to find the police photo. Though buried in the back pages, the article could have been located months before if he'd tried. Now he did, and he regretted it.

Now, her husband not only had a name but also a face. It stared at him from the screen with grainy seriousness. A linebacker's face, thick-boned, heavy-browed, and yet, Sandy had to admit, intelligent. Part Neanderthal, part professor, but in the end, all brute. His first emotion—a stinging jealousy borne of the thought of this man sleeping with Liz—succumbed quickly to a loathing so deep he could barely keep reading. Still, he forced himself on.

He learned little beyond what Saps had already reported. Allan Warhaftig, liberated from Japanese imprisonment, returned to the States to launch a series of businesses, all of them successful. He married, began a family, and showed every sign of happiness. Only behind that veneer lurked trauma. The cruelty that he suffered during the war and later turned on his son. That was the story his wife told the police. Her husband, she said, routinely beat the boy and worse. Obsessed with the culture of his former jailors—a well-known syndrome—he became adept at their weapons. Their impact on a defenseless adolescent could have been lethal, Elizabeth Warhaftig claimed, had she not intervened.

Only one piece of information was news to Sandy. Asked why she had not previously complained of the abuse, the wife cited her fear of retribution. And who would believe that Allan Warhaftig, veteran, philanthropist, feted patron of the arts, was a child beater? A common enough story, albeit with a macabre end. A single blow to the head delivered by a desperate woman wielding for the first and only time an antique Samurai sword.

The journalist was clearly sympathetic to Liz, as were probably his sources in the police. She had no priors, no history of violence—on the contrary, Mrs. Warhaftig appeared the ideal spouse, posing with her husband at events. A responsible parent as well, outspoken in the PTA. "The suspect"— that's how the paper referred to her, never as the murderer—"acted as any mother would in similar circumstances."

So Sandy was not surprised when, reeling forward six months, he found a follow-up piece on the trial. The homicide, committed to prevent an imminent danger to Arthur's life, was swiftly deemed justified and the accused cleared of any wrongdoing. The text was short and all but dwarfed by the accompanying photograph. Not of the dead man this time but of his widow. Clearly taken before her arrest, perhaps at some gala, she looked elegant, coifed and bejeweled, smiling with a full mouth. Pristine, except for the discoloration near her right eye. "Elizabeth Warhaftig," the caption said, "not guilty."

Sandy stared at it for a long time. Leaning into the viewer, face nearly pressed to the screen, he scanned the image for the slightest insight into Liz. He saw many things—breeding, poise, a barely checked sensuality—but one. Buried somewhere between the pixels, perhaps, but otherwise invisible, was a cold capacity for murder.

*   *   *   *   *

He knew from the crack of the bat that the ball was homered. Sure enough, it arced high above the right fielder's head and landed on the track. Sandy pushed up the sleeves of his ratty sweatshirt and applauded while Chrissie cheered on the bleachers. Tossing off his cap, Russel rounded the bases. His hair trailed behind him, comet-like.

The first weeks of spring brought a respite of sorts. No more incidents with Arthur and Rae, no more acts of vandalism. Brooks hadn't returned to weep to him nor Jeanne to confer on love. Though the coffee remained bitter in the teachers' lounge, the conversation sweetened. Less talk of war and more about new movies, Michael Caine and Liza Minelli instead of Kissinger and Nixon, sports in place of politics. Even Wendell Barr seemed mellowed.

A former minor leaguer, he often stopped by practice to shout out pointers to the team and, implicitly, criticism of its coach. But Sandy hadn't seen him in weeks and wondered whether even a curmudgeon like him could resist the season. Surrounded by renewal, it might've been hard to hate.

In school at least, Sandy felt unburdened. But not so at home. His absences, both physical and emotional, diluted what remained of his marriage. Though she said nothing, Esta no longer merely suspected but assumed his infidelity. She still went about her day teaching the dangers of drugs and sex to students all too familiar with both and she still prepared his dinner. But the food was not merely burnt but cremated, the vegetables shriveled, the meat charred. He still fell asleep in his recliner but was no longer awakened by a hand on his knee and a tender, "Come, sweetie, bedtime." By the time he got himself up, the TV programs were over and replaced by an image of the American flag and a recording of the national anthem.

Over on the track, a runner paused to pick up the baseball. A sleek figure, Sandy could not quite make him out, but he certainly had an arm. The ball sailed over second base and bounced in front of third just as Russel touched it. He had to duck and so did Chrissie, as the hop smashed into the bleachers. Both looked irritated, as if the thrower were somehow aiming at them. Sandy shrugged—what else could he do? He squinted again at the track, but the runner was sprinting away.

He turned back to the practice, tried to concentrate on the lineup and found himself, once again, thinking about Liz and his visceral need to see her again. The longer days meant more time to sneak off, more opportunities to explore in hotel semi-darkness the secrets she would never tell him but that her body subtly disclosed. Limberness, wetness, pliancy, knots— they told of an exacting woman who knew how to give but also to take, whether his love or another man's life.

Listening to her physically kept him from asking about the discolored spot near her eye and from letting on about the mugshot or her late husband's photo. She'd never respond to him, of course, but he wasn't certain he wanted her to. *Not* hearing heightened the frisson, the sense of danger both inside that hotel room and beyond. The contradictions were arousing at times but at most others horrific. The same mouth that gifted him so rapturously could, with a single bite, destroy him.

Caught in his own dilemmas, Sandy supervised a round of pickle. A player dashed from second to third while the basemen tried to tag him.

Watching the ball whisk back and forth, he caught sight of the track again, but instead of the runner glimpsed a pair of older women. One of them was tallish, blonde, and dressed in a billowing peasant shirt. The other was much shorter with close-cropped dark hair. They walked very slowly, heads down, shoulders touching, as they turned away from him and sauntered out of view.

Consulting his inside wrist, licking his fingertips, Sandy signaled, "Practice over." The players jogged past him to the showers. Then he was alone on the grass, much as he was months ago on the football field, envisioning himself unleashed. But unlike wistful autumn, spring awakened him not to what had or might have been but rather to the luxuries of the present. He ceased thinking about death, about Allan Warhaftig, and even Joey. Rather than freedom, he relished entwinement. And instead of goalposts, he only saw Liz. He pictured her lying naked before him, with her diamond and its mound, her legs splayed like baselines to be stolen.

2.

The moment Bronowski announced, "Serves 'em right, the slope-heads," Sandy knew the respite was too good to last.

Predictably, McGonnigle countered, "You like massacring women and children like that, why don't you go over there and kill some?"

"Why don't you just go and join the Commies?"

"Earl's right," D'Angelis interceded. He was wooing himself in the wall mirror, grooming his thick black duck's ass. "I say we burn the motherfuckers."

Charlotte Fox berated them—"You make me sick, all of you"—but mostly angering McGonnigle.

"Who asked you, anyway, pothead?"

At issue was the morning's headline about the renewed firebombing of Hanoi. "Phosphorus melts the skin right off, you know. Melts eyeballs, too," Stevens scientifically explained.

"Thank you for that, Ronald," Jeanne remarked from the stained Formica table that held her lunch. "I was trying to eat."

But her sentence was lost in the melee that intensified with everyone shouting simultaneously and loud enough to reach the principal's office. Dr. Steinseifer soon stomped in, followed by his secretary, Mrs. Tannenbaum, with identical indignation. "Have you all gone nuts? The students will hear."

The students, perhaps, but not their teachers who went on battling. Between harangues, Brooks fled the lounge in tears. Sandy, alone, noticed him but did nothing. Silent on the sofa, sipping his bitter brew and pretending to read some files, he had no interest in politics or consoling depressive adults. That is, until someone hollered.

That someone was Miriam Loftus shooting out her chair with an ear-splitting "Shame on you all!" A desiccated woman in horn-rimmed glasses and worsted skirts, a geography teacher as flat and measured as her maps, she was nevertheless passionate about Brooks. Or at least that was the rumor. But now there was no doubt, the truth illuminated by fury. "Have you not one iota of compassion? Do none of you have a heart?"

Her words, though melodramatic, sufficed to shut everyone up. They watched as Miriam stormed from the room, heels clacking the linoleum, and rushed to catch up with the shop teacher. The silence continued even after she exited, only to be broken by Wendell with a single, scornful word: "Pussies."

No, Sandy thought, the harmony of spring could not endure indefinitely. Upheaval, tragedy, even danger would invariably resurge. From this moment on, officially, the respite was over.

*   *   *   *   *

"What was that about?" Jeanne wanted to know. Bolder now, sticking not only her head but her entire bantam frame into the entrance to Sandy's cubicle, her questions sounded more forthright as well. "And who would've guessed, Miss Loftus?"

From his chair, Sandy looked up at her, no longer sheepish and fidgeting with her cross, but exuding a new confidence. A sudden sexuality, too.

"Brooks' son is a draft dodger in Canada," he explained. "The bombing in Hanoi means the war goes on who knows how long more. Years. Not seeing his boy is killing him."

"And Miriam Loftus?"

Sandy rolled his eyes. "Love makes for some strange bedfellows."

"Tell me about it," Jeanne said and plopped down in the chair next to Sandy. Their faces had never been this close, he realized. He could count each of her moles and the strands of dark hair at her temples. Her breath smelled of Life Savers. She gave him a piercing expression. "Actually, I'm coming to you about something else. Arthur."

"The kid in your homeroom class? His last name—remind me?"

"Hard to forget, actually. Warhaftig."

"Arthur Warhaftig. Yes. He's been acting out again?"

"Less so. Someone gave him a Polaroid, which keeps him busy. That and he's got this crush on Rae Henderson."

"You don't say?"

"No, not that…" She slid her chair even closer, kissing distance, and lowered her voice. "I've done some snooping around."

Curious, Jeanne did what he should have back in September—phoned Arthur's previous school. She asked for the guidance counselor, inquiring about troubles at home, domestic violence, anything that would account for the student's erratic behavior and help her better cope.

"And?"

"And what?"

"What did the counselor say?"

Jeanne smirked. "Nothing. He listened to my questions and didn't react. Like he didn't even want to hear them. Eventually, he just hung up."

"Weird…."

"I thought…" Her voice plummeted again. "I thought you could contact the man. That maybe he'd talk to you, you know, counselor to counselor."

Before he could refuse, Jeanne presented him with a slip of paper. "Call him, please," she whispered. "He's hiding something. I feel it."

"Okay. I'll call," Sandy relented and received another touch on the cheek. Longer than the first one she gave him back in the fall and more tender.

"You're a good man, Coop," Jeanne Pagonis said, though he didn't feel like one. His cheeks burned where her fingers had brushed. Of course he'd call the number, but not to inquire about Arthur. The purpose was to ferret out more details about Liz. What she was like before moving to Appleton and did something about her change? Did she ever contact that other counselor, meet with him, entice him to protect her son? And one more question—the real one—was he, Sandy Cooper, unique?

*   *   *   *   *

Hamilton Marsh. A Senator's name or an actor on some soap opera. His voice, though, coming through the receiver after two rings, was anything but stately or theatrical. Weaselly, timid, belonging to a man who Sandy imagined shrinking before anyone stronger and certainly a woman like Liz. A man who pronounced "hello" as "yellow" and braced himself for bad news.

And Sandy gave it to him. "I'm interested in a former student of yours, Mister Marsh," he said after introducing himself. "Arthur Warhaftig."

The response was silence, broken by the faintest of sighs.

"Mister Marsh, are you there?"

Seconds passed before his fellow counselor finally answered. "I have no wish to talk about Arthur," was all he said before hanging up.

Sandy stared at the phone throughout the morning as students entered his cubicle. There were the Jewish kids reeling under pressure to succeed, the younger ones fearful of flubbing their Bar Mitzvahs. The Italian kids who sometimes felt bound to act tough. The hurt and the gripes bled into one another and became one long yowl in his head.

That droning persisted for days, even during lovemaking with Liz. She heard it as well, he imagined, stroking his forehead and asking, "What is going on it there?" She could see the gears churning, she said.

"Sorry. But there're so many questions. So much I want to know."

"Like what, for instance? What do you want to know?"

"Why do we always have to do this in the dark? I want to see you— all of you."

Liz pulled away. "I prefer it that way."

"And why can't we talk about your life for once, not only mine?"

"You'd prefer it that way."

And there the conversation ended, not with answers but Liz's hand delving for another round before departing. No light shed on her body or on her past, only the alarm in his brain clanging louder.

The noise distracted him during handball at the Y that Sunday when he missed shots that bounced at his feet, and later, at Sobotnik's, where he stared at his turkey club. Nothing in the place had changed: that same out of date calendar, the tiny skyline of shakers, the briny corned beef smell. Only Sandy felt different. Not only the ringing in his head but also an emptiness in his gut made him sense that somehow he no longer belonged. As if he'd finally outgrown the place or, more likely, that it suddenly ceased to exist. As though brunching with Saps was not a weekly reality but a memory culled from the past.

"Why do you bother ordering that?"

The question was directed not at Sandy but at his sandwich as the policeman reached for it. His friend barely noticed, though. His eyes, rather, drifted up to the ceiling at the fan frozen at 2:15. "What now?" Saps asked again, garbled by a mouthful of turkey. "Let me guess. Your school's a racist hotbed, your marriage is a mess, and your leg is acting up. And, oh, yeah, you're screwing a woman who axed her husband."

But Sandy only uttered two words. "Hamilton Marsh."

"Plays second base for—let me guess—Detroit?"

Sandy frowned and then told Saps everything he knew about the counselor, his refusal to talk with Jeanne, and his hanging up on him. "Good," Saps said, intelligibly, as he cleaned Sandy's plate and went back to his own. "Now leave it."

"I'm going to go see him. Confront him, if I have to."

"Great, you're not in enough crap as it is, now you want to add harassment?"

Though aimed at Sandy's heart, the pickle spear failed to dissuade him. "I have to, Saps. I have to know."

"And I have to—"

His sentence was cut short by a high whining sound. Sandy thought it was still inside his skull and it took a few moments for him to acknowledge that the source was external. Behind his meat slicer, in a lull between orders for herring, Bernie wept.

Saps and Sandy exchanged looks, then shrugs. Simultaneously, they inquired, "What happened?" but only the counselor got up from their rear alcove table and approached the counter. "Cut yourself?" he asked. "Should I call a doctor?"

With a splotched hand towel, Bernie wiped his eyes. "No. I'm okay. See?" He held up ten frank-like fingers and attempted a smile. Ugly on top of obese, pale with a small, sweaty forehead and huge stubbled jowls, he tried at least to be friendly, remembering each of his customer's names. None of them knew his last one, though—just Bernie—or what life he might possibly have outside of Sobotnik's. From the looks of him, none.

"I'm fine. Really," he repeated and once again burst into sobs. "Sorry, Mister Cooper. Sorry. It's just that...."

"I see, business is slow."

"They've sold the place."

"They?" It occurred to Sandy that he grew up in this town and never met the deli's owner. "Sold?"

"To some burger chain. What am I going to do?"

Sandy gaped at him. Why did people think that just because of his job he knew all the answers? "Something, I'm sure. Don't worry."

Bernie was crying again. He drew his thick wrists across his cheeks and then down over a distended apron as stained as his hand towel. Sandy left him there only to find Saps back at the alcove dabbing the corners of his mouth and vaunting, "What I tell you about all worlds disappearing?"

Not only worlds but the clanging in Sandy's head was gone, replaced by a clarified silence. "There's no time to waste, then," he said while picking up the check and leaving a double tip. "I've got to see Hamilton Marsh."

3.

Another April morning. Trees flaunting their new foliage, a tinsel of dew on the grass. Storefronts blinked open—Herskey's window announcing freshly baked babka, a sale on pork chops at Vinny's. Cars streamed by on tires made, it sounded, of moleskin, and braked for the over-the-hill policeman herding kids. The older ones entered Appleton Junior High, an orange brick building that seemed to swell as it filled. Buses like yellowjackets swarmed toward it. A bell, urgent as a distress signal, rang.

Approaching the double doors, books to her chest, Rae Henderson tried to stay in line. The students in front of her, though, kept standing aside for her. "Go 'head," they demurred, and "Please," some with a half bow. They did not see the blush that darkened her complexion or the tear clinging to one eye. Only when she entered was her discomfort replaced by fear. Positioned at his usual ambush point, Wendell Barr stood gazing at her. Rae looked down, but only momentarily before locking eyes with his. Both pairs said the same thing: *I know what you are, and I know you don't want me here.* The two exchanged nods before Rae pressed on to class.

In the teachers' lounge, silent except for the burbling of yesterday's coffee, Jeanne Pagonis stopped by. She glanced around before mincing toward the Formica table and finding, tapped underneath, an envelope. Surrendering to the urge to open it now rather than later, she extracted its contents. Reading, giggling, she sighed, finally, and hurried off to her homeroom.

Upstairs, meanwhile, in the gym, a shirtless Howard Weintraub climbed rope. Or, more accurately, ropes, each hand clasping a separate cord. He pulled himself up without leg strength, only the arms and shoulders, sinews bulging. Later, after school, he would whip himself through a regime of push-ups and sit-ups, driving himself to anguish. Yet the pain was enjoyable, especially when he remembered its goal. He snorted, he climbed, a now-svelte fourteen-year-old, freed of glasses and zits, ascending toward mysterious heights. His day would conclude, as always, with a twenty-lap sprint around the track.

Through hallways redolent of the janitors' camphor, students surged into their classrooms. Russel Pressman laughing arm in arm with Chrissie Esposito, the band clique and the artsy clique, the jocks and the heads and the nerds. Dr. Steinseifer, shuttered in his office, guarded by Mrs. Tannebaum, could almost feel the bustling. It gave him the most satisfaction in life, ever since his wife of thirty years passed away and their children moved out West. What quiet pleasure there was in imagining Bronowski and McGonnigle waiting with their equations on the board, Stevens behind his Bunsen Burners, Loftus with her maps and Brooks beside his tool chest. The thought of Charlotte Fox dressed like a hippie and teaching those Social Studies delighted him, and D'Angelis showing off his biceps. Education, even of half-crazed adolescents, was an honor, the principal thought, a blessing to those imparting it.

* * * * *

Elsewhere, other blessings occurred. At Temple Beth El, Louis the custodian huffed as he mopped the floors. It was the traditional Passover cleaning and there was so much more to do—scrub refrigerators, wax the pews—in the mere two weeks before the holiday. He paused for a moment, wiping the sweat beneath his *yarmulke*, and for once wished someone would help. And then, as if summoned, another mop appeared alongside his. Furiously it whisked and to the accompaniment of "Me and Julio Down by the Schoolyard," sung off key. Louis paused, straightened, and laughed his bottomless laugh. Right next to him, with his *yarmulke* flapping and aviator glasses slipping down his nose, scoured Stanley Rosencranz. "Elbow grease, Louis," he cheered between stanzas. "Lean into it."

Together they dusted the ark with its Torah scrolls, burnished the plaques and the wrought-iron doors, Windexed the stained-glass windows. The scrawny Rabbi Stan and Louis twice his size, together they sweated and sang. They realigned the Biblical quote about truth. Only the dome remained. Dispiritedly, they gazed up at the plexiglass. Mottled by snow and rain and bird droppings, it was no longer transparent—more like veiled.

"Shame we can't get up there," Louis sighed.

"But, oh, we can!" the rabbi piped. "We just have to keep cleaning."

And elsewhere, too, others tidied and sang. Mrs. Biggs at the Daughters of Jacob Home re-erected the old photographs and holiday cards toppled by her patient's latest tantrum and refreshed the chrysanthemum vase. She hummed and occasionally broke into lyrics, their sadness sweetened with soul.

"Why that?"

"Why what?"

"Why a song about a father who abandons his family? Who drinks and gambles and fornicates? Why not a song about the rain in Spain and mountains alive with music? Why the tragedy?"

"Cause things are not so rosy always." Mrs. Biggs smiled so expansively her features flattened. "Sometimes, they're a bitch."

She pushed his wheelchair toward the window and its effusion of morning light. But Maurice Cooper merely grumbled. A speckled hand shielded his face. "Too bright!" he protested. "Not enough you're poisoning me with your rotten food, now you want to blind me too."

"What do you got to gripe about what with all these fineries?" the orderly chided him, tightening his tie and pin. "With that loving son of yours?"

Maurice's grumble deepened. "You mean that…that…teacher? If you'd only seen him when…" His hand dropped finally, allowing the sunrays to reach him. "Receiving the hike at his own goal line, far behind scrimmage, but instead of passing, he ran. You should've seen him. Dodging this way, cutting that, with nothing but open field in front of him. His whole life…" His rheumy eyes glistened. "The crowd went crazy. His mother too. And even I…even I…until…."

"'Til what?" Mrs. Biggs was wiping the top of his portable table, tsk-tsking him for once again not touching his meal.

"Until what what? What are you babbling about, you *zhlub*?" The crinkly hand was up again. The light drained from his face.

"I know what that means, Mister Cooper, and I do not appreciate it."

"Fine. Fine. Just stop your fussing already. And put on the Victrola."

Music—his music—filled the room. A woman suddenly wondered what she'd be like if she loved someone, the words that would elude her, the confusion. Mrs. Biggs finished sponging and headed to the door, only to pause and glance back.

He sat slumped in his wheelchair, mouth agape, his hand no longer raised but folded serenely in his lap. Sunlight overwhelmed him. "You sleep now, Mister Cooper," the orderly said. "You get yourself some peace."

Stepping lightly in her tennis shoes, she returned to the record player and raised its needle. The room went silent, except for Maurice's snores and her singing. Somebody's father was a rolling stone, a badass man, a sinner, but his children loved him nevertheless. She sang, solemnly, as she smoothed out his lapel and adjusted its Elks emblem.

*   *   *   *   *

That same morning, that very minute, a wheel of dough—the first of the day—whirled above Dominic's head. Passers-by saw it wobbling between the gondoliers on the pizzeria's window and its still-blinking Christmas lights. They marveled, perhaps, at the sight of a pasty disc gyrating in defiance of gravity and the indelible evidence of hate.

At the Appleton Police Station, Sergeant Saperstein prepared for the daily patrol. In his stripes and uniform, his badges and his gun, he cut an authoritative figure—except for the cap seesawing on a head that appeared whetted. Together with the protruding nose, it gave him a canine look, like a pointer hot on a scent.

And the odor he picked up that morning, the stench, was from yet another day-glo inscription. This one was scrawled not on a restaurant or a school but on the door of the First Baptist Church. Between the Jews and the Italians, Protestants were a rarity in town, and their church was commensurately modest. No one paid it much attention before and still wouldn't, least of all Captain Rizzo. Even though the vandal had gone even further this time and defaced a house of worship, there'd be no investigation he told Saps. Not even when the graffiti warned, "Satan is Here."

Not far away, on a side street of row houses, Sandy prepared for work. Though running late, he paused in the upstairs room that housed his old trophies, a megaphone, and the monogrammed bear. Its window looked out over the driveway where his wife, Esta, hurried into her secondhand Corolla.

For once, the previous evening, Sandy had gotten home first—no baseball practice, no furtive stop by some hotel. Forgoing dinner and television, he went up directly to bed. Breakfast he avoided as well, dodged the awkwardness of feeling his cheek pecked icily and having to wish her a good day. Nor did Esta seek him out, but rather grabbed her study guides for drug and sex class, the pamphlets, and sample prophylactics that tickled her too-seasoned students. She rushed out of the door, platinum beehive awry.

Only when he saw her car disappearing down the street did Sandy descend to the kitchen, grab a muffin, and head out to the garage. He crossed the divot of grass, long gone weedy. At least it was free of the lawn statues—the Virgins, dwarves, and black-faced jockeys—that Esta called "*narishkeit.*" Inching past the rusted mowers and bicycles, he squeezed into the Impala and, with barely a glance in the rearview mirror, backed out.

He thought about Hamilton Marsh, his need to question him despite his objections. Getting to his school on the other side of county, waiting for him after class, driving back—it was hard enough finding that hour to see Liz; what pretext could Sandy devise? At this rate, it might take weeks to wrangle it, Sandy thought, pressing hard on the gas. And who knew, even then, whether the man would talk to him or simply storm away?

From gas pedal to brake, his foot flew and stomped. The Impala screeched at the end of the driveway and Sandy's head shot back. But the garbage truck missed him, narrowly, after almost plowing into his trunk. Giddily, he laughed. How fitting it would have been, given the mess his life was in, to be killed by moving trash?

*   *   *   *   *

On the other end of town, Liz Warhaftig gazed through a fancier second story window. She often began her mornings like this, especially after nights when awakened by an engine's growl, a gut-retching sound—the car was famous for it. She waited for it to subside before trying to fall back to sleep. Most times she never did, though, and instead waited for Arthur to come down, wolf a Pop-Tart, and, without a word, scurry off for the bus. And still she gazed—for what, exactly, she wasn't sure. For Arthur's return? A nosy reporter? The police?

Later, she descended a winding staircase to the den. She lit a cigarette and, though not yet nine, poured herself a drink. In her silken robe, she sat and thought about the future. Though scarcely out of childhood, in a mere five years her son would be college aged, and then what? She pictured herself in a condo just off his campus, trying to trail him to class. The nasty frat boys and vicious co-eds, the professors' suspicions—how could she protect him from all that? How would she protect herself?

Five years could still be a long time, though, during which she might have to move again, at least once. The thought of it horrified and exhausted her. Propping her brocaded slippers on the coffee table, hugging her knees, she recalled her flight from the West Coast to the East, the traumas of her previous homes. The arrest, the trial, the fortune she spent keeping it out of the press, and the back-page items that nevertheless slipped through. Nothing helped, not even her involvement with that poor fellow Marsh. In the end, there was no choice but Appleton, a semi-conscious town caught up with football, corned beef, pizza, and petty crimes that didn't even make its *Gazette*. There was no choice but Sandy Cooper.

In an ashtray crammed with red-stained butts, Liz stubbed out her cigarette as she swigged the last of her drink. She patted the pile of her glossy, black hair, and fingered the dark patch by her eye. A good man, Sandy, a sad man, and ever so earnest. Too good to be merely bought off. He had to be emotionally hooked. But how long could it last, really? How long would it be before he, too, was left alone and incurably hurt but never quite knowing what hit him?

Liz Warhaftig peered around her den with its framed kimonos and proclamations, its lithographs and masks. The Tonfa and other weapons. And displayed on the wall behind her, watching *her* it seemed, the sword. The sight of it only raised more questions. Could her husband ever have imagined its ultimate use? Could he have pictured, even in nightmares, the person wielding it?

* * * * *

Call it numbness, but they no longer listened to the quotes. After so many months of love and tolerance, the daily infusions of peace, neither students nor teachers paid any attention to the PA. It still heralded each morning with upbeat passages from Shakespeare and Lincoln, Bob Dylan and Gandhi, but nobody was moved or even educated. In the clangor of bells and locker slam, wisdom now went unheard.

No one noticed, then, when a different announcement blared: "If an injury has been done to a man it should be so severe that his vengeance need not be feared." No one bothered to identify the pubescent voice still crack-ing. "Men take revenge for slight injuries—for heavy ones, they cannot."

Only Sandy, entering late, thought he recognized the reader, Howard Weintraub, but didn't have time to ponder it. Already waiting outside his cubicle were the first of the day's complainers. Others were stampeding to class, jostling, gossiping, hankering over somebody else's new shoes or ID bracelets—a tsunami of jealously, hope, puppy love, and pain. It churned past the lockers as they slammed and the only one of them that remained open.

Like Sandy, Arthur Warhaftig was also tardy. With a Swinger Polaroid slung around his neck, hair draped over his eyes, he struggled to keep his locker's contents from escaping. Still, his wooden weapon, the Tonfa, smacked onto the floor, followed by a flurry of photographs. He tossed them all back in and karate-kicked the rest until at last the door could close. Even then, through the flimsy metal, came the ping of half-empty canisters.

Their echo, though, was squelched by another bell—longer, more definitive—for first period. Arthur's eyes darted from side to side, surveying the empty hall for signs of danger or, perhaps, targets. Then, hoisting his Swinger, swimming in his oversized clothes, he hurried to Miss Pagonis's homeroom. Neither he nor anyone else in school reacted to the voice still breaking through the PA, saying, "It is safer to be feared than to be loved."

4.

The *haggadahs* might have contained evidence of murder. Each page of the paperback prayer books bore the stains of past Seders: red wine, violet horseradish, sanguine splashes of roast. Nobody thought of buying new ones, certainly not the Sapersteins, who were neither rich or religious enough to care, nor the Coopers, whose sole desire was to rush through the ritual parts, get to the meal, and further gore the pages. Only this year was different.

This year, Esta insisted that they read aloud every passage, even those that made no sense to them. Why should anyone care whether there were ten plagues or fifty, or why the parsley is dipped not once but twice in salt water? Why the shank bone, why the egg?

"The bread of affliction, you bet," Saps joked, pointing at his matzah-hardened gut. "Good thing we ate it *after* leaving Egypt." But Esta explained it all as best she could, as Rabbi Stan had taught her.

But there was more to her piety, Sandy thought. A vengeance. The way she glared at him every time slavery and suffering were mentioned but glanced away at freedom. The tortured look on her face while the Saperstein boys, Mark and Gerald, recited the four questions and the story of the wicked son. Prim as always in her buttoned blouse and lacquered beehive, Esta for once was as cold as she looked.

Saps pretended not to notice and kept wisecracking about the Jewish "thing" with bondage. But not his bookkeeper wife, who could also sum up moods. While her husband and his friend guzzled their fifth cup of wine and her sons somehow ended up on the floor racing model Ferraris, Marjorie scrutinized Esta.

"Who is like God our Lord, who sees what is below, on heaven and earth?" she read steadily. "Who raises the poor and lifts up the needy?" Only when she concluded, "Who sets the childless woman in her house as happy as a mother of children?" did her voice finally break.

"*Dayenu!*" With remarkable suppleness, the big-boned Marjorie shot up and sang. "Mark, Gerald, everybody!" Her candied features sweetened as she clapped, "*Day—day—yenu! Dayenu. Dayenu!*" and led Esta, weeping, into the kitchen.

"Happy?" Saps accused him the moment they left.

Sandy contemplated the candles. "Am I supposed to be?"

"This has got to stop!" The demand was punctuated by a pound on the table that set the silverware hopping. "*You* have to stop it!"

Sandy's response, scarcely audible above the "vroom-vroom" racket beneath their chairs, was simply, "I can't."

"Like hell you can't. You're a free man, aren't you?" Not since they were kids, fighting the neighborhood bigots, had he seen his friend so furious. His small mouth widened menacingly, and his nose thrust forward halberd-like. The white polyester *yarmulke*, emblazoned with someone's Bar Mitzvah date, slid from his peak.

"I can't," was all Sandy could say again.

"Bullshit," Saperstein hissed. "Think of that poor woman…."

"Y-y-yeow! Y-y-yeow!" Around both men's shoes, the Ferraris screeched. He swilled the rest of his wine. "I can't."

Then, just as Saps grabbed the handful of bitter herbs, ready to chuck them, the women emerged from the kitchen. Marjorie carried a platter of meat, pre-carved, and Esta a pitcher of gravy. Their smiles were identically forced.

"I'm sorry," Esta began. "You know how this sometimes gets to me. The death of the firstborn."

Saps laughed, equally strained, and toasted, "*L'chaim!*"

"*L'chaim*," the women repeated, and took their seats at the table.

Sandy turned to his wife as she heaped his plate with food. "*L'chaim*," he said, and raised an empty glass.

* * * * *

He never thought he'd be grateful to see the Daughters of Jacob, never imagined himself trotting through its gardens with a tray of leftovers and bounding past the nurses' station. Not even the thought of what awaited him in one of its morbidly cheery halls could dim the relief he felt after driving Esta home. Powered by wine and guilt feelings, the Impala flew.

But rushing into his father's room, Sandy smashed into Mrs. Biggs coming out. She nevertheless managed to catch the tray in one hand and Sandy in the other, hugging him to her bust.

He stuttered, "Jesus Christ, I'm sorry," his face as red as horseradish.

"No worry, Mister Cooper," she assured him, "But, please, respect the Lord's name."

It took him a moment to understand and apologize. By that time, though, the orderly had informed him that the tray would not be necessary. "He's almost there. Almost home."

Again, he looked flummoxed and again she explained. "Where they don't need any more appetite. Can't even look at food." Her features evened as she smiled. "It's a peaceful end, Mister Cooper. Be thankful."

Numbly, he nodded and stepped inside. A harsh scratching noise filled the room. The phonograph needle had revolved through the second act and the finale and now bobbed gratingly on the label. Across the room, in his wheelchair next to the lightless window, his father sat with his chins on his chest, snoozing. For once nothing seemed disturbed—not the old Christmas cards or the chrysanthemum vase. Even the photographs of his late mother and long unseen sister were left to stare placidly from their frames.

Laying the tray on the bookshelf, Sandy selected another dog-eared album—*Flower Drum Song*, a favorite—and was about to lay it on the platter. As fast as he raced into the building, he could scurry out again and perhaps make a date with Liz. But then, just as he lifted the tonearm, he caught a gasp behind him. Only when he half-turned and saw father stirring, did Sandy understand him. "I heard it," he muttered.

"No problem, I'll chose another," Sandy offered. "Here, how's this? *Anything Goes?*"

Another gasp, "I heard it."

"Okay, okay. Then this—"

"I heard it. That day on the field...."

His hand froze mid-selection. Sandy abandoned the phonograph and approached his father. The non-paralyzed side of his face trembled, his glassy eyes ran.

"You couldn't have," Sandy said.

"Like a horsewhip."

"You were too far away. In the stands."

"Like lightning striking a tree."

Could it be true? The sound he heard that day as the tackler lunged at him from behind, clasping his hips and plowing into his thigh. The sickening crack of his femur snapping, the fractured tibia. Yet, even then he was unsure whether he'd heard it really or felt it, the vibrations rifling his body. But here was his father telling him otherwise.

"Mom, too? Esta?"

"No, only me," Maurice Cooper attested. "Only me and you."

"But how?"

The old man's chins again descended, hiding the knot of his tie. A string of drool reached his lapel and gathered on its pin. Sandy was frustrated by the delay—too late now to see Liz—and irked. Surely his father was fooling himself, again indulging his self-pity. Bad enough the limp that reminded his son of the life he missed, worse with that guilt weighing on it. He lifted the tray, thought for a second, and returned it to the bookshelf. Maybe Mrs. Biggs liked *matzah brei*.

"Hopes shattering," his father snored. "That's what it sounded like."

By the exit, Sandy stood, fixed by an urge to embrace him. To tell him "I'm sorry, Dad," and kiss his withered cheek. Instead, he stepped out into the sterile hall and closed the door behind him. But not before a final sigh escaped. "The sound of a breaking heart."

*   *   *   *   *

Heartbreak, that's all these nights were about, heartbreak and humiliation. Pimply boys in Brute and Hush Puppies cowering in far corners, too frightened to move, much less cross the room to where ludicrously coiffed and cosmeticized girls sat stiffly. The strobe lights flashed, illuminating expressions of bashfulness. The throbbing music egged teenagers to "Get it On" and "Go All the Way," but the floor remained empty. Pressed into chaperoning, a few teachers mulled around with their coffee mugs or tried to coax students into dancing. It wouldn't work, Sandy knew. School mixers were not about fun, they weren't even about socializing. They were, rather, about disappointment and loneliness, about preparing young people for life.

From behind a phalanx of soda bottles, Sandy surveyed the cafeteria-turned-discotheque. The strobes exposed Brian McGonnigle, super hip in a tie-dyed t-shirt and jeans, and another burst revealed Charlotte Fox shimmying with Jeanne Pagonis awkwardly mimicking her moves. There was Rae Henderson attempting but failing to dress down, her black patent boots reflecting the leather fringes of her miniskirt. And Wendell Barr, fast by the entrance, searching for violators of dress and consumption, detached.

Squinting into the lights, Sandy picked out Brooks, for once not coated with sawdust but just as depressed, turning down a dance with Miriam Loftus. He saw Russel and Chrissie and any number of students whose secrets he kept along with their parents' thank-you notes pinned to his cubicle. And, fleetingly, he saw himself. Introverted, anguished, unfaithful, and now, according to Liz, strange.

"Strange? What's so strange about me?" he'd asked her earlier that evening, at the hotel.

"Come on, *you*?" She laughed into the sheets. "With your sleeves folded inward and the watch *inside* your wrist."

"It's the way my old coach, Doc Wheelock, wore it."

"And that awful finger licking?"

"For gripping the football."

"And the tie? Like you're incapable of tightening it."

"Ever been strangled?"

"Hmmm," she purred and lifted his hands to her throat.

"And you call *me* strange…."

The music blasted, the strobe lights pulsed. They captured Dr. Steinseifer, who always stopped in at such events but then just stood there nodding, either in approval or disbelief. Saps, too, dropped by, ostensibly to check that all was in order but really to exchange glances with Sandy.

They hadn't seen each other since Passover nearly two weeks before, Sandy skipping their Sunday handball game, Saps eating alone at Sobotnik's. His friend was under the weather, so he claimed, unable to get away. But the sergeant could not be fooled. He resented serving as an alibi, balked at playing the beard. The look he shot Sandy was anything but amicable—fed up and mad.

Sandy's face was penitent, like a child's caught snitching candy, but too blurred by the strobes. And too transient, for a second later it turned back to the floor where he thought he saw Arthur crossing.

His back was to Sandy, but he recognized him nevertheless from the hair and the baggy clothes, and the oddly confident way he marched up to the row of girls. Or rather, marched up to Rae Henderson who shrunk as her classmates giggled. Emerging from behind the soda bottles, Sandy started toward her—not for her sake, he realized, but for Arthur's. Publicly rejected by Rae, who knew how'd he react?

But Rae didn't budge and neither did Arthur. He merely raised his camera and took several photos, their flashes lost in the strobes. The boy waited for the prints to roll out, waved and blew on them. The girls cackled, Rae turned away, and Sandy rushed to get between them. He had to prevent any scene or worse.

"You're strange but, I must say, creative," Liz had complimented him after their second round of lovemaking. "And trustworthy."

She might have been referring to the hands still encircling her neck, but Sandy knew better. His dependability on sexual matters rated a far second to what Liz really cared about. For months now, and despite some close calls, he had succeeded in safeguarding Arthur.

Loosening their grip, his hands fell to her breasts. "Any luck, we'll get through to the end of the year."

"Luck has nothing to do with it. It's your job, Coop. Simple." Her breasts, though petite, were defiant. The angled brows, verdigris eyes, and lips spreading over sharply white teeth could have greeted him in a jungle. "In school and out. And in Washington."

"Washington?"

Liz pretended innocence. "He's going on your temple trip, or haven't you heard?"

The annual youth excursion, four days trudging around the steamy capital, cajoling, disciplining, shepherding disinterested adolescents from one national monument to the next—Sandy dreaded it. And this year, with Esta, would be worse. How, then, could he cope with Arthur?

"I don't think it's a good idea. Maybe you can talk him out of it."

"And maybe you could stop licking your fingers." Liz laughed. "My son is not one to be talked out of anything," she stated. "My son does all the talking."

He was not talking now, on the dance floor, only photographing, aiming his Swinger again and again at Rae. No longer blushing, she looked close to tears just as Sandy arrived and positioned himself between her and the camera.

"I think that's enough, Arthur," he shouted over the music. But the eighth-grader merely stared at him, or so Sandy felt. The lights and Arthur's long hair afforded only a peek of his stone-gray eyes darting. "Did you hear me?"

He barely heard himself. The booming, the blaze—Sandy wondered if this was what war was like. The amplifiers commanded kids to "Hold Your Head Up" only to be blinded when they did. Arthur, meanwhile, didn't budge.

"Please, now, let these girls alone...."

He had lived this moment before, outside the basketball game with South Central, with Rae knowing that he had intervened to save Arthur, not her, and Arthur berating him for interfering at all. The looks they aimed at him, resentment and hate, were identical as well. Sandy braced for curses, even a karate kick, but what happened next astonished him.

The music suddenly went soft, the strobe lights kaleidoscopic. They coated Rae in multiple colors, turning her ghoulish. Whether it was that or the sad strumming of "The First Time Ever I Saw Your Face," Sandy couldn't tell, only that Arthur disappeared.

And the floor tentatively filled. Through the polychrome, he identified Chrissie and Russel dancing slow, hips in tandem, faces close. Another couple, bodies grinding, approached. Through the swirling reds and blues,

Sandy discerned the boy—slim, muscular, but unmistakably Howard Weintraub, with that same calculated grin. It took another second to place his partner as Gina LaValle, a plump, wild-haired girl, said to be the school's most promiscuous. They jived, Howard and Gina, they crunched pelvis to pelvis and knocked into Russel and Chrissie. Sandy glanced at Wendell, wondering if he'd intercede. But indecent behavior was not in the vice principal's brief, only hot pants and beer, and he remained stiff by the entrance.

Others joined, even some of the teachers. Miriam trying but failing to embrace a downcast Brooks, McGonnigle hustling with one of the cafeteria ladies, demonstrating his cool. Jeanne danced as well, with Charlotte Fox, albeit without touching. They didn't have to, the way their thighs and shoulders flowed. Sandy watched them fascinated and confused and even a little envious, but unsure of what and who.

He was observing them still, cowering behind the soda bottles, when he spied an older woman entering. Through the polychrome, he thought he could make her out, the confident way she strode past Wendell and stood erect among the dancers. Sandy froze. What was she doing here? Checking up on him and Arthur, seeing if he was doing his job? The woman, her face still hidden in hues, drew near.

Only when she was directly in front of him did Sandy see the beehive seemingly ablaze. "I know it's not very ladylike of me," Esta shouted, "but can I have this dance?"

Sandy, arms raised, limped forward. He took her hand and enwrapped her waist, far wider than it was in high school, but just as easily gripped. He shifted heavily from foot to foot, chin submerged in platinum hair, and she laid her head on his chest. Once, as seventeen-year-olds, they swayed to "Stardust" and "You Belong to Me," while classmates looked on in wonder. Once, their lives unrolled like a carpet before them. No bumps, no tears, plusher each year. All that was tattered now, but for the moment they didn't care. For an instant, everybody else—Russel and Howard, Jeanne and Charlotte, even Arthur—vanished. So, too, did his worries about the Washington trip. For long as that dulcet song lasted, as long as those strobe lights swirled, Esta was again the queen of the prom and Sandy her consort.

5.

Engrossed in his own fading world, Sandy had almost forgotten there was an America out there, a country beyond Appleton. It streamed past his window, industrial gray and pastorally sprawling, shacks and manors, abandoned gas stations and those new mega-markets called malls. Closer to the capital, barefoot Black children watched the highway and jackbooted Troopers manned roadblocks. A nation of gala openings—Disneyworld, most recently, and the World Trade Towers—but also of shut-downs, protests, and bomb attacks against Federal offices. A nation at war with others and itself. Only in the bus where Rabbi Stan sidled up and down the aisle clapping and leading choruses of "Havenu Shalom Aleichem" were voices raised in peace.

Peace reigned between Sandy and Esta, too, sharing the same seat and occasionally holding hands. The ceasefire of their slow dance at school had expanded into an unspoken truce. Again, he came home to overcooked din-ners, to the taps on his knee that awakened him in his recliner, and even to lovemaking in bed. The word détente was on everyone's lips, what with the President in Russia and China, but cautiously on the Coopers'. They scarcely talked about it at all, what had happened between them and still might, as if the lull were too tissue-thin for weighted words.

Hours passed, the remains of box lunches littered the aisle. Rabbi Stan led the kids in Russian hymns they understood less than the Hebrew but which, he claimed, were sung by Soviet Jews denied the right to emigrate. He taught them the word "Svoboda," meaning "freedom." They chanted it, with power salutes pumping the air, all except for Arthur. He sat at the rearmost seat, the space next to him unoccupied, silently observing the road.

Or at least that's what Sandy hoped as he strained to glimpse the boy in the driver's rearview mirror. "Stop worrying," Esta counseled him with a squeeze of his fingers. "Everything's under control."

Everything but Sandy. While externally composed, even upbeat, inside he reeled with thoughts of Liz—missing her, needing her, suspecting her of meeting other men in his absence. And then there was Arthur, unpredictable enough in school where he was under several teachers' care, now nobody's responsibility but Sandy's. Among the other twenty or so members of the youth group, he'd struck up no friendships, not even casual. A peculiar kid and, Sandy feared, potentially violent as well.

The bus entered an area that resembled the war zones nightly seen on TV. Crumbling houses, trash heaps, mongrel dogs patroling the street. Only the Capitol's dome rising pustule-like in the distance indicated that this indeed was Washington. The doors hissed open and the Coopers took position, counting heads as they passed. Arthur's was the last and Sandy cringed when Esta tapped it. Then they followed the group outside into a heat which, though only May, was brutal. There was no relief from it, not in the hostel lobby and even less in the windowless rooms where fans barely stirred the air. Sandy almost welcomed the task of herding everyone back onto the bus in time for the afternoon tour.

It took them to Washington Monument, the Jefferson Memorial, the Reflecting Pool, and to end of Sandy's patience. While hitching to keep up with the group, he had to maintain eye contact with Arthur. He followed the others disinterestedly, not even pretending to listen to Rabbi Stan's commentary on Washington and the Jews, Jefferson and the Jews, and the need for inner reflection. Sandy also ignored him, pulling on his tie and swabbing his forehead, readying himself for an outburst. None came. The tour proceeded, Sandy sweated, and Esta glowed, or least she appeared to. Once or twice she caught sight of her husband again paying special attention to that strange boy with the long, limp hair and the too-big clothing, with eyes that quivered like watch springs.

She caught him again at the Lincoln Memorial. Rabbi Stan stood at the statue's base and sermonized about the name Abraham. While he paused to wipe his glasses and even Esta grew teary, Sandy anxiously searched. He found him, finally, deep in the building's rear, photographing the frieze of a seashell.

"Jesus…"

Arthur kept staring upward. "Maybe he liked fishing," was all he said.

"This is no joke, Arthur."

"Maybe he surfed."

"Stop it!" Sandy rasped. "Stop it, now." He forced his voice to lower. "You can't keep running off like this."

Arthur finally turned. With his pupils minutely darting and his sculptured features set, he glared at Sandy and asked, "Can't I?"

"Your mother wouldn't like it," Sandy blurted.

But Arthur only laughed. "That's what the others all say."

Echoes of his chuckling reached the front of the hall where Rabbi Stan was interpreting the mystical meaning of numbers. "In gematria," he revealed, "four score and seven stands for mercy, might, and a father's wisdom. Now how fitting is that for Father Abe?"

Several youngsters applauded sleepily but most just looked bored or squinted out toward the Tidal Basin where angry demonstrators gathered. Only Esta remained alert, but to Sandy as he paused beneath Lincoln's boot. His face showed red through the sweat.

"I can explain," his look tried to say to her.

Her nod, nearly imperceptible but nonetheless distinct, disagreed. *No, you can't*, it seemed to reply. *Ever*.

* * * * *

That unsaid exchange continued to separate them even as they sat together in the hostel's dining room. The tables had been cleared away and the chairs aligned in rows for receiving the evening's guest. Esta bustled around keeping everyone awake and silent while they waited. Sandy seemed elsewhere.

Finally, he arrived, a visibly shy, quietly handsome man in a somber suit and crewcut. Flanked by security guards, he strode up to the front of the room and stood. Awkward seconds followed and might have dragged on had Rabbi Stan not leapt from his seat and shouted, "C'mon, everybody, let's hear it for the world's greatest war hero, a man of vision and peace, Israel's ambassador to the United States!" Applauding wildly, he roused the kids to join him in "Havenu Shalom Aleichem" while the ambassador tried to smile.

He spoke finally, in a voice surprisingly reticent for a warrior, roughened only by cigarettes. It was good to greet them, he said, and he hoped they would someday visit his country. A stock speech, delivered blinking into the neon while Rabbi Stan beamed and Sandy fretted. He was thinking about "the others" Arthur once again mentioned, no doubt men with strong faces like Liz's late husband's and hefty incomes. The man who drove the Thunderbird. Positioned in the back row next to Esta, Sandy observed the boy with rising resentment and fear. What if he stood up suddenly and made a scene? Challenged the former general to a duel?

But Arthur was again distracted, his gaze—to tell from the back of his head—fixed on the floor. Nobody interrupted the ambassador, only one of the group members, a chubby kid wearing a bullet-sized *mezuzah*, who rushed to shake his hand before anybody could stop him. The diplomat shook back, reluctantly, as he and his bodyguards trooped out. They passed by Sandy and Esta, who might have stuck her hand out as well if not so distressed by her husband.

The vexation was tangible that night, as the plastic fan hummed ineffectually, and Sandy tossed in the parquet-hard bed. Esta, though, lay straight on her back, motionless and steaming, but not because of the heat. Sandy sensed that she ached to say something and it almost relieved him when she did.

"That boy, Andrew, what is it between you?"

"It's Arthur. And nothing."

The fan buzzed louder, a mosquito whined. "I don't believe you."

Such words, the first ever uttered by his wife, struck Sandy in his midsection. "You're imagining."

"Maybe. But it looks like he's all you care about—not the kids, certainly not me. And for what reason, I wonder? Something about his mom…."

"Jesus, Esta." Clammy drops trickled down his flanks The air had dimension. "Go to sleep now," he begged. "We still have the White House to visit."

"And you've got Arthur, again." Esta sighed. "Arthur Farstig."

"Warhaftig," he nearly corrected her, but didn't. Arthur, the son of his lover, Liz. The woman who had overturned and utterly transformed his life, enchanted and likely ruined it. Who kept him awake on a sweltering Washington night wondering just what might go wrong tomorrow.

*   *   *   *   *

The apex of any youth group trip, the visit to the White House, was going to be extra special this year. It would be endowed with meaning not just for these young teens but for the three million Jewish prisoners of Soviet Communism. "For those denied liberty and rights, we will be their voices. We will be their consciences," Rabbi Stan declared. "*Svoboda*!"

He was barreling through the bus again, not singing this time, but raging against the president's coming summit in Moscow. "Toasting champagne with anti-Semitic thugs while our people languish in gulags—disgusting," he spat. He stomped, the knitted *yarmulke* bouncing on his head and aviator glasses sliding down his nose as he handed out protest buttons. The kids duly pinned them their shirts as did Esta, solemnly. Sandy pocketed his.

"Don't you remember our talk, Sandy?" the Rabbi asked, raising his nonexistent chin. "Responsibility."

He broke the word into six separate syllables, but Sandy replied with one, "Job." His chin indicated the students in the seats in front of him, who relied on him to get them to 1600 Pennsylvania and back to Appleton again unharmed. Sandy was worried. Caught between dozens of political causes, some pressed with more than just posters, a bright-eyed adolescent could easily get crushed. And one fourteen-year-old in particular, peering at the world through his Swinger, seemingly inert but no doubt teeming with mischief. "Du-ty," Sandy said.

* * * * *

Thicker than any summers in Appleton, the late May heat in Washington was viscous. Sandy slogged through it and even some of the teenagers trudged. Only Rabbi Stan seemed to glide ahead of them with Esta skimming alongside, aiming for the gate. Beyond it, a hazy White House shimmered. And something else—shining, sternly aligned, and blue. Slowly, they came into view. Riot police.

What were they doing here? Certainly not to battle a band of pubescents armed with Free Soviet Jewry pins. Though not much of a news follower, he tried to recall the headlines. Another moon landing, the attempted assassination of Alabama's governor, and, in the war, the mining of enemy harbors. But why then police? Why the gear? Something was wrong, he sensed, and could quickly get seriously worse. Striving to keep up with the group, drenched, he strained to keep Arthur in eyesight and away from those shields and batons.

Yet the protest began harmlessly enough. With his back to the president's residence, Rabbi Stan began shouting, "Let my people go!" and exhorting the kids to follow. They chanted, exuberantly as at any football game they cheered, while the policemen looked on bored. But, then, without any order, they sprung to attention. Sandy saw it and wondered what any of them—Arthur?—had done to alarm them.

The answer arrived first audibly, bullhorns blasting. "Stop the bombing!" and "Hell no we won't go!" The first of the demonstrators arrived, long-haired, denimed, and carrying a placard that Sandy couldn't see but which made the officers stiffen. Others arrived, raggedly dressed and hollering. A puckish woman, not much older than the girls in the group, swaggered up to the armored blue line and flashed it the finger.

Within seconds, the space in front of the gate was crammed. More placards appeared, other causes. "End South African Apartheid" and "Free Angela Davis." The policemen closed ranks. Sandwiched, Sandy tried to elbow his way forward to where Rabbi Stan and Esta were still hollering, their words muffled by the din. Somebody shoved him, another punched his arm, but still he pitched, scouring the crowd for Arthur. He didn't see him, only one of the protesters reaching through the gate and emptying a bag of what looked like topsoil. Another released a rat.

At once the scene erupted. The policemen moved in, swinging. Screams, curses of "pigs," the smack of hickory on bone. Everyone was running—officers, protestors, even the fat white laboratory rat scurrying across the lawn. A human torrent smashed into Sandy while struggling to get to the gate. That was the last place he saw Arthur. Indifferent to the mayhem around him, he aimed his Swinger at a cop.

Sandy grappled, he tore, imagining himself for a moment a quarterback again charging the defense. If he passed Esta en route, Rabbi Stan or other members of the group, he didn't notice. Someone yanked his tie off, another ripped his shirt, and still he lumbered. Not even his gimpy leg hampered him as he leapt over discarded placards and reached the gate just in time, as a baton swatted the camera.

"No!"

Arthur was already in a karate crouch and rearing to kick when Sandy pounced and clamped him in his arms. "No!" he bellowed and practically lifted the boy off his feet. He twisted and squirmed and tried to retrieve the camera's pieces while the guard again raised his stick. "Please," Sandy begged him, "Please," he implored Arthur as he heaved him back from the gate.

Many minutes later—so it felt—they emerged from the fray. He still had Arthur in a bearhug, protecting his body with his own even as he tried to break free. Ahead of him, at the park's edge, the group waited. The kids looked frightened and several of the girls wept. Rabbi Stan comforted them, oblivious to the gash on his brow. But Esta, her beehive tattered and blouse stained, merely watched as Sandy and Arthur returned.

If physically shaken, her expression was blank. It glared at the man she had long called her husband. There were other names for him now, all of them too agonizing to mention. It no longer mattered. She stared with the detachment of one who knows that no treatment would help, that all her wounds are mortal.

6.

No one paid attention to the daily reading. Asked whether the voice on the PA belonged to a student or a teacher, no one would have known, or if the quote were Lenin's or Lennon's. The year was too far along, the trees outside the school already summer-bowed, pools and beaches beckoning. Nobody cared about homework or exams or the success of any Appleton team. Hardly anyone fretted at all with the radical exception of Sandy. Sunk in the teachers' lounge sofa, he stared into his mug as if he were floundering it in. Drowning in a brew of worries.

The first was Liz. "Fool, he could have been killed," she excoriated him after learning about the incident at the White House. "You were there to protect him, but did you? Did you? You...*fool.*"

He tried to calm her, assure her that Arthur had lost a camera but was otherwise unhurt. The only injury, he might have added, was to his marriage, sustained precisely because he had been foolish. Idiotic, in fact, for believing that she appreciated all that he had sacrificed and was willing to give up still. He wanted for the first time to say that he loved her, but all that came out was "Sorry."

"Not good enough," she snorted and turned away. In the no-frills motel room, with the lights out but clothes still on, they stood, arms folded. "I have to know that something like that will never happen again. If not..."

"If not, what?" He touched her flinching shoulder. Would she break off their relationship, abandon him as she did that other teacher Hamilton Marsh, or for another—the owner of that Thunderbird, perhaps? Or maybe she'd leave him as she did her husband, lying in his own blood and brains?

"If not…you don't want to know," she responded elliptically. "I hope you never know."

Sandy was stunned, not by her answer but its tone. Not threatening but threatened, rueful rather than mad. Pressing up against her back, he put his arms around her and hugged. Her body, at first rigid, went soft.

"It won't happen again," he whispered into her nape. "I promise."

She revolved in his embrace, bringing her forehead to his mouth. He kissed it where a band of light, escaping through the blinds, cut across. She raised her chin to meet his lips and the beam lowered to her eyes, exposing a triangular scar. He kissed that, too, while pulling down her sweatpants.

"Everything will be okay," he said while lowering to his knees. "Everything will be fine." Her fingers laced through his hair and raked his scalp. "For you. Arthur. For all of us."

He kissed, but Liz didn't react. Her hands merely closed tighter on his head. Still, Sandy worked—what choice did he have? In the dark, in the dank motor lodge air, he labored. The only sounds were his own muffled breathing and the words which he thought he heard her repeat: "If only."

* * * * *

The teachers' lounge began to fill. With McGonnigle and Stevens, Bronowski and D'Angelis, already looking tanned. Jeanne Pagonis and Charlotte Fox sauntered in chuckling and barely paused to wave good morning to Sandy. Only Wendell Barr made a point of calling out to him, if only to disturb his thoughts. "What's you dreaming about, Coach?" he chortled. "Next year's losing plays?"

It would take more than Wendell, though, to erase the memory of the previous night. Returning home after work, Sandy sat through a wordless, overdone dinner, and fell asleep in the den. He awakened in his recliner to snowy static on TV and the frames of black-and-white photos, the Asian vase and the family clock. The newel post was where it was supposed to be, at the bottom of the stairs he nightly climbed. Even the wood creaked as usual. The only difference came at the second floor landing where, instead of turning toward his bedroom, he staggered down the narrow hall toward the door at the opposite end.

Turning on the light, Sandy was almost surprised to see everything there in its place as well. The trophies, the megaphone, all stood precisely on the same shelves along with the stuffed bear, sadly. Irrationally he'd hoped to find it relocated, supine rather than sitting, its button eyes aglow. The stitching would be the same, perhaps, but of a different color, no longer Yankee blue. "Joey" it would have said in vivacious red, "My name is Joey, what's yours?"

He lifted the bear or whatever it was and brought it close to his cheek. The fur smelled of baby powder, he imagined, and musk. Brushing his cheek, it reminded him of Jeanne Pagonis's fingertips that one time they'd touched him, tingly warm. He told himself not to, but he took the toy to the single bed and lay down with it. He cupped it in his hand, football-like, and at some point must've slept.

Because he dreamed. Disappointingly, Joey did not appear to him in jeans and a numbered jersey shouting, "Hey, Dad, watch me go out for a pass!" Rather, to his surprise, on the edge of the bed and looking down at him, in a dappled dress and half-veiled beret, perched his mother. Not shriveled by cancer as when he last saw her, but vital—at least as much as that reticent woman could be—and untypically stern. "How could you?" she asked, with a censorious click of her tongue.

"It's just a bear," he held up the stuffed animal and explained. "Or a chimp or whatever. After all this time, that's the first thing you say to me?"

"Not the doll, Sanford."—She only called him Sanford when cross— "It's as dead as I am. No," she gravely nodded, "it's you."

Sandy sat up on his elbows. "Me? What've I done? Every day I do my job helping these crazy kids. And my duty—to Dad, the community."

"Not to them or your father. To you. You're the one you've failed."

"I don't get it."

She leaned closer to him—so close he could see, hidden behind her makeup, the, cosseting features, the suffering brown of her eyes. "You run, thinking that nobody will ever catch up to you. I was there and tried to warn you. I watched as you ran toward the goalpost and never saw that tackler behind."

"And?"

"I'm warning you again." She smiled now, flashing dentures. "Look over your shoulder, son, just once. Look and take care."

He awakened to the growling of Esta's Corolla backing out of the drive. He was still in his clothes, still clutching the bear, and realizing that the room was his new reality. As much as the megaphone and the trophies, as if his lips were beads and his name stitched across his midsection, he was just another knickknack to be stored and, if possible, forgotten.

Sandy remembered the previous night as he sat slumped in the teachers' lounge. He recalled the dream and his mother's advice. Mulling it over, swirling the coffee in his cup, he scarcely noticed as the rest of the teachers arrived, bickering as usual about politics, schedules, the war. The racket surrounded him but could not penetrate his thoughts. Doing that required the louder, more piercing sound of a woman screaming.

*　*　*　*　*

The woman was Miriam Loftus. As frantically as she could in her skirt and heels, she tripped into the lounge shrieking, "Help me! Help me! Help *him*!"

The lounge erupted with teachers rushing to calm Miriam but without knowing why. Confusion reigned until Dr. Steinseifer appeared at the door with Mrs. Tannenbaum. The secretary looked pale and the principal ashen as he said in a voice no one had ever heard. "To your homerooms, everybody, now. And nobody leaves." He instructed Mrs. Tannenbaum to stay with Miriam and then, with a shivering finger, pointed at two of the teachers. "You and you, come with me," he ordered Wendell and Sandy.

Through eerily emptied halls, they followed Steinseifer down a deserted staircase to the basement where the janitors reposed and the orchestra practiced. Off-key strands of "Hello, Dolly!" echoed as they approached the floor's only classroom.

The smells inside were warmly familiar—cherrywood, cedar—except for one, of unflushed toilet. The workbenches looked unaltered as well with their clamps, jigs, and Miter boxes. Nothing looked out of place in the shop, or at least not to Sandy, initially.

"Aw, shit," Wendell grunted. "Shit."

For a second, Sandy seemed flummoxed. Not until he followed the direction of the principal and his deputy's stare, blinking into raw morning light, did he see the figure dangling. Even then, his first thought was to marvel as this strange student project. Only when Wendell said, "We've got to call the police" and Dr. Steinseifer responded, "I already have," did the reality strike.

Still, none of them moved. They stood among the sawhorses and tool racks and watched as renegade breezes stirred the body but not enough to turn it toward them. Rather, its sawdust-speckled back remained facing them as they waited. "Hello, Dolly!" refrained in the hall outside, Miriam's wailing reached them from upstairs, and from somewhere outside the school, a siren. But the three men stood silently. Sandy, who'd never seen a corpse before, was too sickened to speak, and even Wendell could only manage a half-sentence.

"How do we know...."

"I checked," the principal muttered. "We know."

Minutes passed that could have been hours before the door to the shop class burst open and Sergeant Saperstein rushed in. He stopped, though, abruptly, in line with the other three and gasped. "I've seen it often enough, but never with a belt grinder."

He approached the body, felt for a pulse, and shook his pointy head. "The ambulance will be here soon," he said, "I suppose we should cut him down." The educators stared at each other and then shrugged at Saps. He motioned toward the tool rack. "We're in a shop for chrissakes. Find something."

They did, a coping saw, and cut through the sanded leather. With a sickening thump, the body hit the floor face-up. Its mouth gaped hideously, eyes bulging from purpled skin.

"Just who is this?" Saps, kneeling, inquired.

Sandy gulped. "Brooks."

"And why?"

"He was depressed. Son's in Canada, a draft dodger." The morning's coffee, even bitterer coming up, caught in his throat. "But the war never ends."

Now Saps looked perplexed. "Let me get this—the kid runs away and this guy *hangs* himself?" An ambulance wail drowned out all sound, Miriam's screams and the clarinets' warble. The policeman raised his voice as he eyeballed his friend. "Spray paint on your walls, blood on your car. What is this place, a school or a loony bin?"

* * * * *

The shock of Brooks's death redoubled at his funeral. Not only because Jeanne and Charlotte arrived holding hands or even because the mourners finally learned the departed's first name: Herbert. Most astonishing for Sandy, at least, was the revelation that he wasn't alone—or hadn't been.

He realized that entering the Mount Moriah cemetery with its Star of David gates and cross-less headstones. All those years believing that only he overheard those half-whispered remarks in the teachers' lounge and that he had to be nobler than others. If only he'd known there was always an ally, a fellow-sufferer and soul, maybe he wouldn't have felt so pressured. Or lonely. Perhaps he could have better helped Brooks.

That thought, in particular, haunted him as he lingered in the rear of the service. The shop teacher had come to him heart-in-hand only to be referred to a social worker. That guilt kept pecking at him even as other emotions struck. There was the embarrassment of seeing Jeanne tearful in her lover's arms and remembering how he once thought her crush was on him. There, too, was the pain of Miriam's weeping and pathetic lurches toward the grave, and the seat left vacant for the expatriate son. But alongside regret and tragedy was the delight of seeing Wendell Barr wearing a *yarmulke* and rising for the mourners' prayer.

Yet Sandy kept his distance from Wendell and the others. While the rest of the faculty for once sat in silence, he carefully slipped away. Through the rows of markers, he fled. This was his only chance.

The days after the incident had been intense, with students crowding frantically outside his cubicle. The boys he could understand—all had taken shop—but even the girls were distraught. Sandy at first was nonplussed but steadily realized that it was not Brooks's suicide that rattled them but the prospect of their own. Self-destruction could be contemplated by half-insane adolescents, but never carried out by an adult. He struggled to assure them that Brooks's case was different, a combination of loss and illness, but with dwindling resolve. His own situation was desperate enough not to rule out the unthinkable or to keep driving it out of young people's minds. With only a week of the school year remaining, he had to act swiftly or risk facing that darkness himself.

He reached the Impala and wished it would turn on more quietly. So, too, he refrained from stepping on the gas until he was clear of the Star of David that loomed over the gate. Once on the road, though, he sped. The funeral would give him an extra hour or two, enough to get there in time for the end of school. Beyond the legal limit, he raced, hurling to what he hoped were some answers.

*　*　*　*　*

He didn't have a photograph, but after questioning from students, he knew he didn't need one. There was one man who could fit the description they furnished. It wasn't the height—six-two—or the too-narrow head and gingery hair that stood up straight, the strait-laced clothes of a clergyman. No, there was another unescapable feature. Sandy recognized it immediately, as he exited the school.

"No," he snapped when approached, and his features immediately contorted. His eyes blinked hard and his mouth puckered in, the veins in his neck protruding. An involuntary habit, it surely hindered his ability to give anyone advice, especially when nervous. And Hamilton Marsh was nervous.

Sandy persisted. "No, what?"

"I know who you are, Mister Cooper. And no, I will not speak with you."

He strode across a small lawn and entered a parking lot. Sandy closely tailed. "I only have two questions," he huffed. "What, to your mind, was the problem with Arthur Warhaftig? And did you have contact with his mother?"

Nervously, Marsh fished for his keys. "Arthur had issues," he sputtered. His voice, like his dress, was uptight, his manner as on-end as his hair. "I'm not at liberty to discuss."

"Violence at home? Abuse? I'm asking you as a professional...."

With shuddered eyes and retracted mouth, neck cords popping, the counselor unlocked his car. "A troubled boy," was all he said. "More than you think."

"But how? Tell me, please."

Sandy shadowed him as the tall man managed to contract into his Beetle. He stuck his face in the half-opened window while Marsh stared through the windshield and gripped the wheel.

"Please...."

Gaze straight ahead, knuckles blanching, he uttered a single word: "Evil."

The Beetle began to back up, but Sandy held on to the door. His shirt, even its rolled-up sleeves, were sweat-soaked, his tie looped over his back. Still, he refused to let go. "What about my second question? His mother—"

With a jerk that almost toppled him, the Beetle braked. For the first and last time Hamilton Marsh looked at Sandy but with a mask turned monstrous by his tick. "My advice is run, Mister Cooper," the counselor smiled or grimaced just before accelerating. "Run for your very life."

* * * * *

He neither ran nor walked from the driveway that evening after finally arriving home. Night had fallen, but Sandy did not glance at his inner wrist. The hour did not matter to him nor the fact that Esta would not be waiting for him inside. There would be no meal, scorched or otherwise, or even a snooze in the den. These days, he threw together a sandwich at the refrigerator and rushed it upstairs to Joey's room. His room.

And tonight his retreat would be hastier. The encounter with Hamilton Marsh, his pronouncements on Arthur and Liz, shattered him. What did he mean that the boy was evil and his mother toxic? How had they terrified that imperturbable man, setting him twitching? Could it be, Sandy wondered, that he, too, had been seduced into bodyguard duty in return for the job of lover?

Too impatient for the flagstone path, Sandy cut across his lawn. The grass had long gone uncut and hid the object he tripped over. Cursing, he leaned down and picked up something round, softball-sized, and hefty. Sandy couldn't identify it at first and had to hold it up to the streetlights. Even then, it took a moment to internalize what it was, to drop it and recoil in shock.

Beaming up at him with a bushy beard, pointed green hair, and nose like a ruddy handball, was a gnome. An elf or a brownie, Sandy didn't know which, but the head of one of those statues that proliferated the neighborhood and Esta shunned as "*narishkeit*." But that, alone, would not make him shiver. Rather, it was the other heads—jockeys, angels, puppies, flamingos—similarly seeded in the weeds, all decapitated. As if someone had taken a hammer and knocked them off, which would have been unsettling enough, but shocking when laid on his doorstep.

Yet Sandy could not resist picking up another. Through the blades, its enameled face shone in the lamplight and smiled in his quavering palm. But was that a merciful smile, cold-hearted or sad? All seemed intended for him, the wayward husband, the disappointing son, the counselor who needed counseling. In the late spring night already growing sultry, the Virgin Mary grinned at him, upbraided and forgave him, as he closed his fist on her head.

Summer

Well before he reached the poolside, Sandy could smell it. The coconut aroma of lotion, the smack of chlorine. He heard it as well, the delighted screams mixed in with the cries of purple-lipped toddlers, the *boing* of a diving board followed by thuds and splashes. He could almost feel the blast of the snack bar's air conditioner, almost taste its fries. Climbing the stairs from the entrance of the club, his senses were already saturated but then, at the top, brimmed over. The pinwheeled umbrellas, the swimsuits both colorful and minimal, inflatable balls traversing the air, and most overwhelmingly, the water. Amethyst, unrippled but struck through with light, as if the sun itself were swimming.

Situated in up-the-hill Appleton, the Hartmont Country Club was established in the fifties for the well-to-do Jews excluded from the WASPier resorts. To avoid a similarly snooty image, the members admitted some token gentiles, themselves nouveau riche. He often wondered why they'd want to join—why anybody would, many with pools of their own. For the prestige, obviously, for the status of owning one of the glossy IDs that Esta checked at the entrance and for busying their kids with the activities Sandy ran. And yet, why would people choose to socialize with neighbors they barely waved to and bathe in a communal tub?

Sandy asked himself that again as he squinted into a cloudless noon. He was on his break between capture-the-flag and volleyball and supposed to be grabbing lunch. But he was not hungry today, not even for French fries. Appetite had left him generally, to be filled by a hollow gnaw. Summer, usually a time when he could lose his tie and shirtsleeves, trade in his khaki pants for khaki shorts and replace his gummy shoes with sneakers, had turned nightmarish. True, there were no more teachers around—no bickering McGonnigle and Bronowski, no Charlotte and Jeanne in love. Even Wendell faded. Forced to don a *yarmulke* at Brooks's funeral and stand up for *Kaddish*, he'd retaliated by dumping broken statues on Sandy's lawn—or so Sandy deduced. But that memory, too, had waned, effaced by the reality of a wife who barely talked to him and a lover who kept her distance. And by Arthur, a headache on the few days that he came to the club and a distraction the many he didn't.

Only with Arthur did his schoolyear job continue. He could often see students he knew such as Howard Weintraub, showing off his Coppertoned muscles or jack-knifing off the board. Though popular, suddenly, and self-confident, Sandy questioned whether he still thrived on revenge—against others, first, then himself.

And there, too, was Rae Henderson. Like most early teens, she hid her body behind a beach towel, though in her case, needlessly. But there was no concealing her color as she stretched on a lounge chair surrounded by groupies. She longed to be left alone, Sandy sensed, but he refrained from offering advice. His duty here was to organize dodgeball, not guide young people's lives. He could only see Rae and commiserate.

That and search for Arthur. He rarely participated in the games Sandy organized. The kids were too young, the sports non-violent. He preferred to practice karate alone, in an oversized t-shirt and shorts, behind a tool shed close by the courts. Occasionally, too, he could be spotted ogling Rae, but only at a distance, scarred perhaps by her coolness at the school dance or deterred by the cruelty of her admirers. Most times, though, Arthur simply disappeared—to where, exactly, Sandy was clueless. No sooner did he blow his whistle and consult the watch on his inside wrist than he hustled off looking for the boy and, if lucky, a moment alone with his mother.

Here the nightmare might have been dreamy. Liz Warhaftig of course joined the club, sometimes appeared poolside, tanning and smoking in a floral one-piece and occasionally taking a late afternoon dip. Otherwise, she kept to the courts where by all counts she excelled. With Esta downstairs admitting members, he might easily encounter her at numerous places—behind the snack bar or, better yet, inside her cabana. But in the presence of so much society, Liz kept her distance. Perhaps she feared her affection being noticed. Maybe because Sandy was the help.

So the summer passed, with Sandy chasing Arthur and struggling to glimpse Liz, all the while avoiding Esta. Once home, he went straight up to Joey's room and remained there dozing while fireworks popped in the distance. The weekend picnics with Saps, Marjorie, and the kids were forgotten, even the handball games at the Y. No more Sunday brunches with Saps, no more watching him snarf up both their sandwiches. Even Sobotnik's was gone.

The deli was shuttered. The handwritten signs that once promised brisket and *kishke* were now buried beneath an ad for the coming franchise. Generations of pastrami and turkey triple-deckers, of extra sour pickles and whitefish spread, would culminate in burgers and shakes, and in place of the broken ceiling fan and old Manischewitz calendars, walls of irrepressible orange. Wexler's Drugs and Hershkey's Bakery were also slated for closure soon and replacement by national chains.

No one mourned them or even seemed to notice. Only one figure, round-shouldered and homely, kept vigil. Banished from his counter but still wearing the apron that could barely be tied, Bernie stood outside and wept. Driving to the club, Sandy considered stopping to console him, put his arm around as much of the man as possible and share his loss. But three-legged races and kickball beckoned, the hunt for Arthur and hankering for Liz. Speeding past, the Impala strained up the hill, toward sensory and emotional excess.

* * * * *

Parking away from the Lincolns and Mercedes, Sandy was relieved to spot Esta's Corolla. It meant she was already at work in the clubhouse, already chatting with the ladies who pretended to treat her as equal. He wondered if she spoke to Liz when she arrived or shot her a hostile look. Not like Esta to show her feelings that way. Most likely she glanced at the ID and nodded before going back to her book. Short of red-handed proof, she would never accuse anyone of infidelity, not even a seductress like Liz.

For she was indeed seductively dressed. In a slip-length tennis skirt and lightweight top translucent when wet, she wore her hair in a ponytail that accentuated her slender nose and heightened cheekbones and that watermelon slice of a mouth. Her complexion, milky throughout the year, was now caramel. Jumbo sunglasses shaded her eyes. Women players did their best to avoid her, but not their husbands who waited to watch her bend for a ball or expose more thigh in a serve. Off court, they rushed to light her cigarette and fetch her a sweated Fresca. Shrouded in men's tennis whites, shielded by wooden rackets, she was maddingly inaccessible to Sandy.

But not, apparently, to the pro. She seemed to have limitless time for him, a swarthy, long-limbed man, Hollywood handsome with layered black hair. Spying from behind a nearby tool shed, Sandy watched as the pro positioned himself behind her, his pelvis on her butt, and reached around to guide her in a two-handed grip. Liz's laughter carried across the courts, coquettish and deep.

The scene left him speechless, first with anger and then a vengeful lust. Sandy observed them for an hour at least while the lesson progressed to overheads. Behind her again, the pro placed a hand on each of her armpits and raised her to her toes. If they weren't within earshot, Sandy would have howled.

Finally, with a hug that lasted a split-second longer than perfunctory, they parted. Liz bounded up the trail that led to the cabanas, winding close by the shed.

"Hey," Sandy said as he stepped out in front of her. "What are you doing?"

Fingers on her breast, she exclaimed, "My God, Sandy," and then archly, "Are you spying on me?"

"No. God no. It's just that—"

"Just that what?" The hazel in her eyes turned ferrous.

"You don't seem to have time for us anymore. For me."

"Don't be silly." Already she was peering to the sides and around and about Sandy.

"You have time enough for Jose or whatever his name is."

Liz simpered. "Gordon. His name's Gordon, and you, I believe, are jealous."

"I just miss you…" He moved toward her and Liz practically leapt away.

"Not here," she hissed, but then adopted a chummier tone. "The situation's awkward, I know, but let's just get through the summer as best as we can. In the meantime, please, keep my son out of trouble."

Without another word, she pushed past him and hurried to her cabana. Sandy ached to follow her but didn't. Instead, he cut around the clubhouse on a path that led into a copse near the club's parking lot. There, at the center of a grassless disc, stood a rusty pole with a tetherball tied to its top.

Anyone chancing on Sandy would've wondered why a grown man in khaki shorts and a Hartmount Staff polo shirt would lick the inside of his fingertips, one set after another, then murderously smack that ball. No less curious was the way he kept pounding it as it whirled around in ever-diminishing orbits. Most inexplicably, though, was the abruptness with which that same man froze, the ball and string encircling his neck as he stared out at the lot. Exiting was one of the few remaining cars, bronze and with California plates. The Thunderbird.

*   *   *   *   *

Suddenly, as they said on TV, it all made sense. The T-bird belonged to the pro, that gigolo Gordon, who'd been carrying on with Liz since she lived in Los Angeles. He remembered overhearing that conversation outside of her house, the words "torture" and "love" and "you know I will never leave you." Suddenly he understood why she joined the club rather than traveling during the summer and why she needed him to look after Arthur. It was all a plot to use and humiliate him and then, when no he was longer useful, throw him away.

Fuming, he appeared to supervise an Ultimate Frisbee match between the nine and ten-year-olds, blowing his whistle at random moments while checking the inside of his wrist. Come lunchtime, he would detour around the snack bar and follow the trail to the shed. From there he could monitor Liz and the pro, straining to catch them in some act of affection—a kiss, a caress—to confront her.

With his bad leg pumping, he reached the shed breathless and then, turning a corner, gasped. Rae, sitting cross-legged on the woodchips, beach towel drawn around her, shivered and wept. Sandy bent down to her, asking, "What happened?"

"Arthur. He saw you coming and ran."

"Did he…hurt you?"

She shook her head.

"Touch you?"

Another shake, followed by a flurry of sobs. "Scared me."

Against her judgment but unable to say no to a member's son, not in front of other members' daughters, she'd accepted Arthur's invitation. She followed him to the shed where he showed her his moves, his chops and kicks, barely missing her face. She begged him to stop, even started to cry, but then he did something worse.

"Worse?"

"He said he'd kill him."

"Him?"

Rae's chin lifted in the direction of the courts, to a doubles match between two women players and the mixed pair of Gordon and Liz.

"He'd kill him with karate, Arthur said. With other things, too."

"Boys that way are like that, Rae," Sandy tried explaining. "He was just showing off." His tone sounded unconvincing, even to himself.

"No," Rae insisted. "He said he would kill them all. Including you."

"Me?"

He feigned astonishment only to receive a searing look from Rae. "Oh, please, Mister Cooper…."

How much did she know, he worried, how much did any of them? Reflexively, he asked, "Who are you going to tell?"

First terrorized then frosty, her expression turned bitter. "Who *can* I tell? Who here would believe me? Except for you." She smiled at him. "And you won't do anything, will you?"

She picked herself up from the woodchips, brushed off her thighs, and drew the towel around her. "Because I'm the only Black girl, Mister Cooper, just like at school. Because as everyone knows, all you care about is Arthur."

Turning, marching, she left Sandy alone by the shed. Suddenly, he had to get out of there, go anywhere but the club. But an entire afternoon stretched before him, whiffle and kick ball games. Hours would pass before he could escape to his Impala, the very last car in the lot. No sign of the Thunderbird, thankfully. Only a note folded on his windshield in Esta's curvaceous script. "Quickly," it said, "go to the home." Not home, Sandy noticed. *The* home.

* * * * *

The serpentine drive, the gardens and the pines, suddenly seemed alien. As though he were seeing them for the first rather than the fiftieth time, entering unknown hallways. He nearly asked one of the nurses if this was in fact the Daughters of Jacob and whether a room 35 really existed. Similarly strange was the scene behind the door. No Christmas cards, no chrysanthemums, the family photographs laid flat and the wheelchair empty. And some random man in the bed, in a gown instead of a suit, with no pins adorning his chest but an IV hooked to his arm.

Sandy stood over him and stared. He smoothed the man's comb over and was startled by the coldness of his scalp. The face, a thicket of jowls and age spots, was unrecognizable, the mouth a rictus, the yellowed eyelids closed. Only the expression remained unchanged. Even near death, Maurice Cooper was aggrieved.

Between the burdened wheezes, Sandy heard footfalls behind him. Still, he flinched when Mrs. Biggs touched his shoulder and said, "He's happy now."

"I doubt it," Sandy said, though not to her.

"He was. He is."

He turned to her, his own appearance downcast. Somehow, he'd thought of her as an ally, a fellow target for his father. "Happiness? Him? He didn't know the word."

"Oh, he knew it alright." Smiling, her prominent features leveled. "He knew it whenever he saw you."

"Me? You serious?"

Mrs. Biggs looked insulted for a second but then the smile returned. "You're some big-time teacher, sure, but you don't understand very much."

His look only confirmed it. "*You* were his happiness," Mrs. Biggs explained. "True, he wasn't very good at showing it—not to me neither. But he had love in him, that man. And for nobody more than you."

And still his jaw hung incredulously, his eyes nearly popped. The orderly went on, "You should of heard the way he went on about you. 'My son did this, my son did that,' as soon as you walked out that door. Cheeks glowing. He was so proud."

Sandy gazed at the old man and, with a finger, wiped his spittled lips. "How long?" he managed to inquire.

"No telling. Weeks, couple months, maybe. Depends when the good Lord calls."

Sandy gazed through the window, at the summer twilight outside, and thought about calling his sister in Oregon. She would come while there was still enough time. Meanwhile, he would try to visit more often, sit by the bed and say those things he never could. About Joey and Esta, perhaps even about Liz. Confide and confess with the knowledge that his father couldn't answer but from somewhere, perhaps, could hear.

A pat on his arm and the sound of retreating footfalls told him he was once again alone. Or almost. His father's breaths beat dirge-like. "Oh no you don't," Sandy said to the husk of the man he once thought he knew. "Don't you go dying on me. Not yet."

He went to the bookcase but didn't need to browse. The album cover was especially dog-eared, the record visibly scratched. Yet the song sounded as fresh as the instant of its performance. Someone was young again, like the newborn year, and starlight soft. Someone was heaven and earth, sun and moonlight, to a person he'd only just met.

* * * * *

Labor Day weekend came, but the club was largely deserted. Most of the members were at home watching the Munich Olympics and rooting for Mark Spitz, the American-Jewish swimmer with the gold-encrusted chest. Yet, on the patio between the snack bar and the pool, a crowd gathered. Thirteen and fourteen-year-olds, girls mostly, giggled and clapped, which made Sandy wonder what, besides French fries, they were eating. Only when he limped nearer, squinting into the sun, did he glean the source of excitement.

Russel Pressman had arrived. In his sports camp sweatshirt with the sleeves cut off to show his biceps, with his bonfire of hair and freckles, the incoming freshman bedazzled his younger fans. Music blared—a man was having an affair with Mrs. Jones, meeting her secretly, feeling guilt—and through it Sandy heard terms like "end-around" and "up-the-middle." Russel, he realized, was talking football, but the teens still hung on his words and none more raptly than Chrissie. A working-class girl ordinarily barred from Hartmont, now she was feted. In a skimpy sundress, with big hair bouncing and phantom pom-poms in her hands, she cheered her boyfriend on.

Only Howard remained distant. Abandoned, suddenly, his body displayed on the diving board with no one to admire it, he stood watching the snack bar scene with a look that frightened Sandy. In it he saw the vengeance still smoldering for the quarterback who beat him up in the locker room and the girl who mortified him in front of the school. Junior high fantasies, Russel and Chrissie were the reality Howard hated—what drove him to lose weight, ditch the glasses and the braces, and emerge this adolescent Adonis. And he would get even with them, Sandy saw that, too, even if it meant defeating himself. For now, though, Howard merely catapulted high off the board, drew his knees close to his neck, and cannonballed. He shattered the pool's sapphire surface and showered his classmates with shards. They squawked and tittered and then went right back to ogling as Russel ran on with his plays.

He paused only when Sandy neared. Over the crest of bathing and baseball caps, Russel saw his old coach approaching and called out to him, "What's happening, Mister Cooper?"

Mr. Cooper, not Coach. Sandy shrugged to indicate that nothing in fact was happening then added a question of his own: "What did they teach you in camp?"

"Everything I never learned here," Russel snorted. "Everything nobody ever taught me."

The teenagers chortled and Chrissie practically honked. At that moment, Sandy experienced the shame Howard must've suffered up on that stage, his rage at being pummeled in the locker room. He could understand longing to whack that grin off Russel's face and cut down Chrissie several notches. But he did neither, only smiled in the manner of one whose guts are exposed and managed to mutter, "See you next week in practice."

With laughter crackling behind him and the *thwump* of Howard's cannonballs, Sandy backed away from the pool. He avoided the clubhouse where Esta was working and the tool shed with its view of the courts. Even the tetherball pole was off limits today because of its proximity to the lot. The mere sight of that Thunderbird was enough to derange him. What was this feeling? Depression, a despondency he hadn't felt since Joey's death? Or possibly worse, a sense that, like that ball, he was being hammered around and around on a shortening string and destined to slam into iron.

* * * * *

In diminishing perimeters, he circled the club. With no home to return to, no Sobotnik's to linger in, and even the temple closed for the holiday, Sandy killed the time wandering. He swung by the club's old gazebo and its dilapidated outside bar. He rounded the locked-up Racquet Shoppe and the shuttered dining hall until he finally hit a knoll. From there he could look down on Hartmont's core, a row of pastel cabanas.

Each family had one, a glorified changing room with showers, benches, and storage space for gear. The owner's name was stenciled on the door, but Sandy didn't need it for Liz's. Hers, he knew, was the fourth from the left, Caribbean blue, and the door was just then shutting.

Gordon. He was in there with her. Naked. Somehow, Sandy knew it and his mind wheeled with rage. Instinctively, he reached for a tie to tug on before breaking out in a run. He scrambled down the little hill and sprinted, limp-less suddenly, toward the cabana.

Seconds might've passed, but the time sufficed for Sandy to identify Gordon as one of "the others" Arthur had spoken of. The real one, not like him and that poor Hamilton Marsh who were merely camouflage. Gordon, Sandy surmised, was the reason Liz had moved from California and then kept moving, pausing only briefly in Appleton. Liz's husband was murdered not for her son but for a lover, he concluded. He saw the sword, its hilt gripped not by a woman's hands but by a man's: Gordon's. He saw it all in a flash right as he ripped open the door.

"What the fuck!" Liz was there alone, slipping off her swimsuit. Her shout, echoing in the deserted cabanas, would have sent other members running, but apparently only Sandy heard it. He froze as she turned her back to him and gave him a glimpse of her shoulder blades. The skin between them was marked by a dozen or more discolored patches, replicas of the one near her eye.

"I'm...sorry," Sandy muttered, but Liz kept cursing.

"Fool! Get out! Asshole! Go!"

He stumbled backwards, tripping on his sneakers and regaining his balance just as the door slammed in his face. With a groan, Sandy Cooper tottered and turned to discover that somebody else had heard the commotion. All the way from the clubhouse, she'd run, and now confronted him with an expression more wearied than mad.

*   *   *   *   *

"For years I put up with it," he later remembered her saying. "Can you imagine?"

Her voice was not angry or even accusatory but merely fatigued. What she had endured, he learned, was not jealousy or rage—those emotions were at least definable. "Call it humiliation," Esta explained. "A long, slow-burning shame."

The humiliation of knowing that she was not what he really wanted, even in high school, not the white-gloved debutante at some Naval Academy ball, not one of the many beauties who would later line up for him in the pros. Rather, she was the local girl he'd settled for after his injury, the girl he felt indebted to for caring for him and putting up with this beastly father. The woman who bore him a son and then bore that son to the grave, spending every day since then grieving for him. A booby prize life and even that no consolation. Their marriage reduced, like the meals she once cooked him, to ashes.

No, not jealous, not even of Liz, just tired. "I want to be left alone now," Esta told him in the parking lot, next to her beat-up Corolla. "You need to leave me alone."

He nodded, unable to look at her, at the deflated beehive and the flesh stretching her Hartmont Staff Member shirt. Her eyes reminded him of the water in a paintbrush jar. He stared, instead, at the asphalt.

"You need to leave," Esta repeated as she opened the car door and wedged in behind the wheel. "Tonight."

The Fall

1.

The spittle on his lips flew as far as the pews as he ranted. "Six million Jews were butchered during World War II and the world did nothing! Just this week, terrorists murdered eleven Israeli athletes in Munich and guess what? The world did nothing again! How long will *you* do nothing?"

The *you* were the congregants of Temple Beth El, those traumatized by the Olympic attack and those curious to hear the headline-grabbing professor. A tender-cheeked man with a prophet's pallor and righteous jaw but eyes seething with violence. A professor of what, exactly, no one knew but his students were beefed-up thugs wearing black berets and wielding nightsticks. Members of his Masada Brigade, they patrolled poor Jewish neighborhoods and broke up performances of the Bolshoi. "Not when our women are being raped by gangs and our people imprisoned in Russia, will we ever again be silent," the professor vowed. "Never!"

"Never!" he spumed, and his oath resounded in the sanctuary—off the pulpit with its whiff of Rabbi Isaacson's Scotch and across the walls' memorial plates, amplified by the ark. "Never!" he barked, and the congregation repeated it vehemently. Watching from behind the wrought-iron doors, Sandy swore that the chorus was fierce enough to knock the "All Who Call in Truth" letters awry and steam up the plexiglass bubble.

"And what you do if someone attacked you?" the professor harangued. "What if someone set fire to this sanctuary?"

The audience suddenly seemed stunned—was this a question or a threat? But one person rose in response. His face was scrunched in furor. His receding chin rallied and jabbed. Ever since filling in for the alcoholic

Isaacson, Rabbi Stan had changed. He'd grown more cynical, his innocence supplanted by rage. Causes not only burned in him now, they roared, and the professor was both fuel and stoker. In place of the Save Soviet Jewry pin and the peace symbol *yarmulke,* the rabbi touted the Masada Brigade logo, a fist.

"I'll tell you what we do," Stan hollered. "We fight!"

He bounded up to the pulpit. "We fight!" he declared with both hands above him clenched.

Revived, the congregation repeated the "fight" word again and again while stomping. Yet Esta refused to join. While respectfully attending the event, she clearly bought none of it. Not the spiteful type, she preferred suffering to justice, silence to bellyaching. She sat cross-armed in her pew looking alternately disgusted and bored.

Sap was also unimpressed. Though out of uniform, in a PAL sweatshirt and jeans, he stood akimbo in a corner just inside the sanctuary. He, too, had come to check out the professor, telling Sandy that Appleton had enough troublemakers already and hardly needed another. But mostly because he feared for his friend.

Ever since he moved in with the Sapersteins, Sandy seemed depressed. Listless, he was almost unable dress himself for the first days of school, uninterested in his students, even in football. And despite Marjorie's most fattening dishes, he alarmingly lost weight. Nights he spent lying on his bed beside the box that Esta had given him. Inside were his old trophies, the family clock, and Asian vase. The photographs—of his parents, even of the young cheerleader and quarterback—were thrown in. Everything, except for the bear.

"The Coop doesn't give up," Saps insisted while folding in Sandy's cuffs for him each morning and half-tying his tie. He reminded the counselor of how he once came back from a dream-smashing injury, built a life, aided students. "The Coop takes the football and runs."

So, when he expressed interest in the Beth El event, Saps practically shoved him into the station wagon. Unsuccessfully, he tried to drag him into the sanctuary, getting only so far as its doors. But that sufficed for Sandy. He didn't care about listening to the professor or even glimpsing Esta. He still wanted to oversee Arthur.

And there he was, ogling the vigilantes, admiring their berets and clubs. The professor left him spellbound. His hair thrashed as he cheered, his eyes palpitated. Nearly fifteen now, Arthur was less an adolescent than a bor-der-line adult. Yet he preserved his boyish intensity, his malevolence barely contained.

For that reason, Sandy told himself, Arthur had to be watched. And despite all that had transpired—the lies, the deceptions—Sandy remained what he always was, a guidance counselor. A source of support for young people who needed it, and of direction for those who didn't. Whether or not he was appreciated, even if he was hated, caring for Arthur and teenagers like him was still his responsibility. Still, his duty.

Yet he never stopped hoping that Liz would show up, that the two of them would have the chance to speak. He would beg her to take his phone calls, perhaps even meet for coffee, a single cup. That's all he needed to tell her that he loved her.

But she wasn't present anywhere in the sanctuary, not even behind him when a tap on his shoulder caused him to swerve. He faced not Liz but the custodian Louis.

"What, no bloodlust?" the big man inquired.

"I've had enough of lust lately, thanks. You?"

He raised a rubber gloved hand. "I think I'd rather clean toilets."

Sandy went back to observing, but Louis remained, overshadowing. "Want to go into the kitchen with me? Raid the freezers, play some chess? I've got this wedge of wedding cake…."

"I need to stay here," Sandy said, turning back to the sanctuary.

"You need," Louis replied, "a break."

"Oh, I had one of those. Back in high school, Thanksgiving game. Thank you."

Rubber-coated fingers squeezed Sandy's arm before the janitor padded away. "I'll always be here if you need me, Mister Cooper."

Up on the pulpit, the professor was still fulminating. "In this very town, there have been incidents, here in…" he seemed to forget the name. "Appleton. Hateful words spray painted on schools. And how long will take for those words to become actions? How long before schools become *shuls* and paint becomes fire?" The spittle on his lips now foamed. "And when it does, what will you do?"

Again, Rabbi Stan hollered, "Fight!" and the congregants again took up the chant. But Arthur did more than that. In a high-pitched tone that was still a pubescent's but with a grown man's growl, he leapt up and hollered, "Kill!" With twin fists punching the air, he bellowed, "Kill! Kill! Kill!"

2.

"Kill," he thought he heard the PA repeat while the word reverberated in the hallways. In fact, the announcement concerned cheerleader practice that day and the buzz about that afternoon's Autumn Assembly, rumored to be sensational. But Sandy's mind was elsewhere. In the teachers' lounge, he kept out of the debate over whether, after the massacre, the Olympics should have been cancelled. McGonnigle was in favor, Jeanne and Charlotte, too, but Bronowski and D'Angelis objected. Stevens argued for a pause. "Hebe athletes," Wendell huffed, "couldn't even fend off those ragheads," and Sandy stayed silent.

So it continued in his cubicle where he pretended to listen to the complaints about grades and peer pressure and pretended to render advice. Even when Jeanne popped her head inside the frosted glass door, he barely reacted. Her dark hair, once cropped, was grown out and braided, and her formless pantsuit replaced by a slim-fitting dress. The golden cross was gone. Only the moles remained but scattered as her lips pursed in empathy.

"I know you've been going through a hard time," she said, "and if you ever wanted to talk...."

Sandy managed a nod.

"I mean it. And until then, forget about Wendell, forget about Brooks, even that Warhaftig boy." Her fingers reached out to his cheek. "The world doesn't hang on you, Coop."

Afterward, he sat staring at the phone and the thank-you notes on his wall. The heat of Jeanne's touch diminished. He rose only with the recess bell—it was his turn to lunch monitor—rolled up his cuffs and tugged on his tie before heading out to the yard.

* * * * *

Through the crossfire of frisbees and footballs, he scanned. The conspiring girls, the scuffling boys, cries and curses—the ruthlessness of adolescence once again displayed. But still no sign of Arthur. Last seen, he was wearing one of the professor's black berets and swinging those Japanese sticks, the Tonfa. He was liable to hurt someone or even himself and Sandy was determined to stop him.

He checked the weedy patch where Arthur once practiced Kung Fu and was turning back when someone called out to him, the voice both familiar and strange.

"Yo, Mister Cooper, what's happening?"

Rae Henderson. No longer the demure eighth-grader defined by cashmere, but a brash young woman in dashikis and platform boots, her hair frizzed into an Afro. She was not alone but accompanied by two fifteen-year-olds, hooded, lanky, and contemptuous who seemed to be protecting her—that, or goading her on.

Sandy had heard about them and about Rae, no longer the only Black student in the school. How the three of them had formed a united front demanding, first, an end to those morning PA quotes, calling them patronizing. Dr. Steinseifer instantly relented and agreed to a separate lunch table as well. The time had come to make minorities feel welcomed at Appleton, they insisted. The time had come for pride.

And Rae was undoubtedly prideful. Overnight, she lost all her admirers, those who flattered and doted on her simply to prove they were cool. Their departure was a relief, no doubt, but was their replacement really much better? Or had she just substituted one set of expectations for another, with new pressures and personas? Sandy, himself, was confused.

Now she raised an indignant chin at him and squeezed her eyes into slits. "If you're looking for that crazy Warhaftig kid, he's not here," she said. "And he won't be. Not around me again. Never."

She gestured toward her newfound friends. One of them, hands in his pockets, knocked his shoulder into hers. The other motioned toward the school. Rae had to go. And yet she lingered for a moment, drawing closer, whispering.

"Is this what you had in mind when you said, 'let your guard down?'"

Sandy was speechless.

"This what you meant by 'figure out who you are and go with it?'"

Still, he couldn't speak.

"Happy, now, Mister Cooper?" she asked, flourishing her Afro in his face.

The classmates called, "Yo, Afeni," after the student he once knew as Rae. "Dig it," she said, loud enough for the others to hear, and flashed him a power salute.

* * * * *

And still no sign of Arthur. Not in the cafeteria or in the classrooms where he was supposed to be studying. In the auditorium where the student body squirmed in anticipation of the Autumn Assembly, Sandy scoured the rows. Nothing. Through the welcome to incoming students, the presentation of the varsity team, he continued searching, even when the lights dimmed for the final dramatic sketch. The curtain came up and he half-expected to see a kimonoed lunatic kicking and chopping and swinging his Tonfa like ax-blades.

What he saw, though, was no less horrifying. In place of the kimono was hair—dark, coiled tuffs of it glued over a greasepainted body and piled high in a wig. Instead of kicks were leaps and wild hand-wringing, and in place of Tonfa, a papier-mâché club.

The comedy was Prospero's Magic Cape, a dumbed-down version of Shakespeare, and the woolly creature, Caliban. Most entertaining, though, was the student who played him. With muscles that not even makeup could camouflage, resplendent in his gym shorts, was the same kid who, just a year ago, was a fat and ugly laughingstock. The students laughed this time, too, but *with* him, the outrageously impish Howard Weintraub.

Across the stage he leapfrogged and tumbled, somersaulted and twirled, all the while yodeling. But suddenly, with a change of Klieg lights, the backdrop washed with blue. Caliban bounded off only to be substituted by a couple—a prince in livery and a begowned young lady whose very entrance was cheered.

They waved back, abandoning their lines and characters. Chrissie Esposito, no longer in a maid's costume, but coiffed and sequined, and holding her hand, no less manly in leotards, Russel Pressman. He bowed and far below him, in the orchestra pit, the girls in the marching band swooned. The audience rose applauding, but Sandy remained seated, hands gripping his knees.

He was no longer interested in coaching and even less so in Russel. Haughtier than in previous years, he now seemed unapproachable. Perhaps it was because of the prep school that accepted him for the following season or the scholarship that this rich kid didn't need. Either way, the boy made it clear that Sandy had nothing more to teach him. The few plays sent in from the sidelines went unheeded, along with his hand signals from the bench. Nor did the quarterback have patience for his teammates, especially Tony Metallo, who still couldn't remember the calls. "Retard!" he spat at the bell-headed center as he fled the field sniffling.

But such ruthlessness only enhanced Russel's popularity—Chrissie's as well—and made their reception euphoric. The ovation intensified as the two of them blew kisses and bowed. Neither noticed when Caliban pounced back onto the stage and hopped up behind them. He placed one hairy hand on each of Russel's shoulders and yanked him backward. The assembly erupted in hysterics that Sandy hadn't heard in a year. But the ruckus became an uproar as those same hands wrapped around Chrissie and lifted her off her slippered feet, to a height where Howard could kiss her.

Chrissie squirmed, she tried to scream, but couldn't even grunt with Howard smothering her. Not that anyone would've heard over the bedlam. Sandy saw it, though, as did Dr. Steinseifer, who motioned him to intervene. But Russel acted first. He practically dove at Howard and tried to rip him away.

What came first, Sandy later wondered, the scream or the punch? Probably the latter, a lightning hook that caught Russel's jaw and send him reeling. The scream came from the orchestra pit, loud enough to overcome the din. Curses echoed through the auditorium as the quarterback rose, shook his head clear, and charged again only to be felled by a jab. Howard went back to kissing Chrissie, grinding his furry pelvis into her gown, while Russel managed to crouch in a three-point stance and lunge.

Howard pounced back at him and clasped his body so tightly the audience couldn't tell them apart. It staggered, this half-boy, half-monster, and pitched across the proscenium. Dr. Steinseifer was on his feet and flicking his fingers at Sandy.

And still, the counselor sat. He watched mesmerized as Howard and Russel tipped over the lip of the stage and together plunged into the pit. A cacophony ensued—crashing cymbals, twanging strings, and the clang of brass on wood—but through it all a sound that only Sandy could discern. Retrieved from his harrowing memory, the crack of breaking bone.

3.

For most of members of Temple Beth El, Yom Kippur was the only time they prayed or at least appeared to. They asked for forgiveness for all their sins and be inscribed in the Book of Life again. They beat their breasts and recalled the many ways that people die—by sword, by fire—and the solitary path to salvation. And they listened to the shofar blowing with a sound like the wail of frightened woman or the whine of a spoiled child.

Yet even those rituals proved too debilitating for many, and by mid-morning, they had gathered outside the synagogue on the lawn. They complained about the length of the services and the rabbi's firebrand speech, but most of all they gossiped. About that terrible incident at school, with Howard Weintraub indefinitely suspended and Russel Pressman hospitalized in a half-body cast, unlikely to ever play sports again. There were whispers about the new pornographic film being shown in family theaters and rumors of a break-in at Washington's Watergate Hotel. There was yearning for the food denied them this one day and that would remain off-limits until nightfall.

Sandy stayed outside as well. It was not only his fear of running into Esta that distanced him, or his inability to visit the kitchen, closed for the holiday. Nor the fact that Louis was too busy setting up chairs and Rabbi Stan spoke his call to arms against vague but gathering antagonists. What ultimately drove him, rather, was the dread of fidgeting for hours in his pew, pickling in old whiskey vapors, and reading the name plaques of the dead. How could he bear an entire day being told by that quote that God would be near to him but only if he called out in truth?

Sandy refrained from praying but neither did he mix with the others. He hung back wearing one of Saps's old seersucker suits, his tie typically half-knotted, with a polyester *yarmulke* on this head. He considered slipping off to his Impala, visiting his comatose father in the home, but in the end just lingered. He couldn't resist Arthur's lure.

Like most others his age, he needed real light, not just the disc of the plexiglass bubble, and air not soured by fasters. But while his classmates flirted and horsed around, Arthur handed out fliers. In his black beret and clenched fist pin, he spread the professor's word: defend your community or die. The message now went largely ignored, though, and the leaflets unread, but still Arthur preached. Above the peals of holiday mingling, Sandy heard his high-pitched voice and hoped it would summon his mother.

It did. Shortly, Liz appeared in a tight linen suit and broad-brimmed sunhat, and discretely exchanged words with her son. They had no effect that Sandy could see other than to give her an excuse to step away when he approached.

"Please."

She angled the hat brim over her face. "Go away."

"I've lost it all—my marriage, my job—for you."

"Oh, not for me." She turned her back to him and waved nonchalantly at Arthur. "Hurry up, honey," she chimed. "Time for home."

"I'm sorry about what happened at the club. Sorry about everything. One more chance, please."

She waved again and called more urgently now as some people had started to talk. "You see how they're staring," she rasped. "Leave me alone."

"You can get away from all this—we can. I can take you." Was he really saying this finally? "You, me, and Arthur. A new town, far away where nobody knows us. A new life."

"You're making a fool of yourself," Liz snapped and stepped yet further away. "At least have some dignity."

But Sandy gripped her arm. "I love you."

Pivoting, wrenching her elbow free, she faced him. "Love? That's what you think this was about?" Her mouth, once alluring, was ghastly, the scar jagged beside her eye. "You really are a fool, aren't you? A poor, deluded fool."

With another cry of "Arthur!" Liz strutted off.

Many hours later, lying in darkness, he tried to remember if he heard her right. Through all the laughter outside and the temple's distant prayers, he thought he heard her say, "Go, Sandy, while you can." More a plea than a warning. Or maybe he was just imagining it, the closure he needed to believe.

He was deliberating it still when the door burst open and the lights snapped on. "Get up!" Saps shouted at him.

"What? What?"

Khaki pants, a button-down shirt, flew at him. "Get dressed! Quick!" The keys to the Impala followed. "It's burning!"

* * * * *

The flames formed a grotesque geography—triangles, trapezoids, polyhedrons, stars—enveloping the temple. Beth El was on fire, not just the reception hall and the kitchen, but the entire structure was engulfed. The sanctuary with its pews and pulpit roared fiercest. Baked behind wrought-iron doors, flags and curtains incinerated. Plaques dripped down the walls.

Into the whorls Sandy saw firemen plunge, some emerging with prayer books, others bearing scrolls. But they could not contain the conflagration. Steadily it drove them back, with a shattering of stained-glass and the crackle of a collapsing ark.

Saps ran to offer assistance but Sandy, dazed, stayed back with the other congregants. He recognized many of the faces but failed to find Louis's. An irrational fear struck him, that the custodian was somehow trapped inside. He asked around if anyone had seen him, at first casually but then with mounting panic. If Rabbi Stan was there or even Esta, Sandy didn't notice. His only concern was Louis. He pictured his chess pieces flickering like candles, the freezers melting. Wildly, he fought the urge to dash past Saps and dive headlong into the blaze.

Instead, he just witnessed the inferno. The lights on the fire engines flashed like Eternal Flames and smoke rose in an acrid offering. Sandy imagined it forming words in the sky. Call to God, they advised him, be near to Him in truth. "Call in truth," he said out loud as if reading the gold-painted letters, but none of the onlookers could hear. Extinguishing his voice was the gunshot-sharp pop of the plexiglass bubble exploding.

* * * * *

Near dawn and exhausted, he first mistook it for a renegade flame. The way it burst from somewhere behind the smoldering temple and streaked by the lawn where Sandy stood. Squinting, rubbing the ashes from eyes, he made out the hatchback roof and beveled grill. The glow of brake lights further revealed a bronze exterior and blue California plates. And, for an instant that nevertheless sufficed, Sandy identified the driver.

With his mouth ajar and eyes distended, he scampered toward the Impala. He finally understood what Liz meant by crying, "All you do is torture me," and Hamilton Marsh's one-word warning: "Evil." At last, Sandy understood his own offenses and the terrible contours of the truth.

Down Union Street he sped, past the hamburger joint and convenience store going up in place of Sobotnik's and Wexler's, past the darkened school, screeching through the intersection, uphill. The Tudor houses, the Hartmont club, whizzed by as the Impala climbed to a height where he could see the nearest city glimmering. Still, he ascended until the asphalt ended abruptly in woods and his wheels crunched onto gravel.

The crescent driveway was empty—the T-bird not back from its spin—and the mansion's windows black. The nymphs and cupids no longer judged or mocked him but reflected his own cold resolve. He didn't buzz the intercom but pushed through a door purposely left unlocked.

The marble floor, the post-modern chandelier, both were as abstract as the art on the walls as he stormed through the hall and down three steps to the den. The light from the reading lamp showed that nothing had changed. The kimono was still displayed along with the masks and the proclamations, the titillating prints, and the Tonfa. And, grinning above the sofa, the sword.

Sandy lifted it from the brackets and drew it from the lacquered sheath. Steel shimmered in his open palms as he weighed it.

"Light enough for a woman," a voice behind him commented.

"Or for a child."

He turned to find her no less obscured than the first time they met and yet visibly altered. In place of the silk-and-jade beauty, Liz appeared well beyond her prime or even middle age. Skin sallow and sagging, hair bedraggled, lipstick smudged on her once-tempting mouth. Ice jiggled in her glass.

"You *are* crazy," he said.

"I told you, never call me that." She tugged the folds of her terrycloth robe and angrily puffed a cigarette. Its ember illuminated the scar. "I told you I'd do anything to protect him."

"Even cover up for him? Vandalism? Arson? Even…" The blade, now clenched, threatened to slice Sandy's skin. "Murder?"

"Anything."

The sigh of brakes, the whirr of a cutting engine, penetrated the den. The outside door opened and slammed. Footsteps resounded in the hall.

"You didn't kill Allan Warhaftig, and yet you took the blame."

Liz merely simpered and shrugged. "What difference did it make?"

"You used me, and others before me, to stop it from happening again."

"Didn't quite work out, now, did it?"

"You let him have all this." A sweep of the sword in his palms took in all the mementos. "You let him drive—"

"He insisted. They belonged to his father. Also, the car." As much as any of the demon masks, her face was wrought with fear. "And, believe me, driving is the least he can do."

The footsteps stopped on the stairs. Sandy saw the desert boots popular among junior high schoolers, and the baggy pants stained with what smelled like lighter fluid. But the lamplight didn't reach his head, not until he descended and removed the set of Tonfa from the wall. And then, in an offensive crouch, he confronted Sandy.

"I know everything, Arthur," he said.

The Tonfa spun, first forward and then in reverse, a bone-breaking orbit. Their angular tips could easily have left the scar near his mother's eye or the many across her back. Through a curtain of hair, pupils darting, Arthur grinned at him. "So?"

"You aren't going to say anything, are you Sandy?" Liz interjected. "Not to that police friend of yours…."

He didn't respond but only kept staring at Arthur. At his belt. An old quarterback trick—the tackler's buckle always signals which way he'll move. Sandy lifted the sword.

"No," Liz pleaded.

"Don't worry, Mom. He's not going to tell anyone." The highness of his voice complimented the feathery steps he took across the den as the Tonfa swung faster. Sandy's hands found the hilt and raised it over his head. Arthur's was a saber-slash away. Yet, still he came, weapons whirling, and the counselor prepared to strike.

"No!" A cocktail glass shattered on the floor. "No!"

Sandy froze for a moment before releasing his grip. The sword clattered among shards. He no longer looked at Arthur, certainly not at Liz, but merely groaned, shortly, grievously, as he fled the den, the hallway, the house. On gummy soles that felt leaden for once, he lunged for his car and raced it out of the drive. Down the hill, he plummeted, to the center of what had once been his life.

4.

"We Shall Overcome," they sang, and "Oh, Freedom." In a half-circle ringing the embers of Beth El, they stood and praised brotherhood, held hands and bowed their heads in mourning. They swore solidarity against the hatred that animated this crime, provoked—so people believed—by the vigilante professor and his Masada Brigade. The September sun showed mercy on the thousands of townspeople gathered, led by clergymen from all three faiths, Protestant, Catholic, and Jewish. They marched singing up Union Street in the direction of Appleton Junior High.

Sandy staggered among them. Salted in the crowd were faces long known. Dom from the Starbright pizzeria and Bernie from what had been Sobotnik's, Saps and Captain Rizzo, who finally pledged to investigate. Esta was there as well, though Sandy could not see her face. It remained pressed into a handkerchief as she sobbed for a loss of much more than her marriage, as she hadn't since Joey died.

They were all there except for Stan. Ashamed, suddenly, of his support for the professor, he chose to stay away, perhaps permanently. In his place teetered the senior rabbi Isaacson, whom no one had seen in years. Wizened, whiskey-cured, and held up on each side by a priest and minister, he swam in his black clerical robes and struggled against the weight of his *yarmulke*. Still, he strode doggedly, righteously, toward the school.

And Louis. Sandy searched all morning without finding him or identifying anyone who cared. Not even Saps, eager to collect any evidence in the case and hold Rizzo to his promise. "Most likely in a bar somewhere getting soused," was all he snapped. "I know I'd be." Through the demonstration,

Sandy kept scanning, resisting the urge to call out his name. Maybe he feared getting blamed for the fire. Or may he mourned for the temple.

Eventually, the people reached the double-door entrance and quietly filed into the auditorium. The faculty served as ushers—Dr. Steinseifer and Mrs. Tannenbaum, Bronowski, and McGonnigle, D'Angelis and Stevens. Jeanne and Charlotte distributed programs, Miriam Loftus handed out tissues. There was no arguing, for once, no rancor. Each at some point approached Sandy with a look of mixed condolence and contrition. As though he, alone, were bereaved by the incident, as if he needed their apologies. They shook his hand and took their seats among the Elks Club and the scouting troops, the PTA and war veterans. All of Appleton, Sandy noticed, but Wendell.

The ceremony began with the "Star Spangled Banner" and proceeded to benedictions and prayers. The mayor, who few seemed to know existed, spoke about tolerance. Meanwhile, in the pit, the marching band played the theme from the movie *Exodus* and a pair of guitar-playing freshmen, a girl and a boy, performed ballads. The audience sang with them, rising in applause. What began as a memorial blossomed into celebration with teachers and students embracing one another. Even Rae Henderson forgot herself and dragged her new classmates into a *hora*.

Retreating backstage, hidden in curtains, Sandy observed the rite. He no longer felt part of it—not the sorrow, not the craze—or even a resident of the town. Nor did he bother to look for Arthur. He and his mother were no doubt packing up, the artwork and chandelier already in boxes along with the Tonfa and sword. In the Thunderbird, they'd drive to another county, perhaps a different state, there to begin the process anew. Fear and duplicity, seduction and death.

There was only one more job for Sandy to perform, a final duty. Slipping out of an emergency exit, he descended two floors to the basement and the abandoned shop class. The memory of Brooks suspended there chilled him for a second but no longer. His finger ran across the tool rack and settled on a claw-head hammer. He removed it and returned upstairs, to the rows of identical lockers.

His was unmarked but Sandy had no difficulty locating it. Inserting the claw through the bolt, leaning on the handle, sufficed to break inside. As if disemboweled, the contents spilled at his feet.

First, there were the photographs. Polaroid prints of the Lincoln Memorial and riot police outside the White House. Mostly, though, there were snapshots of Rae—Rae at the dance, Rae at the club, Rae clutching her head that had just been beaned by an iceball. And still the innards poured out. Spray paint, a half-dozen cans of it and in colors Sandy recognized. Flamingo Pink. Mind-Blowing Blue, the Green from Psycho Hell. Karate books, Masada Brigade paraphernalia. A kitchen knife with gore and fur still stuck to it and a mallet coated with the dust of lawn statues.

Sandy bent and retrieved the items, reinterring them within the locker. Slapping his hands, he closed the metal door only to find Wendell behind it.

"And you protected him." With white teeth bared, leathered face crinkling, he smiled. "You protected that little Hebe bastard, blaming it on everyone else, and for what?" His hobnail eyes drilled. "Pussy."

Sandy's fist flew. It collided with Wendell's face between his upper lip and nose, opening them both. Blood was already spraying across the hall when the vice principal struck back, a punch that split Sandy's eyebrow. Yet he felt nothing, saw nothing, only the blackness that was Wendell Barr's presence, which he kept pummeling, right-left, left-right, even as his own face was battered.

* * * * *

He couldn't remember whose scream it was, whose arms were prying them apart. He only recalled the blood, a shocking amount of it, bright on the floor, and the sound of someone—Saps, maybe—shouting, "Jesus Christ, Sandy!" And the faces. The pimply ones and the unblemished, the hideous and the cute, hundreds of them gawking at him, stunned.

Somehow he found himself seated in front of Nurse O'Shanassy, gazing over her hump, as she swabbed the meat of his hands. His head throbbed—a butterfly cinched his brow—and teeth ached, but the worse pain gripped his gut. It felt like an entire team had tackled him. As if he had already been sacked.

The pain intensified as one by one the teachers stuck their heads in to see him. Some whispered, "Way to go, Cooper," and "You pretty much knocked him out," while others merely winked. Wendell had it coming to him, they intimated. Only Jeanne Pagonis looked different. She positioned herself behind the nurse and opposite him. She did nothing, not even blink.

Rather, she stared at him with a crestfallen expression that darkened the moles on her face. They traded looks, the former apprentice and mentor, for several moments before Jeanne turned slowly and left.

No one visited him after that. No more faculty members, no students certainly. The nurse was almost through swabbing when Mrs. Tannebaum whiffled in. In her cat's eye glasses and steel-wool hair, the secretary looked as perfunctory as usual as she informed Sandy that Dr. Steinseifer wanted him in his office. "Not in five minutes," she added. "Now."

He thanked Nurse O'Shanassy for patching him. He tried, unsuccessfully, to wipe the stains from his shirt and settled for folding in its cuffs. He glanced at his inner wrist, but the watch must have broken off. Then, with a tug on his half-knotted tie, Sandy stood and began limping, straightened his back and strode, as if to take the field.

*   *   *   *   *

At twilight, he emerged with nothing but the thank-you letters plucked from his cubicle. The parking lot was empty except for the Impala, waiting for him under a megaphone of light. He started for the car that could not take him home anymore or even to Saps, but somewhere else, far away perhaps. Short of the door, though, he stopped. He turned and rounded a corner to the sprawling gridiron behind.

Practice had ended and the team was already in the showers. The season would be played, with games won and lost, and the seasons after that. From autumn to autumn, fall to fall, the cycle persisted, impervious to war, indifferent to upheaval, much less the loss of one coach.

He hitched, gum-soled shoes springing on the turf. A slight wind worried the grass and bruised the purplish sky. The air ripened with cleat-pierced soil and the lingering sweat of adolescents. He halted to the fifty-yard-line. There, sloppily in his absence, the players had forgotten a ball.

It lay shimmering, laces up, inviting him. But to what? To where and for which purpose? He wasn't sure he knew anymore or even had the energy to answer. And yet, he found his hands opening. The letters scattered and flew. Licking his fingertips, Sandy reached down and retrieved the elliptical, raised it, and clasped it to his heart.

Peering downfield, he made out the goalpost. The uprights like a referee's arms signaling "touchdown" or a broken man's arms raised in surrender.

He scanned around for any tacklers who could again clip his leg and his life. He imagined the cheers, the pom-poms, the drums. He once more pictured himself unshackled, but uncertain now who was unleashed. A monster or a sufferer, a victim or a saint? Or maybe just a typical man trapped in his time, weighed down by the past and pinned by fallibility, deciding whether to run.